To River and Goulet

*I totally get you; I was a birdcage and
you were meant to fly.*

Brian Sella

KEROSENE

<u>BEAR</u>

He always had with him a jar of kerosene, a lighter, and his black German Shepherd.

Even if he had no money in his pockets, or was stripped of the clothes on his back, he'd have those three things – from the golden coast of southern California, to the flat plains of Illinois.

They were with him now, snug in his jacket pocket and trotting along by his knees as he made his way towards the towering Big Top. A gust of vile wind cut through the Fairgrounds and he buried his chin deeper into his collar, breath visible in the chilly April morning. The air smelt of stale popcorn and fried food, the scent hanging in the air like a rain-heavy cloud. Another bought of wind caught his tail end as he ducked into the safety of the red-and-white tarps.

While outside was still bitterly cold, clutched by winter's lingering grip, underneath the Big Top it was warm and dimly lit. Standing in the middle, the Ringleader directed carnies to hang more lanterns in the darker corners, especially around the aisles in the bleachers. He was a heavier set, upper-middle aged man with a waving finger and a booming voice; he was so involved with shouting instructions, he didn't notice the dog running up to greet him.

"Atlanta!" The Ringleader greeted, pleasantly surprised by the wet nose that nudged his hand. He knelt down to rub the thick fur around her neck and under the leather collar to the itches she couldn't reach herself. As her owner approached behind her, he rose. "Barrett, welcome back." His tone was warm, rumbling almost into a purr, as he pulled the younger man into a hug.

"You know I hate when you call me that, Roy," Barrett complained as he pulled back from the embrace. "Just call me *Bear*, everyone else does."

Roy waved that conversation off and turned to walk in the other direction; Bear became his shadow and Atlanta became his. They walked in unison around the wide diameter of the center ring, footsteps silent on the recently packed-down dirt. The Circus' carnies moved like a colony of ants to set everything up, a fixed routine perfected hundreds of years ago and passed down through generations of workers. Bear greeted them all by name as they scurried around him.

"Did you find what you were looking for?" Roy asked, stopping to inspect a palette of folding chairs for any damage done while traveling.

Bear nodded. "Five gas stations within walking distance."

"I told you New Hampshire would be impressive."

"In gas station numbers, at least."

Outside, the sun was finally beginning to gather its strength up, preparing to sprinkle the tiniest hints of warm weather upon the fairgrounds. The dew would disappear, the grass underfoot would dry, and divots of water trickling down the tent would dissolve. Summer would be arriving soon. The weather wouldn't truly relax into Spring until mid-April, a grueling aspect of New Hampshire's climate. Leaves were picked up and spun down the pathways between newly erected kiosks by eddies of wind, twisting and twirling as if to say, *Look at us! We're acrobats, too!*

The fairy lights still needed to be hung, the wires connected to the massive generators. Signs needed a fresh coat of paint, Murphy beds needed new linens, rides and games needed dozens of hands to be dusted off and set up. The rides were the best and worst part for the carnies, always saved for last; they got to safety test them after all the grueling labor of setting them up. Their cheers could be heard for hours as barkers began to set off into town with flyers and stories of exceptional performances.

Bear watched them design their posters, eyes on the flashy oranges and reds of a firebreather contrasting against a sheer black background. "When will we open?" He asked, fingertips already buzzing. He could hear the applause.

"Early May, I think," Roy responded. Could he hear it, too? "That'll give us enough time to settle in, set up, and send the barkers out."

Flicking his lighter, Bear said, "I'll fill up," and slipped off, leaving behind the lingering smell of gasoline.

* * *

<u>BEAR</u>

One day everything will fall into place. Bear looked up from his varying array of torches, smacking his lips. The taste was stinging down his throat, under his tongue, behind his teeth. The Clown was applying makeup in a mirror, covering up smooth skin with layers of colorful paint. *I hope we fall together.*

She did not notice him watching her, or if she did, she ignored him. Triangles above her eyebrows and below her bottom lid, the twisting path of red from the corners of her mouth, stretching her smile up to her cheeks. The makeup was different every night. It was like watching an artist paint or a photographer shoot, each move was made with practiced ease and every finished product was unique. She could've been more than this.

They all could've been more, but they chose to be here.

It was the second weekend in May, and true to Roy's schedule, the Circus was debuting to the public tonight. The murmur of carnies and barkers moving around outside their trailer buzzed in Bear's good ear, individual voices faded together into one indistinguishable jumble. He must've become visibly irritated, his body twitching with the overload of senses, the suddenly invasive craving to brush his teeth and scrub his tongue, because Magnolia turned in her seat.

Her wrist was poised half way to her face, about to apply her final touches.

"You good, B?"

He could hear her voice perfectly. Maple syrup on pancakes, the first roses of spring, a pale olive color, Magnolia's voice stole Bear's attention back from the hectic outdoors and the vile taste in his mouth. Green eyes were blown wide with worry and her frowning lips countered the large smile painted onto her face.

Bear shook out his head. "Yeah. Tastes bad."

"It's gasoline."

The boy kissed his teeth once more, grimacing at the additional spark of burning taste that zapped on his tongue. Magnolia watched him for a lingering second, her eyes flirting south to the jar of kerosene that was dwindling down in contents. Their dog whined in the corner, ears pricking up at the door as more people passed and shouted just beyond it.

Putting the finishing touches on her face, Maggie cleaned up methodically: washing brushes, setting them up to dry, wiping up any splattered paint. She then stood and crossed the camper, rummaging through a cabinet and then the freezer, and returned to sit crisscross on the floor in front of Bear.

Not a trained nurse, Magnolia the Clown picked up tips from online searches and elders. A Styrofoam cup full of ice cubes and a travel sized squeeze bottle of burn ointment she swiped from a pharmacy is all she needs to ease Bear's pain. This was a well-practiced tradition of theirs: costume, make up, clean up, ice on the blisters.

The sores were worse around his mouth where the flame kisses the most sensitive parts of his face. They were an ugly and invasive species, some shriveled and dried up, but the fresher ones were still puffy and leaking. Maggie applied ice to the ones on the surface and popped a cube into Bear's mouth for those hiding within his throat and on the walls of his cheeks.

The ice worked its magic, numbing the pain of the blisters as it melted and rant in trickles down Bear's neck and Maggie's wrist. She applied the ointment after dabbing his lips down with a soft towel, careful to avoid getting it where he could taste it.

Bear grimaced at the thought. "Tastes worse than the gasoline."

Maggie leaned back and smiled. "I sincerely doubt it."

It was nearing showtime, and the sun was dipping below the trees. The Fairgrounds were beginning to come alive with fairy lights and the faint twinkling of ambient music; vendors were setting up the remaining touches on their kiosks, game attendants were fluffing up their stuffed animal prizes, and cooks were dazzling the air with the wonderful smell of fried food.

Maggie streaked red eyeshadow under Bear's eyes with her thumb, dragging out the last syllable in *Simba* to make Bear giggle into her palm. Then she got into her clown outfit while he gelled his own hair back, braiding the fiery red-orange locks that went past his shoulders, and adjusted a black headband to hold back the loose strands on his forehead. He was particular about this part; any loose hair caught by a flame would set everything up.

"I should just shave it, huh?" Bear said, looking over Maggie's shoulder at his own reflection in the mirror. "Save myself the time."

"I like it long," Maggie pouted. "Don't shave it."

"Okay. I won't."

As if to punctuate his sentence, Maggie reached up behind her to cord her fingers through his hair. Bear leaned into the touch, nearly purring as she scratched her long fingernails into his skull and dragged them down to his cheek. Long fingernails skimmed over the raised scar tissue that marred his left ear. She always made sure to stand to his right.

They stepped out of the stuffy bubble of their trailer into the refreshing, cool air beyond it. A gust of wind whistled through the rows of mobile homes, picking up Maggie's skirt as it went. Blushing, she held it until the bought died down.

"That's going to pose to be an issue tonight, huh?" She said, readjusting her costume.

Bear watched her. "Anyone glances up there, you call me. I wouldn't mind bruising some of my knuckles tonight."

"If someone looks up there," Maggie said, "I can handle them myself."

"Oh, I know." Bear shot her a grin. "I just want to get some licks in, too."

Their trailer was in the furthest corner of the Fairgrounds, where early guests and prying eyes couldn't bother them. Blocking off the senior performers' trailers from the rest of the lot were gutted out semi truck trailers. Bunks lined the metal walls for newer Circus comers to sleep on top of each other until they reached a level of seniority that earned them a more private arrangement.

The performers' area was usually bustling with pre-show excitement at this hour; today, there was an eerie stillness about it. By routine, Maggie and Bear were the last ones out, but there should have been the stray loiterer, someone who overslept or couldn't get their make up right. There should've been someone responsible for the noise Bear could hear from within his trailer.

It was a ghost town.

Ignoring the unease beginning to settle in his belly, Bear led Maggie towards the midway. They spared the clown alley a glance, and still saw no signs of life. Only a few paintbrushes stuck in murky, blue-green water.

Maggie frowned at the absence of her comrades. "Are they already at the Big Top?"

"Possibly."

In the main lot, the workers were scurrying around chaotically, trying to put the finishing touches together while guests filed in.

A group of carnies hunched over a plate of fried food. They inhaled it, barely sparing Maggie and Bear more than a polite wave as they passed at a brisk walk. One of them had time to throw Atlanta a scrap of meat, though.

They rounded a corner so fast Bear crashed right into someone's chest. Or, rather, being a few inches shorter, they slammed in *his*.

Maggie and Bear were suddenly face to face with the trapeze twins.

"Watch where you're going, jackass," The taller one hissed, shoving past Bear with pointed irritation.

The smaller one smiled apologetically: "See you guys under the Top!" and followed his brother beneath an arching line of fairy lights.

"What's his problem?" Bear grumbled, brushing off the shoulder that had been checked.

Maggie smirked towards the direction of a row of ten-by-ten poster of Bear's face hanging across an assembly of kiosks. "That, probably."

"Jealousy is a disease."

Another gust of skin-raising wind cut through the Fairgrounds. Tucking their tails like dogs, they broke into a brisk jog to get to the corner of the lot that had attraction tents and game vendors.

In a lonely corner, blanketed in darkness, their destination, the psychic tent, promised shelter from the wind.

Magnolia ducked in without hesitation but Bear stopped at the entrance, kneeling to pick up the sign outside that had been knocked over. He dusted off each side with his hands, careful to avoid catching on a splinter, then slipped through the curtain after Maggie, accidentally colliding with her back before his eyes could adjust to the low light.

"Sorry."

She smirked over her shoulder at him.

A voice from the back corner greeted them: "Good evening, children."

Mavis was a paradox: elderly while maintaining youthful charm, shaky in her movements but sturdy in her voice, and vaguely wise. Her tent was the oldest one, still the same from the earliest days when the Circus still traveled by train and brought animals with it. It smelt of mildew, yet the air was still and dry underneath the black canvas. Only a small, circular lamp was omitting a small halo of light.

Mavis remained sitting at her table when they approached, her cane leaning up against her chair, within reach. Maggie sat down opposite of her while Bear remained standing and Atlanta trotted up to greet her.

"Such a good girl," The psychic purred, scratching underneath the Shepherd's black chin. As if from thin air, she produced a treat for her, and then three more. "You can see her brains through her eyes you know – her heart, too. She's a smart one."

Bear smiled. "Sometimes too smart."

Mavis clicked her tongue. "Ah, but that's the breed, my dear boy. Go on, you know where it is."

Shelves were lined with various bottles and potions. She waved him off towards the furthest one, nestled away between two book shelves that were overflowing with peeling covers and tea-beige pages. A single can of kerosene perched on the highest shelf. Bear grabbed it with the care of a man scooping up a newborn, tracing his fingers over the blank label.

Occasionally, Mavis took payment in the form of favors or groceries. She'd put out a registry of sorts, which the barkers would pass out with their fliers. The promise of a more detailed, accurate future telling was gifted upon anyone who brought something from her shopping list. If anyone from the Circus needed something that was a mild inconvenience to obtain, it went on Mavis' list. Like kerosene.

"Thanks for holding onto this," Bear said, returning to where Mavis and Maggie were seated.

"How are you feeling today?" Maggie asked. She had reached across the table to place a gloved hand over Mavis' bird-boned fingers, and her eyes were soft with concern. Breaking down, traveling, and setting back up was stressful for even the youngest, most vibrant workers. For the frailer ones, it was hell.

Mavis waved her off. "I'm fine, honey. How does it look out there?"

Bear and Maggie shared a brief, heavy look. Mavis must've known there was something up: she'd normally be able to hear the excited commotion of the performers practicing and warming up. There was nothing but bleak silence outside her tent. Bear rolled an answer over his tongue before responding.

"It's quiet."

The palm reader's eyes went empty and her body relaxed. Maggie leaned back in her chair while Bear took a step closer to the table. Atlanta's nervous whine was the only sound for what felt like an hour, but couldn't have been more than a minute.

When she spoke again, her voice was softened.

“I just have a bad feeling.”

“About what?” Maggie asked, hushed.

Mavis shook her head, looking worried. “All of it.”

“Pre-show anxieties,” Bear butted in, both of his hands resting on Maggie’s shoulders. The touch startled her enough to make her jump in her chair and flush with embarrassment. “I get them all the time.”

He hoped Maggie would have the decency to carry out the lie with him. Bear didn’t get anxious before shows anymore – he fed off the energy around him, though. Tonight, he felt an unfamiliar tug in his heart that took him back to his beginning days at the Circus.

Thankfully, Maggie stayed silent, although he suspected it was due to the eerie nature of Mavis’ reservations rather than backing Bear on a white lie.

Deciding enough was enough, he tugged on Maggie to encourage her to stand. “We better get going,” Bear said to Mavis, offering her an apologetic smile. “Don’t want to sully our on-time reputation.”

Another lie. Bear was always late.

“Goodbye.” Mavis’ voice sounded far away and she didn’t even spare them a glance as they moved towards the exit of her tent. She seemed transfixed on the world beyond her walls, where she could hear crowds beginning to gather. "And good luck."

"Best not to question her," Bear reminded Maggie gently, the hand gripping her arm loosening once they were back outside. The Clown nodded, eyes lingering on the tent for a moment longer. Bear pulled her into his chest and spoke into her hair. "She gets confused, remember? Don't think about it."

He pulled a torch out of his backpack and tucked it under his elbow while he unscrewed the lid on the kerosene. Fingertips tingled with excitement and muscled vibrated in anticipation – he wanted to eat fire. It was a craving he couldn't ignore, like the itch for nicotine or the ache for alcohol. Maggie watched him tip the bottle and soak the wick.

The wind was unrelenting. Kerosene dripped off the torch and onto the ground at Bear's feet before he could light it, and once he managed to, the flame was extinguished within an instant. A single puff of smoke was yanked violently away in a gust.

"Shit," He murmured, and snubbed the torch off in the dirt.

Bear picked at the healing blisters around his mouth; Maggie smacked his hand away. "You'll make them worse."

He kicked a rock and watched it skip across the dirt walkways and into the dew-soaked grass. "I don't think that's possible."

"It's possible."

Magnolia kept her eyes on where the rock disappeared, even after Bear started walking towards the Big Top. She just stood there, let him go on ahead of her, until their dog stopped and looked back at her, questioning. Bear paused and held a hand out.

She must've felt the dark aura that was pulsing from the tent in the center of the Fairgrounds; Bear could almost see it, the little tidal waves of forewarning that made their destination unwelcoming. It was always like this before a show – any performance could be the one where someone cracks their head open or sets their face on fire.

But Bear could feel something different about tonight, and no doubt Maggie could, too.

"C'mon," Bear urged, honeying his tone into something softer. "It'll be okay."

Maggie finally looked at him. "Promise?" This was bigger than whatever lukewarm prophecy Mavis thrust upon them moments before, this was bigger than the Circus itself. Bear's heart was under a hydraulic press.

"You know I can't do that."

"I know. Can you say it anyway?"

"I don't like lying to you."

"I'm asking this time. Please?" Maggie's voice cracked. Tears were beginning to leak out of her bright green eyes, threatening to ruin the makeup she just worked so hard on applying. Bear closed the space between them and wrapped her up in strong, scarred arms.

"It'll be okay. I promise."

Shouting from across the Fairgrounds broke them apart.

Roy was making his way towards them at a light jog, down through a corridor of kiosks that casted strange, dancing shadows onto his form. Bear and

Maggie watched him approach instead of meeting somewhere in the middle.

"Hey, you two." Roy's breathing was on the heavy side when he got to them, and he took a moment to readjust his flashy red ringleader jacket against his square torso. "Why aren't you under the tent?"

It wasn't accusatory, if anything mildly curious, but Bear felt the need to defend himself and Maggie. "We had to grab gas from Mavis."

Roy's eyebrows shot up. "You saw her today?"

"Yeah, just came from there." Maggie tilted her head back towards the psychic tent. "Why?"

Roy shrugged and in unison they started walking towards the Big Top. "Jump days are getting harder on her, did she seem okay?"

Bear lied without looking at Maggie. "Yeah, she seemed fine."

The Fairgrounds were far removed from the ghost town state it was in previously. The energy was beginning to swell as groups of guests started to trickle in, loitering around kiosks and games, casting excited glances towards the Big Top.

Kids ran around, free of their parents' commands, gripping the limbs of stuffed animals so tightly all stuffing was shoved to either side of their fists. They were the first winners of the night and boasting to younger siblings, unaware of Maggie breaking off from Roy and Bear and skipping over to them gleefully.

Her male and canine companions kept on without missing a beat, leaving her to *literally* clown around with the visitors. Bear hoped she'd soon forget the uneasy interaction with Mavis.

On their way to the Big Top, Roy and Bear were stopped a few times, bombarded with questions they were happy to answer. Atlanta loved the attention, too, eager to show off the many tricks she practiced with her owner. She'd jump through Bear's arms when they formed a hoop, weave through his legs as he stepped backwards, forwards, side to side. The applause was as pleasing to her as it was to him.

"What do you do?" A bright eyed preteen asked Bear, mouth already sticky and blue from cotton candy.

"I'm a fire breather," Bear said.

Somehow, those eyes went wider. "Like a dragon?"

Roy couldn't hide the snort of laughter that left his nose, despite how quickly he threw an elbow across his face to stifle it. Bear ignored him and tossed the kid a wink.

"Yeah, just like a dragon."

"You enjoy that a little too much," Roy chuckled when the boy was eventually dragged away by his parents.

Bear didn't argue – because of course he did – as they finally managed to slip away from the ever-growing midway crowds. They walked within the shadows behind the vendors, where the twinkling lights didn't reach and Atlanta's fur blended in with the ground.

"It's going to be a hay show tonight, looks like," Roy said, referencing the old and outdated term used to describe sold out shows. The seats would get so full, the carnies would bring out bales of hay for people to sit on. But not here. Their bleachers were big enough.

"It usually is on the first night," Bear murmured. He swatted away a mosquito that lingered in front of his nose. "And we've been around long enough for word to get out."

Roy glanced at him sideways. "Doesn't hurt that the barking team has been plastering your mug on every flat surface in town."

"Every flat surface, huh? Does that include your ass?"

The Ringleader pinched him on the bare bicep.

Behind the tent was a trailer that opened into the back of the center ring, so performers could enter without being seen by the audience first. Bear, Roy, and Atlanta crowded in through the rear door where the rest of their comrades were gathered to each amp other up for show time.

Dozens of bodies filled the small place; the air was stale and hot, the energy buzzing with anticipation, and a series of whoops erupted when Bear's presence was noticed.

"There's the man!"

"I knew I smelt gasoline!"

Bear pushed through their pressing bodies to get to the front, leaning into pats on the back and knuckles to the top of his head. He was smaller than most of the men who worked with him, well-muscled but still lean and standing at five feet, ten inches: he barely came up to the shoulder of Andreas, one of the Strongmen.

Even Bear's outfit was bland compared to those his friends were clad in. He kept his image simple to up the effect of his act.

Andreas put a heavy arm across his shoulders, squeezing once with an ounce of his effort. "You ready, boss?"

Sharp, crooked teeth peaked out as Bear flashed a lopsided smile. "Always."

"Make me proud, kids," Roy shouted above the pre-show commotion, standing with his back to the curtain, poised to be the first to burst through it. At the sound of his voice, the performers quieted like well-trained dogs, and through the newfound silence they could hear the hushed chatter of patrons just beyond the barrier, as eager to see their acts as they were to perform them.

The Ringleader's hand found the back of Bear's neck and his thick fingers weaved and twisted a grip into the baby hairs loose from the braid as he asked: "And what do we always say?"

Together, in perfectly rehearsed unison, the Circus responded: "The show will go on."

FOOD CHAINS

<u>BEAR</u>

Bear sat in the middle of his own private, sought out corner of backstage, eyes closed and spine straight. Each inhale, exhale, and seconds between them were calculated with practiced care. He did his best to block out the sounds of the sword swallowers performance just a few yards beyond the curtain; Atlanta sat at his shoulder, eyes half lidded, one ear angled towards the stage.

Someone cleared their throat.

Peaking open one eye, Bear saw the Circus' assistant manager, Dee, peering around the corner. She waved at him and stepped fully into view, her hands clasped behind her back and a contrite look on her face.

"Sorry to interrupt," She said.

Bear shrugged. "It's fine. What's up?"

Dee had bright blue eyeshadow streaked above her eyes, a color that popped against her dark skin. "Some men requested to speak with you before show time."

"Some men?" Bear echoed, pursing his lips. The movement pulled on some dry scabs around his mouth.

Dee merely copied his shrug and gestured behind her.

Two men in matching, expensive-looking three-piece suits appeared as if out of thin air. They each had a pair of sunglasses over their eyes that, in one synchronized motion, they shifted up onto their heads as they greeted Bear.

"Bear!" The taller one exclaimed. "What a pleasure to finally meet you."

The other one, a short and pudgy troll-like man, said to Dee: "Can we have some privacy?"

Dee bowed her head. No one spoke until she was gone and out of ear shot.

The first man snorted. "I know we're at a Circus, but what's that man doing in that ridiculous get up?"

Not off to a great start.

Bear stood, brushing off his pants and glaring daggers. "Dee's a woman."

"Wasn't she some sort'a bearded lady here?"

"Decades ago." This conversation was rapidly reversing the meditation Bear just finished up with.

"Well," Sniffed the troll, "we're here for you anyway. I'm David, and this is my partner–"

"*Superior.*"

"– Greg."

"We're recruiters, or agents, if you will," Greg explained. Bear wondered if, in the right lighting, he could see his reflection in his balding head. "We work out of some of the larger circus' in the world. I'm talking *Ringling,* kid."

"Ringling's been shut down," Bear pointed out.

"We worked with them for many years before."

Bear huffed. They were boring him already. The crowd's uproar of impressed applause sent a jolt of excitement through his nerves.

"But enough talk about skeletons." David stepped closer. "We've come to talk to you about your future."

Bear tried to contain a bubble of laughter from escaping. This was their pitch? Professional recruiters – sorry, *agents* – and they couldn't sell water to a fish.

"Let's cut to the chase, kid." Greg leaned against a support pole, his hands out like he was presenting Bear an invisible gift. "With your skills and image, transferring to a bigger, higher volume circus could be your big break. I'm talking Hollywood big. Your face will be on every taxi cab, every screen in Times Square."

"Everyone wants to be rich," David pushed, "but not everyone gets the opportunity. You could go the easy route – have a sex tape leaked or whatever. Or you could get famous for being *you*. Which is the cool way."

They both cut off like they use all of their allotted time on air. Bear looked at each of them in turn, arms folded over his chest, waiting to see if they had more to say. Atlanta sneezed as if she were covering up her own snort of laughter.

Greg sighed when he realized Bear wasn't moved by their half-assed speech. He kissed his teeth and dug around in his suit pockets.

"Can I smoke in here?" He asked, pulling out a pack of Marlboros.

Bear raised an eyebrow. "Are you asking me if you can smoke in a tent?"

The pack was slowly returned to the pocket. "You're smart, Bear. And incredibly talented, and I'm not just saying that because the commission I'd get from recruiting you would put me a whole lot closer to retirement. You have what we call the 'Circus Gene'."

"It means you're naturally good at what you do – so good, in fact, that you can't be picture doing anything else," David added. He narrowed his eyes at Bear. "Can *you* picture yourself doing anything else?"

They knew the answer to that question, hence why they asked it.

Bear didn't have anything else. He tried to live within "normal" society and failed miserably. He hadn't experienced true belonging until he found the Circus and had zero intention on trying again.

Greg got a wicked look in his eye. "Fact of the matter is, Roy can't maintain this place for much longer, Bear. His refusal to add animal acts or sideshow attractions costs him a lot of money he could be making. In an already dying industry, you're swimming in shark invested waters covered in seal blood. You're not reaching your full potential here, kid, and if it keeps up like this you never will."

"Think about it." David handed Bear a business card. Bear didn't miss the way his eyes shot nervously towards the Shepherd that was watching him. "Give us a call, okay?"

Bear held the card gingerly. "Alright." He shoved it into his back pocket. "We'll see."

Winking, Greg shot him a pair of finger guns. "Honored to finally meet an urban legend. Have a good show, Bear."

They left, shooting Bear one last glance over their shoulders like he'd call out for them. Unfortunately for them, this wasn't a Hallmark movie. Bear watched where they disappeared, half-expecting Dee to return.

Urban legend. The term felt weird where it rested unspoken on Bear's tongue. It wasn't the first time other circuses had approached him for recruitment, but it was the first time any of them had offered him such promises of fame and fortune. He chewed on the inside of his cheek.

Atlanta whined and began pacing. Roy's booming voice came over the intercom, announcing the departure of the sword swallowers and the beginning of the next act. Bear shook out his head to empty it, calling his dog to his side so they could sneak out from their hiding spot.

Bear found an empty seat reserved for him in the front row of bleachers, next to other performers who stayed to watch the remainder of the show. His thigh brushed against the hard plane of Andreas; the strongman was panting like a dog, trickles of moisture traveling in rivets down his bulging neck and shoulder muscles. Sweat or a result of chugging a gallon of water, Bear wasn't sure.

He was up after the acrobats, a pair of sixteen-year-old girls who were exceptionally skilled for their young age. Whenever a night allowed it, Bear tried to catch their act. Sometimes he'd even watch them when they were directly after him, and he'd nurse his wounds and blisters from the front row instead of hidden behind the curtains.

Onlookers wouldn't know where to look: at the acrobats, or at the fire breather who stumbled off the stage only to sit back down in front of it and cough up blood onto the back of his hand.

Tonight, he got the pleasure of being after them so he could watch them twist and dance thirty feet in the air without distraction. Quinn and Callie wouldn't return the favor. The fire show scared them. They'd cool off by stretching and fooling around with the clowns out on the midway, entertaining children not much younger than themselves.

A lot of performers used their free time after their acts to wander around the Fairgrounds instead of getting well-deserved rest. Bear joined them every once in a while, but the fresh reek of gasoline and the sight of peeling, oozing blisters were never enticing to patrons. Teenagers and preteens wanted to talk to him but their parents would pull the younger ones away with a sideways glance in his direction and their nose wrinkled up to their eyebrows. He was far easier to interact with before the show.

More often than not, Bear spent his post-show hours doubled over the tiny sink in his trailer, scrubbing his mouth and tongue and gums with the strongest mint toothpaste he could pull from a pharmacy. He brushed until his mouth bled, until the bristles of the toothbrush were flattened and sporadic. He didn't mind the taste of gasoline anymore – it was always there anyway – but he knew his companions did. He brushed out of curtesy.

The can of kerosene he took from Mavis was leaning up against Bear's tapping leg. Atlanta sat calm and collected between his knees, and together they watched the acrobats swing and twirl amongst their silk. The dog's brown eyes followed them through the air, mouth hanging open and ears alert with herding dog levels of focus.

Bear turned around for the hundredth time in five minutes, running his eyes across the sea of faces behind him, judging each reaction, calculating each *ooh* and *aah*. Across the stage, barely distinguishable through the bright lights, Magnolia loitered with the other clowns, laughing and picking on people in the crowd.

To his delight, Bear caught the eye of the boy from before who asked if he was a dragon. He was sitting a few seats down from Bear, a few rows up from the stage, clutching a can of soda in one hand and a cone of bright red cotton candy in the other. When he noticed Bear watching him, he sat up and waved excitedly, almost losing his cotton candy in the process. Bear waved back with an easy-going smile and mouthed: *I'm next!* and hoped he could read his lips from so far away. Judging by the way the child beamed even brighter, it was safe to say he did. Bear tilted his head back to the acrobat show to say *pay attention.*

As he continued to scan the crowd, something caught his eye: a face in the masses that shouldn't be there.

Mavis.

Bear straightened in his seat, confused. She never left her tent, much less during open hours when people were flooding her with questions about their futures, sticking their sweaty palms under her nose and demanding answers. Yet there she was, in the center of a stack of bleachers, just a few rows above the boy with his cotton candy, watching the acrobats with empty eyes.

Bear hovered on her long enough for her to turn her gaze just slightly, eyes locking with his. She nodded.

Atlanta leapt up and started barking like mad – but not at Mavis, nor at a patron that was acting out of turn. The Shepherd was still facing the acrobats in the air.

And then the wire snapped.

Bear couldn't move. No one could, not even Atlanta. Not fast enough.

A tiny blur, a sparkly full body suit that was designed to be seen from distances, a loud, awful thud of shattering bones against the packed ground. The crowd went silent, Atlanta ceased her barking, and then from thirty feet in the air, someone let out a gut-wrenching screech of horror.

"Quinn!"

Bear wasn't sure what made the screaming sound so dull and distant: his bad ear, or the sheer shock he was experiencing. His legs moved on their own accord; he followed Atlanta over the stage rail and into the ring. He vaguely registered the kerosene knocking over without spilling, and the torches dumped on the ground next to it. He didn't care. He needed to get to Quinn.

Atlanta had made it to the center of the stage in two bounds, throwing her body over Quinn's and resuming her hysterical barking. A wet nose shoved into the aerialist's neck to seek a pulse.

The hard floor ripped the knees of Bear's cargo pants when he slid up next to his Shepherd, hands shaking as he reached for Quinn's face. Her tiny, youthful face gazed up at him in horror like a cow in slaughter barn. She seemed to be looking straight through him with glassy eyes. Her limbs were twisted in a grotesque way and her spine curved out to the side unnaturally; Bear told himself he'd seen worse in the war, this was nothing.

Those private assurances were for naught. He couldn't even convince himself.

Before he could even touch her, someone yanked him back, and he could barely make out Roy's outfit through tear-blurred vision. Atlanta pressed in close with the Ringleader. Bear wasn't needed – Bear couldn't help.

Callie's wails cut through the jumbled mess of overlapping chatter.

She was in a dead sprint towards Quinn's body, but Maggie had hopped the railing and caught her around the waist before she could get too close. She pulled her in, cradling her against her breast while the acrobat's body gave out into a crumpling heap of sobs. Maggie's knees buckled with the sudden need to support another body and they both sank to the ground. That beautiful make up was streaking.

Bear didn't notice the EMTs flooding in until they were barking out orders to back up. Roy did so reluctantly, and had to pull Atlanta back by the collar. The dog was grieving as badly as any of the humans were: she had tried to warn them, and her years in the Army didn't provide her the skills to heal the small child. While emergency response workers were coming in, the patrons were being herded out by pale-faced carnies who seemed to be struggling to remain calm.

Quinn's body was limp when they picked her up gently despite the harshness of their voices. Bear caught sight of her face and noticed that her eyes had closed and the terrified expression on her face had faded into a slack-jawed, empty one.

A stretcher was brought in and she was laid across it, strapped in safe and snug, and wheeled out. Just like that. Gone.

Callie was leaning out of Maggie's hold, her body trying in vain to follow her partner's. "Roy," She sobbed. "Roy, I don't know what happened. One minute she was holding on and the next–"

"Little one," Roy knelt beside her in the dirt. Normally he would've reached for her, or cupped her face tenderly, but both hands remained limp at his side. Bear noticed the blood on them and hoped Callie didn't. "It's not your fault. Accidents happen."

A slight shake of her head – Callie was losing the will to fight. "No, we rehearsed that move so many times."

Bear's heart ached, not just for Quinn, but now for Callie who would blame herself forever. He caught Maggie's eye over the head of the wailing child. The clown's face was a canvas of grief and confusion, still trying to process the tragedy she witnessed.

Movement over her shoulder caught Bear's eye and he saw Mavis leaving out of the same exit they wheeled Quinn out of.

* * *

<u>MAGNOLIA</u>

Eventually, the skies opened up.

Roy warned them New England weather would keep them on their toes: sweaters in the mornings, peeling off layers by noon, cowering under an umbrella by evening.

Underneath the Big Top, the performers huddled together in a vibrating mass of nerves while the carnies and grounds workers struggled outside to save kiosks and displays from the sudden downpour. Bear was one of the select few broken away from the group; he paced like a caged lion along the outer rim of the center ring, underneath posters that displayed his face in colorful affair. An unlit cigarette hanging from his mouth that he chewed and worked down until the rolled tobacco was limp and soggy. His anxious habit stole their purpose.

Wasn't it funny? Cigarettes – the puny things – could take down the toughest sailors, blacken their lungs and shorten their breath until it ceased all together, and here was this simple boy, taking all of that power away with his molars. That's all life was about in the end. Food chains. Magnolia's father always told her that you are never truly at the top of one.

Perched like vultures a few feet above the rest of their heads, the pair of twin brother trapeze artists spoke amongst each other in low voices. They were still in their full body cat suits, striped red and black like angry bumblebees, and every now and then, one of them shot a weighted glance in Callie's direction where she still sat cradled against Maggie's chest. Maggie held her chin high, daring one of them – *Wes* – to say something, to break this heavy, bone crushing silence.

In the end, it was Callie who finally did.

"Will she be okay?" She craned her neck to an awkward angle to stare at Maggie's face, her way of catching any change in emotion that might give away what her words would try to hide. Atlanta was curled up with her head in Callie's lap, providing comfort with the heavy weight of her body.

"Yes. She'll be okay." Maggie prayed the clown make up did its job and hid the sadness behind the painted grin. It was a well-practiced charade that she used to fool even herself. When Bear was leaning over their tiny sink, coughing until blood splattered like paint against the beige plastic bowl, she stared down her reflection in the mirror and promised them both: it'll be okay.

The child in her arms sniffled and nuzzled back into her chest, staining Maggie's costume with the last of her own grease paint that hadn't yet been sobbed off, and dug her fingers into Atlanta's thick, body fur.

Many pairs of nervous eyes blinked in the shadows, but no one was brave enough to speak up with their own attempt at optimism. Even Bear stayed silent on the matter; he had ceased his pacing and was fiddling with his torches and cans of gasoline.

From the same slit in the canvas he left from hours ago, Roy slipped back under the Big Top, followed by his second in command. Dee was a powerful presence; she walked like she owned every room she occupied, but her personality was gentle and sound. Roy stood a few inches shorter than her as shook out the umbrella they had taken cover under, careful to avoid splashing water droplets on his companion's long, black coat.

"The carnies told us we'd find you all in here," Dee said, her voice tight in chastising nature. "Why are you lot not in bed?"

"How could we sleep?" Maggie's murmur was muffled by Callie's hair.

She had no idea how late it was or how many hours had passed since the guests were herded out of the Big Top, and then asked to leave the Fairgrounds all together. She had tried to keep track of how many breaths Callie took or how many times Bear had paced from one side of the ring to the other. Each hour had bled into another at a painfully slow pace. How *could* they sleep?

She didn't realize Roy had walked over to her until his hand gently brushed against her back as he crouched down. His age-hardened face, crisscrossed with wrinkles like roads drawn on a map, was soft and sad. When he spoke, it was weighted with exhaustion.

"We won't know of her condition for a few hours," said Roy. His hand left Maggie's back and found a loose strand of Callie's hair that had clung to her cheek, glued down by tears. Pushing it back behind her ear, he continued: "You must sleep. All of you."

He punctuated his demand by shooting a pointed look in Bear's direction. The fire breather held his stern gaze with a chin tilted towards the roof and dark, hooded brown eyes. He wouldn't sleep, probably not until a few days from now when his body would eventually cave under the pressure of exhaustion. He would keep up until there was no other option but to drift into dreamless sleep.

Roy lost the staring contest to turn back to Callie and Maggie, his expression softening again. "Calista." He used her full name rarely, less even than he used Maggie or Bear's. "Do you think you'd be better off staying with me and Dee tonight?"

"She can stay with us," Maggie offered, but Roy shook his head.

"It's too crowded in that trailer already," He pointed out. "And Bear will use that as an excuse to avoid sleeping." Roy leaned in closer so what he said next was only audible to Maggie. "You can't take care of both of them."

Maggie wanted to argue, though there was no point. Callie would be more comfortable in a larger, less crowded trailer that didn't reek of gasoline or buzz with Bear's anxious energy. With uncharacteristic ease, Maggie gave in.

Roy was already coaxing Callie out of Maggie's arms. The sixteen-year-old went without a fight, her body limp with exhaustion and sadness, and Roy scooped her up in his arms princess style. It was hard to tell, but Maggie was pretty sure she was asleep by the time he stood up. Dee lingered behind as the Ringleader exited the Big Top, scanning the small bunch of sorry-looking Circus performers with a terribly sad expression on her face.

"Good will come from even this, my loves," Her voice was flat and gentle in the poor acoustics of the tent. "Sleep now, for tomorrow's sake."

From his perch still above the rest of them, one of the trapeze brothers murmured: "The show must go on."

Dee ignored the hint of sarcasm in his voice as she nodded. "And it will."

Then she too was gone and the performers were alone in the silence of the Big Top, surrounded by glittering lights and the sound of support beams creaking in the wind. For a long time, no one moved or spoke, terrified to disturb the peace; but eventually, one by one, they started to get up despite their stiff bodies groaning in protest. There were quiet exchanges of pleasantries and swift comforting touches as they filed out, numb to the world by this point and just hoping they'd make it to their beds before their legs gave out.

Maggie, Bear, and the brothers were the last ones remaining.

The first twin jumped down from their perch.

Wes was more built than his brother Judas. Their faces were identical but Judas had dyed his blond hair a pale shade of purple and kept the sides shaved. Wes let his grow longer to curl just above his shoulders.

The four of them stood like a scatter graph in the middle of the stage. Wes looked restless like Bear, while Judas and Maggie were tucked in on themselves, weary and tired – but like Bear and Wes, neither of them would be able to sleep.

To Wes, Bear asked quietly, "Did you get approached by recruiters tonight?"

"Recruiters?" The aerialist echoed, confused.

Bear shrugged. "I heard whispers that there were some floating around."

Maggie eyed him. There was something in his body language that was suspicious: he angled his shoulders away from Wes and chewed on a fingernail, staring down at his dog instead of the person he was addressing.

"I didn't hear anything about that." Wes' voice raised to an offended pitch. "And I think if recruiters of any kind came through here, they'd look for *us* first."

Bear rolled his eyes. "Yeah. True."

"What, are you doubting that?"

The boys stood chest to chest now, Wes forcing himself into Bear's bubble with a sudden burst of aggression that Maggie wasn't prepared for.

Bear was taller than Wes by a few inches and broader in every way. His muscles, more bulk than lean, bulged in rage when the trapeze artist stood so close their noses nearly touched. If Bear got mad enough, he could squash Wes like a irritating bug.

Knowing this, Judas stepped in quickly.

"I don't think Bear was insinuating that he doubted your – *our* – talent, Wes," He said anxiously.

"I wasn't." Bear shrugged. "He just has a very fragile ego."

"Watch it, gas breath," Wes hissed.

"The fuck did you call me?"

"Okay!" Maggie shoved her way between them now, confident that nothing would escalate if she was in the middle of it. "Cut it out. What are you guys, eighteen again? I thought we were past this."

Ever since Maggie joined the Circus three years ago, those two could not leave each other alone. There was too much testosterone. If Wes pushed, Bear pushed back. If Bear went hard, Wes tried to go harder.

Fucking boys.

Bear looked between them in a contemplative way.

"Ferris wheel?" The fire breather offered. It sounded like an apology.

Outside, the rain had ceased but the wind kept on, urging them to run down slick pathways in between kiosks. Their boots splashed muddy water up onto the backs of their calves and into their shoes, but it made the whole situation almost comical.

Maggie found herself giggling as Bear stomped into a particularly deep puddle, the splatter of water reaching Wes' legs which earned him a string of muttered curses. They paused at the twins' trailer so they could change out of their stage attire and into warmer clothes.

As a last-minute thought, Judas swiped a bottle of Jack Daniels that was almost empty.

He bit back a grin at Maggie and Bear's quizzical looks. "We were saving it for a rainy day."

Wes grabbed it from his brother. "Rainy night is good enough."

And they were off again, back tracking to the front of the Fairgrounds, passed the Big Top and through the vendors, more mindful now of the puddles. The Ferris wheel towered over the western side of the park with the rest of the rides, all of which were covered in tarps to protect them from the rain.

The wheel alone stood mighty and bare against the storm, and the four performers (and Atlanta) hovered at its base, calculating.

The worst of the rain and wind had subsided into nothing more than a drizzle that was unnoticeable against their soaked skin.

Wes stuck the liquor in his jacket's inner pocket, safe and sound, as Bear knelt down in the soaked grass to hoist Atlanta up on his shoulders – safe and sound. Maggie and Judas waited as they tested out the metal bars first, finding a way up that wasn't too slick. They climbed it so frequently that the task was easy enough, and within a few minutes they were all crammed into the tallest most pod, passing the bottle around and taking tiny sips to conserve what little remained.

The idea to scale and hide out in the Ferris wheel was Bear's from his first summer spent in the Circus.

It was the year before Maggie arrived and, spare Atlanta, he had no one. He would sneak out at night or early in the morning and find his peaceful solitude high up above everyone else, where no one could reach him, and he could sit in silence and watch the sunrise or gaze up at the Milky Way.

Maggie was surprised he ever let her come up with him, and even more so when he started inviting Wes and Judas. She was sure everyone else knew by now, but no one chastised them or invaded the moments. Somethings, she found, were better left alone.

Atlanta snored quietly at Bear's feet, and Maggie spoke around the whiskey-burn in her throat. "We can come back from this, right?"

Wes looked across the car at her. "Yeah." He took the final swig and tapped the empty glass bottle against the metal seat. "We've come back from worse."

Bear and Maggie weren't around when Wes and Judas' parents died in a trapeze accident; the twins were only thirteen at the time. Bear wouldn't come around for six years after that. They were world renowned trapeze artists and were bringing their boys up to be the same, so Wes and Judas didn't know a life outside of the Circus. They were born and raised in this life, indebted to their parents now, and unable to even comprehend an existence not surrounded by red and white tents.

"We shouldn't *have* to keep coming back from it," Judas murmured, staring off into the sky, where the beginnings of dawn's light were starting to creep up over the horizon.

The storm clouds were far in the distance, dark against the growing light like a majestic mountain range. Maggie blinked in groggy surprised: *where did the night go?*

Judas continued: "This shouldn't be the normal."

"Well it is," Wes snapped. "It was Mom and Dad's normal, too."

Judas didn't argue, he seemed to have no energy left to even speak again, so they all fell silent once more. Bear chewed on his unlit cigarette and scratched behind his dog's ears rhythmically, trying to curb the anxiety Maggie could feel through the tiny vibrations going through his body. She leaned in closer, hoping to provide comfort.

"I've had a lotta normals," Bear said. "I had a habit of running away from them for a while there." He laughed even though there wasn't a damn thing funny about it, Maggie knew that. There was only so much a twenty-three-year-old could go through before he had to just start laughing about it. "Somehow, this is the best one I've found. And I'd like to keep it, 'cause quite frankly I don't have much else." The fire breather looked at each of them one by one, a scowl on his face. "We come back, so we don't have to *go back*."

Back to what the Circus was an escape from. For Wes and Judas, that didn't exist, but it could – and Bear was preaching to the choir. None of them wanted to leave or witness the Circus shut down, so all they could do was put on brave faces to the public and keep on performing, even though any night they could easily be Quinn.

Bear tossed his cigarette over the edge. "I'm going to take the kid out this morning. Talk to her, make sure she's good."

"Maybe Roy will bring her to the hospital," Maggie said. "To see Quinn."

"He won't."

The sky was becoming lighter, and soon the carnies and barkers would be waking to start their morning chores. They made their way back down the Ferris wheel.

Wes left the empty bottle of Jack on the base and Bear knelt down to let Atlanta off his shoulders and pull up a couple dandelions. He stuck them in the mouth of the bottle, stepping back to examine his work. Wes rolled his eyes and nudged him; Bear had to grab onto the trapeze artist's shoulder to stop from stumbling sideways and they were both giggling like school girls, weak-kneed from exhaustion and alcohol.

Moments as brief of those reminded Maggie that at the end of the day, they were twenty-somethings, just barely adults, who shouldn't be so used to seeing terrible things. The death of both parents, a handful of years at war, and whatever other childhood traumas that led them all here. At what point does it stop?

They said goodnight – or rather, good morning – to the trapeze twins quietly amongst the trailers and tents, mindful not to wake their sleeping friends who wouldn't wake until far later.

Bear pushed open the door to their home, grimacing at the loud squeak of the hinges that desperately needed oil, and held it open for Maggie and Atlanta to enter first. Maggie flopped onto her back on the Murphy bed and only then realized she was still in makeup and costume. She was too exhausted to care, prepared to just sleep how she was, until she felt Bear untying her boots.

He slipped them off one by one and placed them neatly by the door, then disappeared into the bathroom only to reemerge seconds later with makeup wipes and a glass of water. He handed her the cup to drink and got to work removing the color on her face, paying extra attention to the crevices of her nose and around her eyes, humming the twinkling Circus tune that played in between acts in the Big Top. Only once he was satisfied, Bear moved on to removing the many layers of her costume: tutu, fishnets, knee high socks, corset, elbow gloves, until she was just in her underwear. He placed a light kiss on her forehead and stood to grab a sweater of his own and PJ shorts.

Maggie shrugged them on with his help, barely maintaining consciousness as he tucked the blankets around her body and continued humming a lullaby. Their windows had black out curtains so they could sleep late into the morning, and the trailer was a dim and warm. The last thing Maggie could recognize was Bear swapping out his outfit for a nearly identical one and stepping back out into the world.

As badly as she wanted to chase him down and beg him to allow himself to rest, her body wouldn't move, and a dreamless sleep consumed her.

WHEN IT'S SUNNY

<u>CALLIE</u>

It was early when Bear came to find her but Callie was awake anyway, having admitted defeat on her restless hours of tossing and turning. She was sitting outside Roy's mobile home fiddling with a pocket knife. The fire breather, trailed loyally by his German Shepherd, hovered nearby. He looked exhausted but rosy in the cheeks, and there was a tiny hint of a slur that accented his southern drawl when he spoke.

"I'm takin' Atlanta for a walk, you wanna come?"

Bear waited a millisecond before setting off towards the Fairgrounds exit, not pausing or waiting to see if Callie was following – she was, of course, but he would not slow his pace for her so she had to jog briefly to catch up.

Eventually she was able to match his speed. They walked down the dirt road that led to the Circus lot, winding through a small forest glen. Atlanta ran about freely, never too far from her owner, but still fetching the sticks he tossed her and bounding in and out of the trees on either side of them.

The morning was sunny but brisk in typical spring fashion, warming with each passing minute. Dew sparkled on the grass in its final moments before dissolving underneath the sun, and the baby leaves on the trees were bright green against the sunrise.

Callie was comfortable in an oversized sweater and leggings that Roy had given her and she relished in the lack of wind. Bear's style didn't change: he was clad in cargo pants and a off-white wife-beater (what a truly awful term for an article of clothing) and had his long, red hair in a fishtail braid past his shoulders.

"Where are we going?" Callie finally asked after twenty minutes of silence. Bear shrugged nonchalantly.

"Wherever we end up."

The fire breather walked with confidence, having explored these trails and country roads for weeks since the Circus touched base in New Hampshire. Through neighborhoods, past two gas stations, a pocket-sized town center that had a library and a vet, alongside fenced in pastures with horses that Atlanta stared down.

Callie watched the sky brighten in the East, chasing out away the last of the stars. After some time, it became easy to clear her mind of everything but the way Atlanta walked so close to Bear's hip.

They turned left at a railroad crossing, walking parallel to them for another five minutes before the forest opened up to a small patch of wildflowers nestled next to the tracks. Only then did Bear stop and stand in the direction they came.

As if on a cue, a blaring horn cut through the peaceful birdsong, and a locomotive came crawling towards them.

Bear stood so close to the tracks the gust of wind from the passing train picked up loose strands of his hair. Callie sucked in a worried breath from where she stood a few paces back, hoping Bear didn't pick up on it. The fire breather was fearless on the surface. Below the blistered top layer of skin was a different story.

It took extended, dragging minutes for the entire train to pass. You forget they're miles long until they're right in front of you, somehow fast and slow at the same time. Before Callie and Bear's time, the Circus traveled via train. Elders told stories of loading the boxcars up with everything from tent tarps to wild animals. Now the only animal at their Circus was Atlanta, and just like the rest of them, she was there on her own accord.

The ex-army dog was waiting patiently at her owner's side, paws tucked underneath her ebony body as she sat still, unflinching. One of Bear's hands had drifted towards the top of her head and stroked the tips of her ears lightly. Callie noticed some patchy black polish on his nails, curtesy of Maggie, that was blending in with the dog's fur.

Atlanta stood when the caboose finally went by; Bear stepped up to the tracks.

"My sister used to tell me," The redhead said, kneeling as he spoke, "you could tell how recently a train has passed based off of how warm the tracks are."

Callie lowered herself down and placed a hand gently on the metal beam just centimeters from Bear's. The metal was vibrating just barely, but it was cold to the touch. The longer she held her palm against the surface, the temperature climbed minuscule amounts until she gave up and sat back on her heels, glaring at her older companion. He watched her, emotions unreadable, as she dusted her hand off on her black pants.

"She was a liar." Callie stood, irritated.

She was exhausted, hungry, and still in a shock-induced trance; nothing felt real or permanent in this state. It felt as though she could step into a bank with a semi-automatic weapon and walk away with all cash and no repercussions. Is this how Bear felt all the time? This daring and adventurous? The boy before her wasn't the same one she knew back at the Fairgrounds. There was no fire in his eyes, no lopsided grin. He was stoic and quiet.

"Sometimes people don't mean to be," Bear said gently. He neglected to look at Callie and instead focused on the metal tracks, as if hoping his gaze could warm them better than the train could. By now, the caboose was disappearing around a distant bend, a simple dot at the edge of the horizon. A period at the end of the sentence of their vision. "Sometimes life has a way of making us into liars when we had every intention of telling the truth."

Bear's eyes were cloudy as he looked off into the distance, and at some point, he pulled out a cigarette to gnaw on.

Truth is, Callie didn't want to talk about it. She didn't want to be lectured or spoken to like a damaged child, she wanted to go back in time and not mess up. She wanted Quinn here, not Bear, talking to her about train tracks and life before the Circus.

The fire breather had moved to kneel within the dusty, withered plants that grew determined next to the train tracks, defying the sun that burnt their bulbs to a crisp. Exposed to the elements like this, the flowers Bear was collecting were small and pitiful and bland in color: mostly white and off-lavender. Still, Bear plucked them with careful calculation until he had a bouquet of some sort. He let Atlanta sniff, and then glanced over his shoulder to meet Callie's confused gaze.

"They're for Quinn," Bear explained around his cigarette. "Figured she might want something other than bland hospital walls to look at, you know?"

"Do you even know if she's alive?" Callie snapped. When Bear didn't respond, she continued just as aggressively. "And if she is alive, she'll probably never walk again – she'll definitely never perform again. What kind of life is that, Bear, for anyone? Let alone a *circus performer*."

Bear was glaring at her now. "I thought you knew better than to base one's worth only by what they contribute to the fucking Circus."

Callie snorted. "Do you see the irony in you saying that, of all people?"

Bear's entire body went rigid; Callie struck a nerve. For perhaps the first time in front of company, Bear brought his lighter up to the end of his cigarette and lit it. Thin wisps of smoke danced out of his open mouth, twisting and dispersing in the gentle breeze. Stray bright red hairs followed their pattern. He didn't speak as he sucked it down to a nub held between two fingertips, the lingering heat just a centimeter away from burning his lips and adding to the many abrasions already scoring the soft skin around his mouth.

When the first one was gone, Bear stuck another one in his mouth and sparked it up; he remained knelt amongst the weeds, which framed his tense body like a floral casing. He could've been stuck up on a wall somewhere in some forgotten about hallway of an art gallery, and people would stroll right by him on their way to the paintings that caught their eye. This smoke lasted a bit longer than the last one. A third one was lit, and finally he spoke again.

"I'm worthy outside of my craft," Bear said, although there was a tinge to his tone that showed he didn't believe it himself. It disappeared when he steered the conversation away from himself: "And so are you, and so is Quinn." He stood, holding his cigarette in one hand and Quinn's bouquet in the other. "And nothing gets better through becoming cynical."

Callie watched him stuff the flowers into his back pocket, all the care and attentiveness sucked out like the last of the tobacco leaves in his cigarettes. "So, how does it?"

Bear shrugged. "I don't know. Try running away from home and joining a circus."

Trying to hide the smile that was tugging at the corner of her mouth, Callie shifted her attention to Atlanta sitting sphinx like on the tracks, watching the wooded glen beyond them in silence. There was something about that dog that made Callie want to follow her into the forest and sit amongst the trees, guarded by a loyal companion, safe to close her eyes and feel nothing in every direction. But she was stuck here in the wide-open wound that the track tracks created through the trees.

Callie thought about the day of her mother's funeral; the sun was out and it was sixty degrees in Ohio. In her mind, funerals always happened on rainy days. Your black clothing would be soaked through and heavy, you could blame your runny make up on the downpour; when it's sunny, everyone knows you've been crying. That was the last time she's felt as exposed as she did on the rails. It may as well have been her on the morgue table, her open casket funeral, her face on a poster board, displayed in front of a weeping crowd.

But Bear was not her widowed father, and Bear wasn't her distant relatives looking upon her from a distance, just sympathetic enough to cry for her, but not enough to reach out to her.

Bear's hand skimmed her shoulder, asking for permission. Callie's body moved before her brain could process what was happening and she leaned into it, allowing herself the silent gesture of comfort she so badly craved without knowing it. The aroma of gasoline crept up on her nose and burnt the roof of her mouth; she must've made a face, because Bear backed away in an instant.

As Callie opened her mouth to apologize, something different came out: "Teach me."

Bear blinked, his face a perfect picture of confusion. "What?"

"Teach me." Callie's gaze had drifted south to where the torches were hanging by his belt loops. "I'm tired of just being an acrobat. I want to learn fire."

"Did you fall, too? Knock a few screws loose?"

"Come on, Bear. I'm going to try and learn anyway, might as well be taught by the best," Callie reasoned, taking a step closer to him. He matched her with a step back. "You know, to limit the chance of me burning my face off."

Atlanta had stood now, starting to circle Bear slowly, having sensed her owner's distress. "Cut that shit out, Callie," Bear grumbled, and his dog sat between his legs; a finger blackened by ash jabbed towards his ugly mouth. "Even if you're good at it, you're going to burn your face off."

Since joining the Circus about eight months ago, just four months after her mother lost her battle with cancer, Callie had been taught through social cues to not stare at Bear's mouth. It was easy to abide by – no one *wanted* to – but unavoidable when the fire breather spoke to you or sat across from you.

Those blisters, old and new, dried and leaking, were a haunting reminder of the physical toll this life style took on their bodies. They were different than the aching joints and pulled muscles of acrobats or Strongmen: they were visible, *raw*, and staring defiantly back at Callie now.

With every act, there was more than one of them performing it. Callie and Quinn alongside other duos of aerialists, Wes and Judas – the trapeze brothers, Andreas and the other Strongmen, Maggie and her band of clowns, pairs of knife throwers and swords swallowers alike. Even Roy had assistance as a Ringleader in Dee, who came up with him from the earlier days of the Circus.

But Bear was their only fire breather and the only one who bore the marks to prove it, the only one who reeked of gasoline, the only one who stood alone on stage. It was the solo act, the individuality he possessed, that set him apart from other performers worldwide. He did not dress in flashy costumes, he did not use magic or illusion to make him seem better than he was: everything he did was his own, which made him even more phenomenal.

Callie wasn't after the image, she was after a sense of borrowed power, something that could make her feel in control of her own life again. Fire was the key.

"Okay," She agreed, still determined, "then I'll burn my face off."

Bear blinked in surprise. "No," he repeated, "you won't. Besides, you'll slow me down."

That hurt more than anything else he had said.

The fire breather snubbed out his last cigarette and laid a heavy hand on the top of Atlanta's head, scratching behind her ears as she lifted her chin to stare adoringly up at him. The Shepherd had battle scars of her own that marked up her pretty face; Callie had never asked how she got them. She knew Atlanta and Bear met in the Army and got discharged for medical reasons. She could figure the rest out.

Callie deflated and tried not to let Bear hear the desperation in her voice, "Please," she whispered, "I can't do the acrobatics show alone."

While that wasn't true, and there were other acrobat duos she could join, there was a weight to the way she said it that must've resonated with Bear. He

looked up from his dog and into Callie's eyes, searching
for something she couldn't figure out; a long, heavy
moment passed, dragging on like the train for miles and
miles, no caboose in sight.

But finally, when he spoke, his rough voice was
hinted with honest sympathy.

"I just don't want you to get hurt."

"I'm here," Callie pressed, "it's inevitable."

"I know."

The snap of a chord, the slick feeling of fingers
slipping from her own, the flash of falling glitter: Callie's
breath caught in her throat. She knew she was asking a
lot, but she knew he was the right person to ask.

"You want to be known, right?" Callie continued,
figuring she'd aim low with her persuasion. Bear's face
changed. "What better way than to take on an apprentice
who can keep your legacy alive when you inevitably..."
Die? She couldn't picture him retiring. "I might slow you
down at first, but think about the potential!"

Bear picked at a scab.

Callie wished she could read that beautiful mind.
Before today, she hardly talked to Bear. In passing, he
was friendly and supportive, and watched their shows
whenever he could. But he kept a wall up

"I'll teach you," he said, and a slow, lopsided smile
crept up his face. "I bet you chicken out first day,
anyway."

Callie couldn't even respond at first, taken aback by
his agreement *and* his sudden change in tone, and then
she realized: he was antagonizing her on purpose, daring
her onward. This was a fire breather's first test. She
matched his coy smile, sticking her hand out.

"I bet I don't."

Bear's handshake was rough and calloused, and smelt like gasoline.

* * *

<u>MAGNOLIA</u>

Maggie woke later into the morning than she ever had, and she probably would've slept more had she not become aware of how hot she was getting under all of their blankets. The sun beat through the heavy black out curtains that absorbed all the heat and spit it back out on Maggie three times hotter. She sat up, feeling a thin layer of sweat underneath her clothes, and threw the covers off. She glanced around the tiny trailer. Still no Bear.

Determined to take her mind off of the incident last night Maggie stuck closely to their normal morning routine: shower, a cup of tea, and line up her face paints for the show tonight, ten minutes of stretching and meditation. She was stuck on that last one, unable to clear her mind enough to properly meditate, so she found herself sitting crisscross on the floor staring blankly at her tea until it turned lukewarm and undesirable. Like her expectations for the day, she poured it down the drain.

"Okay," Maggie said to the framed picture of her, Bear, and Atlanta that was sitting on their bookshelf. "Next step."

She pulled off her PJs and threw on a pair of black jeans and a black t-shirt, tying a light jacket around her waist just in case it was cooler out than she thought. The door squealed again when Maggie pushed it open and she grimaced. Making a mental note to track down a carnie for some oil, she stepped out into the day, one hand up to block the initial sunlight from blinding her.

The performers were still stowed away in their beds, but the ground workers were busy bees per usual. Maggie peered at their faces for a specific one as they hurried past her; she spotted him by the generators shoving a Twinkie in his mouth. He looked up as she approached.

"Good morning, Magnolia."

"Hey, Cody," Maggie greeted, politely declining his offer for a bite. "Do you have any grease for our trailer door? It's protesting something fierce."

"You got it, honey bee." Cody shoved wiped his mouth off on the back of his hand and brushed the crumbs off of his chest before continuing. "By the way, Roy wanted you to go see him whenever you can."

Maggie frowned. "Why?"

Cody said, "I don't know, he wasn't mad or upset or anything though. Tell you what, I'll go get that grease for you and leave it by your trailer."

"Thanks, Cody."

The sunlight felt good against Maggie's bare arms as she made her way across the Fairgrounds, taking her time on her way to Roy's office. It was the biggest trailer on campus because it doubled as his living quarters, although he frequently gave up his bed to his staff if they needed it. He was a good man, far better than the Ringleaders before him from the stories Maggie heard. Roy spent decades trying to make up for the mistreatment of Circus performers and workers that was the norm for so long, both in other Circuses and his own when his father or uncles reigned before him.

Maggie knew it took a lot of guts to be a good person in this industry, and the financial blow he suffered would've been enough to change a lesser man's mind. To Roy, it was worth it to cut out animal acts and eliminate the idea of "sideshows" that exploit disabilities. His predecessors wholeheartedly disagreed.

The Ringleader was outside when Maggie approached, sitting on the steps of his trailer and whittling the end of a long stick. He was dressed in normal clothes – jeans and a band t-shirt – and was so focused on his task that he didn't notice Maggie until she greeted him with a quiet hello.

"Ah, Magnolia," Roy said, squinting up at her. "How are you today, my dear?"

"Good," She was nonchalant with her response. "Cody said you were looking for me?"

"Yes." He put down the knife and wood and reached into his back pocket. "A letter came in for you."

Maggie's eyebrows shot up in surprise. "A letter?"

Roy shrugged and handed it to her, then shifted over so she could plop down next to him. The envelope was official-looking although crumpled around the corners from being in Roy's pocket. Her name was written on the front with flowing calligraphy; there was a return address – some law firm – but no mailing one, as the Circus didn't even *have* an address.

"Someone dropped it off on one of the barkers this morning," Roy said as if he could read her mind. "Some fancy looking dude in a suit. Travis said he looked like a tool."

Maggie couldn't help but laugh. An image of a put together man in a three-piece handing off such a formal piece of mail to one of their grease-stained, laid back ground workers was pleasing to her. She just hoped this one was less creepy than some she'd received in the past. It wasn't terribly uncommon for them to get letters from people following shows: Bear got a lot from star struck kids, Magnolia from boys (or girls) asking about her love life, Wes and Judas got their fair share. But this one seemed different. This one seemed planned. Waiting for her.

She didn't want to open it yet, so she put it down on the step next to her and tilted her chin towards Roy's project that he had resumed. Judging by the fresh and old cuts on his fingers, he wasn't very good at it.

"It's for Quinn," Roy explained. "I have to go to the hospital later. I thought maybe I could carve out a dolphin. It seemed easy enough."

At that point, it was an indistinguishable blob, but it was coming along.

"It looks good so far." Maggie smiled. "She'll love it."

Roy shook his head but got back to work, speaking again without looking up. "I saw Bear leaving with Callie."

"He wanted to talk with her."

"You didn't go?"

"I was asleep. Unfortunately, I couldn't convince Bear to do the same."

"Right."

They fizzled off into a comfortable silence, accompanied only by the gentle scratching of knife against wood. Enticed by the sun light, performers were starting to peek out of their trailers and join each other out on the midway. Dee and Judas were out by the food vendors, helping the cooks make enough pancakes to feed an entire army (or Circus), while Wes stretched out in a sunspot next to them. Everyone waved to Maggie and Roy as they passed, following the smell of buttermilk and maple syrup, and Maggie's own belly started to rumble.

She waited patiently by Roy's side while he carved that dolphin, watching the distant entrance to the Fairgrounds for a familiar head of bright red hair. The urge to read the letter was growing stronger as she lingered, so she picked it back up and held it in her open palm, tracing her own name with the tip of her finger. Roy glanced up at the sound of her ripping it open with little to no care for the precision it was stamped down with.

Maggie read it closely, growing more and more uneasy as she went. It became more evident what it was with each handwritten word. When she got to the end, her appetite was gone completely, and she could damn near feel the rotation of the Earth beneath her. Roy nudged her, voice frantic with concern.

"Hey, you okay?" He didn't reach for the letter and instead placed a hand on her forearm, coaxing out a respond. "What is it?"

She handed it to him, desperate to get it out of her own hands. "It's from the judge that sentenced my father."

WHAT THEY CALL YOU IS NOT YOUR NAME

<u>BEAR</u>

"I thought you were afraid of the fire show?" Bear asked Callie. They were heading back to the Circus at a slower pace than when they left it, taking their time up the shady dirt road that led to the entrance.

Callie shrugged. "Quinn was, mostly. I always wanted to watch you but I didn't want to leave her alone or make her feel bad about being afraid."

She kicked a particularly large stone that was in her way; it sailed into the woods and Atlanta, ball driven as hell, went chasing after it. Bear called her back and she turned on a dime, trotting happily back to his side with her tongue lolling out and her tail wagging.

Bear greeted her with a scratch behind her ears. "I don't think she liked being in the Army," He said, a sly attempt at changing the subject away from Quinn just in case. "I think it was too much death for her."

Callie glanced sideways at him. "Do you think she knew what was going on?"

"Of course." Bear watched his dog trot on ahead of them. "I think she was more sensitive to it than I was."

"Why'd you two have to leave?" Callie asked, sounding cautious. He smiled at her to reassure her he didn't mind talking about it.

"See these?" Bear gestured to the ugly scars that adorned the left side of his face, from the sharp corner of his jaw line, up to his ear, and down to his collarbone. "I got them when I was younger, and it affected my hearing in this ear. Army made it worse 'til I was pretty much deaf in it, so they kicked me." He glanced down at his dog. "Her original handler died in combat and she became bonded to me."

"Did she see him die?" When Bear didn't answer, Callie's bottom lip jutted out. "She got to leave with you."

"Where I go, she goes. And vice versa."

They shifted back into a peaceful silence. The sun was taking its time climbing up in the sky, and the trees around them were sporting newly blossomed bright green leaves that went translucent in the sunshine. Bear always had a soft spot for springtime: it was a returning reminder that life starts over and rebuilds itself, even after the fiercest winters.

They rounded the final bend in the dirt road and the arch that marked the entrance to the Fairgrounds game into view. A handful of barkers were up front with a carnie, listening intently as he gave them specific instructions. In their hand were stacks of fliers, some to hang up on poles or on bulletins, others to shove under the noses of people who dared step to close. Bear admired their tenacity. Cody, one of the head carnies, seemed to not be totally impressed by it.

"Listen, Ed," The tall boy was saying, leaning in to one of the smaller barkers until their noses were almost touching. "You just gotta throw 'em at people. Drop them and run. Hell, throw 'em on the ground! People hate littering, they'll pick it up."

"That's a solid plan," Bear greeted as they approached, unable to hide the biting smile on his face. "Let me know how it works out, Eddy."

Cody smirked as they grabbed each other's hands and half-hugged. "Hey, just trying to make sure as many people as possible see that handsome face of yours."

Bear took a few fliers from Ed, fingering through them one by one. All but a select few had a picture of his face plastered with poorly photo shopped fire and big, block letters announcing: **"THE WORLD'S GREATEST FIRE BREATHER"**. Bear looked at them for a fleeting second before handing them back to the barker, nose scrunched in distaste.

"Am I the only one who works here?"

"According to them–" Cody lit a cigarette and waved Ed and the rest of the barkers off to town, "– yes, you are."

Bear looked at Callie, who was trying not to smile, and rolled his eyes. He beckoned her onward, but Cody called after them as an afterthought.

"Hey, you might want to go find Maggie."

"What?" Bear asked.

Cody shrugged, taking a long drag of his smoke before answering. "I dunno. Roy wanted to see her and I haven't heard from her in'a few hours."

Without waiting for him to continue, Bear was heading back toward the trailers at a jog, weaving around ground workers who cursed him out. Callie kept pace with him while Atlanta sped far ahead, no doubt reaching Maggie several minutes before Bear could.

During the day the Grounds were hauntingly desolate. Even in the brightness of mid-morning, everything was empty and still: the skeleton of a once-mighty carnival. It was a safe place, but only for those who were brave enough to scratch beneath the surface of its outer layer. Bear could sometimes imagine being left to die here, his body gutted and stuffed into some taxidermy oddity for people to point and gawk at, to argue over if he were once a real being or just a mannequin. They got rid of pickled punks a while ago, but they still haunted him.

The aroma of bacon and pancakes floating through the air momentarily threw him.

Bear slowed down just as he made it to the performers' common area, where Dee and Judas were standing behind a huge griddle with beaming smiles on their faces. Stacks of pancakes teetered on flimsy paper plates and piles of bacon left puddles of grease on napkins; Atlanta had skidded to a halt with her nose inches away from one, and even from a distance Bear could see the string of drool coming from her mouth.

The fire pit had been lit and grey smoke was drifting up towards the blue bird sky, and sitting beside it with a mug of tea in her hand was a very subdued-looking Maggie. Bear ignored the hunger pains that gnawed at his belly and went straight for her. Callie stayed by the pancakes.

"Hey," Bear murmured, sinking to his knees next to her camp chair. He nodded his head towards her mug. "Do you need that warmed up?"

Maggie's face brightened when she saw him. "Hey, you! No, it's okay." Her happiness seemed forced, and she was an exceptional actress. Bear frowned but didn't push it. Whatever was bothering her, she'd talk when she was comfortable. "Are you hungry?" She asked, and then continued before he could respond. "Don't answer that. Of course, you are."

Under Maggie's watchful eyes, Bear filled a plate with food and far too much maple syrup for his own good, cackling evilly as he poured it until Dee chastised him sharply. Maggie got her own (smaller) plate of food and they joined Wes and Callie at one of the far picnic tables. The trapeze artist had a deck of playing cards out that were getting sticky with syrup and was teaching the younger performer how to play Rummy.

With the sun warming his back, alongside the gentle cadence of Wes and Callie going back and forth, and now his fully belly, the affects of skipping a few hours of sleep were rapidly catching up to Bear. He rested his head on Maggie's shoulder and was prepared to let himself drift off when the background noise cut off abruptly. He shot his head up and turned, seeing Roy standing with all eyes on him next to the fire pit.

No one spoke. They were waiting on their Ringleader.

Roy scanned the crowd as if seeking someone specific out, and when his eyes landed on Callie, Bear knew what was going on. He felt more exhausted than ever.

"I'm going to the hospital to see Quinn," Roy announced, tearing his eyes away from Callie, who sucked in a breath. "When I return, I'll gather us all together before the show and tell you everything, okay?" He sighed and shook his head, his fingers pinching the bridge of his nose. "I hate that the show must go on in these instances, but I know you all need it, so it will. Be well, rest up – *Barrett* – and be ready to give these guys a show, alright?"

Bear huffed, annoyed at the call out.

Maggie tugged on Bear's arm as their boss turned and walked away. "Come on, you know he's right."

"You need to sleep," Wes agreed.

Callie stayed silent.

Bear knew it wasn't worth it to argue because he didn't have the energy to. He stood, said goodbyes to his companions, and called for his dog that was still begging for bacon scraps. Atlanta pressed against his legs as he dragged them towards their trailer. He noted offhandedly that the door didn't squeal when he opened it.

He flopped face down on the bed, inhaling the comforting scene of Maggie and Atlanta that lingered on their sheets. The black shepherd went to pulling his boots off as if she was playing a tug of war game with his feet. She hopped on the bed afterward, curling her body against the curve of his spine, and they were both asleep in seconds.

* * *

<u>MAGNOLIA</u>

With Bear sound asleep, Maggie mulled over the letter under the Big Top. Beneath its towering ceiling, she felt small and meaningless, an ant in the middle of a sand box: it put things into perspective. She sat crisscross on the hard-packed stage floor; the letter was placed neatly in front of her.

Roy knew why her father got arrested, as did Bear and Dee, but no one else. They just knew that his incarceration left her alone with an abusive mother that drove her so crazy that she ran away to a Circus the second she turned eighteen. It wasn't a unique story, several of her comrades shared a similar one. It wasn't noble like Bear, or a life she was born into like Wes and Judas. She just had to get away.

Her new friends were quick to assure her that getting away was reason enough for seeking out refuge here. While they all had heavier baggage and nowhere else to turn, Maggie had just been feeling impulsive and defiant against her mother.

Bear's calm words of validation echoed on the edges of her subconscious: "*We're all trying to get away.*"

Away from all talk of her father, of the murder, of her uncle, of the... Maggie couldn't even bring herself to say it. That fucking *r* word. You say it and you either get an overwhelming amount of doting sympathy, or you get the rare sour apple that jabs an accusatory finger at your chest and sneers, "*Well, what were you wearing?*"

What was she wearing? She couldn't even fully remember. Something appropriate for an eleven-year-old girl, no doubt.

She knew why her father had to be given a life sentence. Maggie grew to understand it. She perfected the art of burying it deep down, but it was always there, like the itching of a new tattoo. It took a few long, very angry years, but she learned how to accept and forget about it – and now the judge who made the final call had contacted her and was asking to take her out for breakfast to "explain some things".

Maggie glared at the letter on the ground in front of her like it might blow up on her.

"Oh, shit, sorry. I didn't know anyone was in here."

The voice ripped Maggie out of her intense focus enough to startle her into jumping. She whipped her head around to see Wes powdering chalk on his hands, already in his show time get-up. Maggie blinked in confusion.

The acrobat shrugged. "Was looking for extra practice time. Pointless, anyway, 'cause Roy's back and everyone's gonna be flooding in here in a second."

Maggie heeded his warning and stood, brushing off the dust on the back of her pants and stuffing the letter into the pocket of the jean jacket she was wearing. Wes was watching her with some level of interest, and she praised whatever higher power when performers started filing in and he lost his window of opportunity to question her.

Bear was at the head of the group with Atlanta and Callie, rubbing sleep from his eyes and blinking warily in the low light of the tent. Workers of all trade followed the performers in and they all climbed up onto the bleachers, sticking together in one huddled mass with their heads bent low. Maggie and Wes joined Bear and Callie in sitting silently until Roy and Dee took up the rear, and all hushed voices ceased.

The two Ringleaders stood in the center of the stage, a half-halo of their loyal performers surrounding them like an orchestra without instruments.

Roy laughed dryly to start himself off. "I hope one day I can stand in front of all of you and announce that we've all won the lottery and I'm moving this operation to Costa Rica for good. Maybe someday." A chorus of chuckles followed. The Ringleader continued more seriously. "I love and respect you all, you're my pride and joy and my reason for living, so I'm going to give it to you as straight as I got it." He paused, letting his words sink in. Callie whimpered next to Maggie. "Quinn is alive, and was chipper as always when she saw me. You'd think it's been weeks since I saw her, not hours."

A collective sigh of relief came from the crowd like a single exhaled breath, and a voice called out from behind Maggie: "So she's going to be okay?"

Roy's mouth was a straight line. "She's alive," he repeated, "but her spine is shattered. She's paralyzed from the waist down. Not to mention a concussion and a broken arm. But, she's alive." He must've heard Callie swallow a sob because he turned in their direction with a broken expression on his greying face. "Her spirits are up, despite everything. We have to continue on the same, it's what she wants. We're extending our stay in New Hampshire for a few more weeks, just until she can be admitted and we can figure out what to do."

Wes spoke up. "She's going to keep traveling with us?"

Roy met his eyes sternly. "It's what she wants. She's still a member of this Circus."

There was a terrifying break in conversation where Maggie feared Wes might say something completely out of pocket. It passed, thankfully, and the acrobat tipped his head back to the ceiling. Bear was quiet and still as a statue.

Roy calculated their faces a minute longer, as if daring anyone else to speak up. When no one did, he started towards the exit with Dee, pausing to glance back. "Magnolia, Bear," He said, and they both straightened to attention. "Give me an hour, then meet me in my trailer. I think we need help with something."

Although the Circus wouldn't be open for another forty-five minutes, there was already a growing line up people purchasing tickets when Maggie and Bear slipped out of their trailer. They were decked out in everything but their face makeup, which Maggie was hesitant to slap on too soon.

It was difficult to navigate around the Fairgrounds at this hour. Everyone was outside their trailers tossing each other around or trying to find a piece of flat ground to stretch out. Marijuana smoke hung heavy in the air and the barkers, worn out from a long day of gathering the impatient crowds out front, were the culprits.

She followed Bear into Roy's trailer, careful not to let the door slam shut. A gentle click, and they could hear soft spoken voices coming from the office; Bear rapped his knuckles against the wall to alert Roy of their arrival.

"Come in!" Came his shout.

Bear guided Maggie with a hand on the small of her back, equal parts politeness, protection, and anxiety. Atlanta slipped ahead of them to make it into the room first and they followed her closely, just incase the newcomer wasn't a fan of strange dogs running up to lick their face - especially one as intimidating looking as Atlanta.

But the Shepherd had stopped short in the doorway, body stiff and head cocked to one side, as if confused about what she was looking at. Maggie traced her line of sight and had to bite back an involuntary sharp breath of surprise.

The boy could not have been older than some of the younger performers, anywhere between fifteen and seventeen, yet his face was completely covered by long, hazelnut colored hair. You could see his lips, the outline of the ridge of his nose, and one brown eye, and one blue eye. He was hunched in a chair, staring at Atlanta with eyes blown wide in fear, accompanied by a tall man standing on one side of him, and Dee kneeling on the ground a few feet away. Roy was in his chair behind his desk.

"Atlanta, easy." Bear stepped up without missing a beat, seemingly oblivious to the uniqueness of the child in front of him. At his command, Atlanta melted into her true form: tail wagging, ears back, nose forward as she stepped up to her new friend.

Dee smiled and wrapped one arm around the neck of the Shepherd, accepting a plethora of kisses from her wet tongue. "This is Atlanta," She said to the boy. "Our favorite member of the Circus." Despite how badly Atlanta was begging for love, he did not reach out to her. Dee continued. "And those are her parents, Magnolia and Bear."

Maggie smiled and took a few paces forward, extending her hand. "It's a pleasure to meet you, what's your name?"

The child did not answer, his older companion did, in a tone that made Maggie's blood boil. "They call him The Dog Boy."

Before Maggie could process where he was, Bear was closing in on the guy, but addressed the boy with a calm, even voice. "What they call you, is not your name." He stopped moving when the man's back thumped against the wall and he took a nervous gulp, and then in an instant the nerves on his face turned sour. Bear was a mere inch from him, and the wafting aroma of gasoline hit Maggie at the same time. The boy did not flinch at it.

The boy looked a bit taken aback by Bear's readiness to come to his defense and the kindness Maggie was speaking to him with. Her heart shattered. She knew she could barely imagine the full extent of bullying and name calling and mistreatment he must've suffered, even from this adult in his life. Straining to avoid showing the rage that was overtaking her in effort to not startle him more, she turned back to the boy.

Maggie asked again, quieter now, kneeling down in front of him. "What's your name?"

Perhaps feeling safer to answer now that Bear had the man literally backed into a wall, the child spoke so quietly Maggie barely heard. "Paris."

She smiled. "Handsome prince."

"What?" Bear glanced her way, confused.

Maggie looked up at him. "Paris. The name means 'handsome prince'." She turned back to Paris and reached for his hand. They were covered in hair except for his palms, and he did not pull them away when she placed hers on top of his like she expected. She gave a gentle squeeze. "I think it's very fitting."

Satisfied by the man's lack of snark, Bear had come to Maggie's side but stayed standing. Maggie noted that Dee had joined Roy at his desk and they were both watching silently, and the reason behind them asking for her and Bear became evident.

Bear, because this asshole needed someone to bounce him, and Maggie, because while the fire eater was standing guard, she could get Paris to talk.

It worked. Smart duo.

"So, what can you do?" Bear asked, hands on his hips and dog between his knees. She was panting and looking expectantly up at her owner, ready for any command.

The man spoke for the boy, again. "What can he *do*?"

"Yeah," Bear said. "What can he do? Roy tells me y'all want him to join the Circus - what can he do?"

"You're kidding, right? Have you seen him?"

Bear rounded on the guy again, Atlanta following his movements like a puppet attached to strings. They flowed like a single entity. It was scary to even witness.

"Who the fuck *are* you?" Bear hissed in the man's face, muscles bulging and teeth clenched.

"Mr. Sweeney. Headmaster at the orphanage –" The man attempted to snap back. He had shoved his finger against Bear's chest and Atlanta growled low and long, but by the time he registered the mistake he made, Bear grabbed his wrist and twisted downward, pulling out a sharp yelp of pain from Sweeney's throat. He stole his arm back and rubbed the stinging skin that was already a bright angry pink.

"Don't touch the merchandise," The fire breather snarked, "And I'm insulted that you think we just accept anyone here, regardless of talent, based off of something as shallow and insulting as looks." Bear stepped back again. Atlanta stayed put, frozen in the classic three-point stack of a German Shepherd.

"I agree." Roy rose from his seat and broke his silence. "Mr. Sweeney, how about you step out for a moment. I'd like to speak with Paris alone and understand what he wants to do." When Sweeney hesitated, looking like he might argue, Roy cut in: "If you'd like, Atlanta here can follow you and keep you company?"

The man shot the Shepherd an anxious glance and left without a further fight. Dee slammed the door behind him.

"Ugh," The woman said, wiping her hands off on her shirt like his presence had dirtied them. "What a waste of oxygen."

No one spoke. Maggie's brain was still trying to catch up and process the reeling events of the past minute and a half; Bear was fuming, Roy looked like he was contemplating something as he scratched the patchy five o'clock shadow on his chin, and Paris appeared to be shell-shocked.

Trying to gage his next action, Maggie kept her eyes on Roy. A few Ringleaders ago, Paris would join the Circus only to be deemed the same life of humility he was trying to escape from. His face would replace Bear's on every flier, he'd be stuffed in a cage and told to bark and act feral towards the people sick enough to humor the money-hungry ploy.

But this was Roy, and Roy looked so, so sad.

His next words were straight out of Maggie's expectations. "I know what Sweeney thought I would do to you." Roy didn't continue until Paris glanced up from his hands in his lap and into his cornflower blue eyes. "The olden days of the Circus industry would be unnecessarily cruel to you. But these are not those days, and those were not my Circus."

Bear had calmed down and was kneeling with one arm around Atlanta's shoulders and his face buried in her neck. Dee joined Maggie on the floor next to Paris.

Roy went on: "My first priority is giving kids, young adults, *anyone* sanctuary from a life they can no longer live in. That's first and foremost what this place is about. If you decide your passion lies in stage acts, and the bright and colorful costumes and make up tugs at your heart, then you are more than welcome to apprentice. If you have a nasty bug of stage fright but still wish to pull your weight, we always need extra hands on the carnie or barker team. And if you just need a roof over your head, we'll find an empty bed and you can travel with us for as long as you like, free of charge or expectation."

The boy's mouth was slightly agape as he took in Roy's offer. His gaze went from Roy, to the Shepherd and fire breather, to Dee and Maggie as bookends on either side of him. Those heterochromatic eyes started to water and his bottom lip quivered. Bear stood and let Atlanta go and she was at his side in half a second, nuzzling Paris' hands until he succumbed to her attempts at comforting. Mimicking Bear, Paris wrapped her up in his arms, her front paws up on his knees, and hugged the dog in silence for several minutes.

Finally, just when Maggie was starting to worry about being late for the Circus' open, Paris spoke.

His voice was wet and shaky, but louder than when he uttered his name. "You guys are so much nicer than people expect you to be."

Much to Paris' surprise, and admittedly everyone else's in the room, a sharp laugh came from Bear in the corner. All eyes went to him, pleasantly shocked to hear him laugh.

"You haven't met Wes yet," Bear said, shooting the boy a wink. Paris blinked slowly than started to laugh, catching the humorous note in Bear's rough drawl.

Maggie stole Paris' attention back by reaching for his hands again. "The Circus is opening soon. You can watch everyone perform, see if you get inspired!"

Dee nodded. "We'll find you our own private corner to sit in. No one will even know you're there."

Roy stood from his desk and threw an arm around Bear's shoulders. The fire breather fake fought the embrace for a second and then seeped into it, allowing his Ringleader to ruffle the loose strands of hair that found their way out of his braid. Magnolia and Dee rose to their feet too and Atlanta dropped back down to all fours, striding loyally back to her owner and walking circles around Bear and Roy's legs.

They looked like a perfect postcard for the Circus.

"You know," Maggie said gently, "I spent some time in the system, too." And she had: her mother disappeared on a bender for many weeks and when the school found out, they shoved her in a girls' home until Mama Mendoza pitched a fit and got her back.

Maggie never understood that. Her entire life, her mother acted like she wanted her gone, but when she was finally somewhere else the woman acted like someone had stolen her property.

For his sake, she hoped Paris' parents were dead. Ending up in the system as a last case scenario was better than what the reality was: he had been dumped – abandoned and left to navigate the world wondering why he wasn't good enough. Not here, she wanted to promise him. Here there are no grey walls and tasteless meals. There is love and colors and a bed of your own, and people who will love you with an intensity you've never felt before.

A tinge of hopefulness snuck into his voice as Roy asked: "So, what do you say?"

Paris looked more comfortable, the smallest ghost of a smile hiding beneath the overgrown mustache curtaining his lips. He looked at Maggie when he nodded, just a barely-there tilt of his head.

Maggie smiled proudly and declared: "Welcome to the Circus."

JUDGE, JURY, CLOWN

<u>BEAR</u>

The first day Bear ever met Maggie, they escaped the rambunctious environment of the post-show Circus and snuck into town to a 24/7 diner. The Circus had set up just a few towns over from her home city in New

Jersey, so she knew where to go and which side streets were the best short cuts.

He saw her for the first time at a gas station in Jersey, sucking down the last cigarette in a pack. And then she found him again, ember green eyes watching him from the bleachers. Bear had always felt watched – it wasn't until her that he finally felt *seen.*

So, he gave his dog to Roy for the night and followed this strange girl through alleys and over bridges that crossed rushing rivers. Muscles screamed for rest, gasoline-stung mouth begged for toothpaste, but Bear didn't listen to anything except the girl's lilac flower voice.

Bear never cared much for girls. He didn't care much for sex at all, but he dabbled with people of many genders. Any encounter was initiated by someone else sliding their hand up his thigh, whispering in his ear about how they love the smell of gas. He complied because it was easy to.

This was easier.

Maggie wasn't a *girl;* she was something else entirely to him. Their friendship was brand new and unsure on its feet like a newborn filly, yet somehow Bear felt as though he knew her and had been searching for her.

Illuminated by the bright neon open sign, Magnolia held the door for Bear with a daring grin. He brushed past her into the air conditioning.

They were seated at a booth near the back by the big bay windows, two of the few patrons there that late.

"I ran away," Maggie had said. There was a mischievous glint in her eye. Bear would come to find out that it wasn't really a truth, and it wasn't necessarily a lie.

Bear raised an eyebrow over the rim of his coffee mug. Back then, the patches of blisters on his mouth were just forming and he could stand to drink hot coffee. He leaned forward; maple syrup was on his fingers and the sleeve of his denim jacket trailed in his left-over waffles.

"Are your parents looking for you?" For comedic affect, Bear glanced warily out the window into the night, as if sirens were going to go off moments before the building was surrounded by cops demanding Maggie to walk out with her hands up.

Maggie tipped her head back and laughed. "Definitely not."

At this, Bear flashed her one of his crooked-teeth smiles. The aroma of gasoline hadn't yet started following him around like a dark rain cloud, and he could get into people's personal bubbles without receiving a look of disgust. The girl across from him, fresh out of her mother's home with a black eye and a cut over her cupid's bow, mirrored his smirk, those green eyes piercing with teenage defiance.

She sent shivers down his spine and his heart thumped so powerfully for the first time ever, like the epicenter of an earthquake, that Bear half expected to see ripples dancing in their coffee mugs.

He didn't believe in love at first sight.

But he believes in *knowing* at first sight, whatever that means.

"You belong with us," Bear said confidently.

For the rest of his life, he would wish he had been right.

* * *

<u>MAGNOLIA</u>

The clowns always made sure to sneak into the Big Top in time for the fire show. They didn't mind missing other acts if they got caught up on the midway, but Maggie was passionate about watching Bear every night. Equal parts proud, equal parts worried.

Tonight, it was just her skipping across the Fairgrounds towards the tent. The others were preoccupied teasing a grown man who was terrified of clowns in front of his wife and kids. She would've hung around herself if not for the anxiety gnawing at her belly. Callie was with the clowns, opting not to perform tonight and instead stay far away from the Big Top. She seemed to be enjoying herself a lot so Magnolia didn't feel too bad about abandoning her.

She made sure to weave through the less crowded patches of kiosks, determined not to get too caught up with patrons that would make her late for Bear's block. She was making good time until she caught sight of the psychic tent. Her feet stopped moving as if on their own accord and she hovered a few meters away from where a short line was trailing outside waiting for Mavis. The older woman hadn't been seen since Quinn's accident, and Maggie all but forgot about the eerie way she had predicted it.

A fleeting surge of misplaced resentfulness fired up in her belly. Maggie shook herself out of it, settling on the whole situation just a freaky coincidence and a senile old lady. If it still bothered her later, she'd talk to Bear or Dee about it.

She kept on, making a quick stop at their trailer to grab Bear's ointment and a cup of shredded ice. He typically refused both after a show, too sick and in pain to even think about putting anything else near his mouth. Maggie still brought both, just in case.

The knife throwers were up when she slipped through the back of the Big Top, almost on top of Dee and Paris who were hunkered down behind some unused props. They grinned and waved, sharing a large bucket of popcorn and each sipping on their own sugary sodas that were turning their tongues blue. Maggie settled in next to them for the time being, watching the back of the throwers and their wheels.

In synchronized breaths, the crowd *oo'd* and *aah'd* and even gasped in fear when a knife got too near to someone's limbs. Paris' eyes were wide with awe and he jerked back nervously in tune with the people in the bleachers at each close call. His admiration was touching; Maggie hoped it was enough to make him consider picking up an act of his own, preferably one that wasn't completely life threatening.

Whitney, the lead knife thrower, caught Maggie's eye and winked before tossing her final blade against the spinning wheel. Her long hair had been braided into colorful box braids, red and white to match the Big Top, and her costume clung to her curves while exposing her toned midriff. The crowd cheered loudly for the group of throwers, some even raising to their feet for standing ovations, and while Whitney and her crew bowed, Roy stepped out on the stage. Carnies flooded out behind him to clear the area completely.

"Up next is a handsome face I'm sure a lot of you will recognize from the fliers." Roy was clad in his Ringleader get up, which was comedically flashy compared to the man's usual low-key way of presenting himself. A hushed sound of excitement aroused from the bleachers. Roy waited for it to settle. "The flames you are about to witness are one hundred percent real. If the smell of gasoline is bothersome to you, I recommend stepping out for this one. Please give a warm – pun intended – welcome to our fire breather: Bear!"

Maggie said hurried goodbyes to Dee and Paris and slipped around the stage to the front of the bleachers, posting up in the aisle between two sets. Costumers hardly noticed her as Bear stepped out from behind the curtains with Atlanta walking between his legs, her feet stepping high and her chin raised to stare adoringly up at her owner.

In front of a crowd, the Shepherd presented herself like a proud dressage horse.

The two of them seemed not to notice the eruption of cheers and applause, or the sudden shift in energy that zapped through the Big Top like a bolt of lightening. Atlanta was only focused on Bear, and Bear was practically salivating over the sight of his kerosene cans placed neatly in center stage for him. Roy waited until they joined him in the ring, covering the head of the microphone to whisper something in Bear's ear. One sharp nod from the fire breather and the Ringleader stepped off, catching sight of Maggie and joining her.

"Is he okay?" Maggie asked, referencing their quick exchange of words.

Roy laughed dryly. "Yeah. I just asked him not to burn us down."

Bear performed with no secrets to the crowd. It made him more authentic, and in that sense more desirable. He stepped out from around Atlanta, saying a command in German that sent the dog bounding to the right end of the stage and dropping down to her belly, ears forward and tail straight out like an ebony snake.

Bear lit his first torch and left another one plain.

After showing the audience the flame on the end of the torch, he lowered it into his mouth and touched it to his tongue, not closing his mouth to extinguish it, and pulled it back to reveal the flame alive and well in his mouth before he transferred it to the previously empty torch.

With two lit, he barked another German word and Atlanta sprung up as if on a pressure plate, crossing the arena to her owner in impressive strides. She wove in and out of his legs as he stepped, juggling the torches with expert precision.

The audience absolutely ate it up.

He embodied fire.

The flame was an extension of his being – the torch was beyond just a simple tool: it was another limb. It seemed to breathe with him, expanding and sinking in rhythm with his chest with each precious breath. Bear reveled in the danger of it – he reveled in being dangerous. When you're so accustomed to being the prey, you become drunk with power of becoming the predator.

The first time Maggie watched him work, when she was no more than a member of the audience herself, she didn't breathe for his entire block. She just watched, struck silent with anxiety and marvel alongside the entire audience as he danced and brought his soul to life through the fire. Such a special gift to be granted, she thought. To bear witness to the rawest form of one's soul.

It went on like this for his entire twenty-minute block: Bear doing various transfers, breathing out flame bursts that made him look like a dragon, or simply tossing up flames that he would catch behind his back. Atlanta assisted when allowed, doing Bear low risk tasks like fetching extra torches. They danced, spinning and weaving and she jumped through the hoops he made out of his arms. Maggie watched, chewing nervously on a fingernail. She knew Bear made up every act as he went, so there was no way for her to predict what he'd do next.

Maggie's lungs finally released when it ended. Roy stepped back out on the stage, brisker than any one before or after Bear. Atlanta, panting and happy, greeted the Ringleader with a bark and howl, but Bear looked glassy eyed and was staggering. It was if when the fire went out it took its master with it, fading in a puff of smoke.

Standing ovations and shrieking cheers, some even begging for an encore, flooded Maggie's ear drums. The trapeze artists were up next and the carnies were hurrying to clear the area of Bear's equipment.

Wes somehow appeared at Bear's side before Maggie could get her brain to move from her spot hidden among the bleachers. The boys leaned against each other, Wes cupping Bear's face and whispering something and lightly punching his chest. Bear was laughing and nodding, nuzzling into his friend's neck, allowing himself to be assisted off the stage.

Maggie met them at the stairs, kissing Atlanta between the ears and then letting Bear lean against her. She thanked Wes and wished him luck. He nodded and planted a sloppy kiss on her cheek, at the same time giving Bear and Atlanta one last pat each.

"Hey, beautiful," Maggie greeted, hugging Bear tightly. "You did so well."

"Thank you." Bear coughed, careful to do so away from Maggie so the splatters of blood went on the ground and not her.

"I brought ice," Offered Maggie, showing the cup of ice and ointment on her open palm. Bear shook his head as she expected and stumbled off behind the curtains where Dee was waiting.

The woman was ready with a bucket which Bear promptly gave everything up to, sinking to the floor against a crate full of extra folding chairs. His head lolled back against the sturdy surface and his eyes closed, his breathing shallow and slow. Atlanta curled up on his lap.

Paris was watching with concern. "Is he okay?"

"Yes," Dee said without hesitation. "Just tired. And that gasoline tastes bad, that's why he threw up."

Convinced, Paris turned back to watch the trapeze show. Dee and Maggie exchanged worried looks. Dee had been in the Circus long enough to know most fire breathers don't react that badly, but then again, Bear was not most fire breathers. He went over the top for too long to make up for the fact that it was just him alone on the stage instead of a group of fire artists.

Maggie thought about Quinn, alone and fighting for her life in a hospital, and wondered how many nights Bear had left until he joined her.

Bear slept late into the next morning for once. His body was heavy like a stone on their stiff and lumpy mattress. He didn't even shift when Maggie clambered out at dawn and threw on leggings and her father's jean jacket that she ran away in. She braided her long brown hair into pigtails, not even bothering with the baby hairs that stuck out defiantly against her hairline. Atlanta was awake, big black ears erect and expressive brown eyes peering out from around Bear's body.

Maggie stared her dog down as she pulled on her boots and tied the laces around her ankle. On a second thought, she stuck Bear's pocket knife into her sock. She stuffed a wad of cash into her bra and slipped a cigarette behind her ear like a pencil, patting herself down to ensure she had a lighter. Satisfied, she shot one last glance towards her bed. Atlanta had settled back down, but her eyes were still open and curious. Maggie blew her a kiss.

Thanks to Cody, the door didn't give her away with an obnoxious screech. The sky was still dark although the beginnings of dawn's light were beginning to creep over the horizon. Maggie glanced around the trailers, searching for any sign of life as she set off at a brisk jog. The letter in her breast pocket was burning a hole.

At the exit to the Fairgrounds, she saw the silhouette of a person lingering. While she assumed it was an early rising ground worker didn't bother reaching for the blade, her heart fluttered with brief anxiety; it wasn't until she heard Roy call out to her that she fully relaxed.

"Magnolia."

"What are you doing?" Maggie questioned, fully aware of the irony.

"Waiting for you," Roy said simply. Maggie cursed inwardly; she forgot he had also read the letter. "You're going to meet them?"

"I think so." Maggie glanced down the road where it spiraled into dark shadows. "I might lose my nerve."

"I hope you don't," Roy sighed. He was smoking a cigarette and flicked the ash off the end to punctuate his sentence. "I think you should do it."

"Is that why you were waiting for me?"

Her Ringleader nodded. She waited for him to say anything else but he just gestured down the road.

Maggie hesitated and then hugged him quickly, whispering a thank you. Roy's hand cupped the back of her head and he squeezed her tightly once and then released her. Starting off down the road, she glanced over her shoulder to see his dark outline waving before he turned and disappeared into the Fairgrounds. Maggie tried to imagine heavy metal gates slamming down behind him, blocking her from following.

No backing out now.

The letter gave her a designated diner and time to meet this person, and she stuck the address into her phone when she got to the end of the first road. She cut the time down by jogging, ignoring the way her lungs screamed for a break and her sleep-deprived brain became hazy.

New Hampshire towns were small and unimpressive, and hauntingly quiet at this hour. The Denny's was the only building that had its lights on aside from the few gas stations she passed.

Maggie stopped outside the door, bending over with her hands on her knees to catch her breath. She checked the time on her phone. Ten minutes late.

The diner was nearly empty and it was sending her back in time to her first meal with Bear. Clinging to the comforting memory, she glanced around the booths and tables. She realized she had no idea who she was looking for. The passing of time had caught up to her, and what she could remember about the trial and judge was blurred and buried deep within her amygdala.

Then, she caught sight of an older woman sitting alone in a corner, sipping on a cup of coffee and reading a book. The shape of her face, and the way she maintained a professional posture even in a Denny's at five in the morning, told Maggie all she needed to know. The woman glanced up as she approached and her eyes blew wide with shock.

"Magnolia?"

"Yeah." Maggie slid into the booth across from her without waiting for an invitation.

A waitress skipped over before they could say anything else. "Can I start you off with something to drink?" She slid a glass of water and a straw across the table.

"Just the water, please," Maggie said politely. She reached for the straw, peeling it out of the wrapped and immediately going to work on the paper, ripping it nervously, a habit Bear found quiet endearing.

"It's a pleasure to see you again," The judge sounded genuine. She was smiling. "You've grown into a gorgeous young woman."

Maggie blushed; it never got easier to accept compliments. "Thank you."

"I'm pleasantly surprised you came."

"Me, too."

"My name is Adele, by the way." She closed her book and reached for a handshake. "I'm not sure if you remembered."

Laughing nervously, Maggie accepted Adele's extended hand. "I didn't, to be honest. I don't remember a lot about any of that."

Adele pulled her hand back. The book was cover up on the table. It was a Virginia Woolfe novel that Maggie had been wanting to read herself. Good taste. The waitress, a scrawny blonde little thing, returned to top off her coffee and offer Maggie some once more. Maggie denied again and shredded more of her straw wrapper.

"I'm sorry I didn't go into much detail in my letter," Adele said when the waitress left them alone once more. "There was so much I wanted to say, but none of it felt right to say through writing. Face to face seemed far more appropriate."

And anxiety inducing. Thanks, Judge.

Maggie thought about Bear asleep in their bed and the way his hair fell across his face, and the gentle cadence of his quiet snores. The town was starting to wake up outside and Maggie remembered it was a Monday morning; headlights shown through the window behind Adele's head, illuminating the frizzy hairs that had escaped her low ponytail. Her bottom lip started quivering against her will.

"Why did you write at all?" Maggie asked, frustration manifesting into anger. She worked so hard to bury this just for it to be dug up before she was ready. The last thing she was interested in was being a pawn in some forgiveness game.

Adele took a long sip of her black coffee before setting the mug down and remaining deadpan. "He wants to see you."

Fuck my life.

"How do you–"

"I visit him often," Adele explained. "And, no, I don't do that with everyone I sentence to life in prison. He's a good man, your father. I never wanted to do this to him."

"But you did," Maggie growled. The paper straw wrapper was completely shredded now and littered the table like a snow globe had exploded.

"He murdered someone. Violently, and with intent. If he didn't plead guilty, he would've gone to death row."

Maggie sniffed, turning away to watch the servers move from table to table, from register to coffee brewer. She zoned out on the muffled, distant conversations between the few patrons around them. An older couple was walking in, holding hands and smiling while they waited to be seated. She didn't want Adele to see her cry – but she already had, hadn't she? Ten years ago.

A deep sigh, a sip of her coffee, and Adele leaned on her elbows, extending herself over the table. "As a judge, I can only throw out guilty verdicts. Many members of that jury wanted him to walk, but he *confessed*. Turned himself in. There was no trial there."

With heavy eyes, Maggie watched her sit back in her seat, back thumping against the booth cushion. There was something about that day that stuck the most vivid in her memory, and it wasn't the moment of sentencing. It was the silence. The lack of arguing amongst jurors. More than anything, she remembered how loud the quiet was.

"Will you come?" Adele asked again.

"Right now?" Maggie raised an eyebrow as she turned her attention back to their table.

"He's at Mohawk Correctional Facility in Rome, New York," Adele reached into her pocket and pulled out a pamphlet, sliding it across the table under Maggie's nose. "Its about five hours away."

A brick building surrounded by tall, barbed wire fences stared up at Maggie. The paper had a glossy finish. The name of the prison was printed in bold white letters on the front, and she flipped it over to see the visitation hours and rules.

Roy would want her to go. Bear would be worried but when she got back and explained her absence, he'd understand. He could spend his day quietly with Wes or Atlanta or Callie and she'd be back before dinner if they left now. There was an opportunity to get some life changing closure or ruin every shred of progress she'd made. Or thought she made, at least. She read somewhere about fooling yourself into believing you've healed from something when really, you've really just buried it and continue to let it quietly hurt you.

Her brain was rambling again.

Maggie realized she had been staring over Adele's shoulder out of the window, tapping her foot so hard it was trembling the table. The judge just sat silent and took occasional sips of her coffee. Maggie checked the time on her phone; it was nearing six o'clock now, and her window for making this a day trip was closing.

Involuntarily, a dry laugh escaped her, before she even processed finding it funny.

Adele raised a curious eyebrow. "What's so funny?"

Maggie waved her hand, taking a settling breath before answering. "Nothing. It was just... so easy to run away and join a Circus but so hard to run away from it for a day."

The woman across from her smiled over the brim of her coffee mug. She finished her last sip while Maggie chugged her water, then the judge threw a twenty-dollar bill on the counter and stood up. Maggie swept up the ripped-up straw wrapper, mindful of the mess she made, and stuffed in her back pocket to throw away later. Bear always loved that she did that.

"Okay," Maggie said, mostly to herself. "Let's do this."

THE DRAGON, THE ACROBAT, AND THE WOLF

BEAR

Bear woke with a start. The fragments of an already forgotten nightmare were clinging to the corners of his subconscious, ghostly bits of information that were quickly becoming nothing at all, like eye floaters after staring at the sun for too long. He tried for naught to grasp at them, to have some idea of what had plagued him while he slept. Giving up after a few frustrating moments, Bear registered Atlanta's heavy body curled up next to his head, and the empty space Maggie normally occupied.

He sat up, rubbing the sleep from his face and glancing around his empty trailer. It was late morning, later than usual, and since the air was still, he could hear jumbled voices speaking in low volume a few yards away from his trailer. His bad ear was ringing so he couldn't make out exactly what was being said, but the tone was light and not call for any concern. The haze refused to clear and Bear wished he could stomach coffee for a quick caffeine boost.

Bear glanced towards the brewer and imagined the steaming hot liquid pouring over the open lacerations in his throat. His stomach turned over.

Atlanta whined behind him, reminding him that they were late for a very important morning ritual: breakfast.

While the Shepherd wolfed down her high quality, raw mixed kibble, Bear brushed his teeth over the kitchenette sink, noting that he needed to get into town to get a new back of toothbrushes. "That'll be our day today," Bear declared to Atlanta. She looked up briefly and then went back to work on her food. "Glad you agree."

Blood and water swirled slowly into the sink in a whirl pool spiral, momentarily hypnotizing Bear where he stood. It was a struggle to breath this morning. There was a weight in his lungs like someone filled them with wet cement, and his lips were a sickly shade of blue that he'd never seen before. Bear blinked, reaching up to trace the skin around his mouth, feeling each blister like there was an answer there written in braille.

Clicking his tongue, Bear stepped away from the mirror. He shucked out of his clothes and ran the dinky trailer shower, waiting for the water to turn lukewarm before he stepped underneath the weak stream. Out of its braid, red hair fell past his shoulders, still leaking dye from the last time Maggie applied it for him. The shampoo and conditioner were almost out. Another thing added to his shopping list.

The temperature was mild from what he could tell, so Bear threw on a plain black t-shirt and his only pairs of black jeans. He tied his long hair up in a bun and called Atlanta to his side. A forgotten red rubber band sat out on their counter, catching his eye. After a moment of careful consideration, Bear slipped it onto his wrist.

The voices he had been hearing turned out to be Cody and a rag-tag looking group of newcomers that he was addressing. Cody always had a way of looking like a dick when he spoke to others, especially when he was in an authority position. The kids he was talking to all looked to be in the mid-twenties, some buff, others short and scrawny, a couple thicker set and taller.

They were called Drifters by the Circus folk: kids who were drawn to the Fairgrounds more in the day time than the nighttime. Most looked for work and a fun job that traveled, where they could smoke shitty weed and drink away from the shelter of their parents. Some, like Cody, stuck around. Most didn't last more than a few weeks.

Desperate to slip by the newcomers without being dragged into an introduction he could put off for a few more hours, Bear ducked around the back side of the neighboring trailers. He wasn't exactly looking for Maggie, but he did expect to see her in one of her normal spots. She sometimes liked to sneak out early on the rare occasion Bear slept later than her – she valued her alone time to read or draw or write poetry.

He went towards the food vendors, where the aroma of breakfast still clung stubbornly to the air. There were a few late risers who arrived just before Bear; they were settling down at picnic tables with paper plates sinking in at the middle with piles of greasy eggs and bacon.

Whitney looked up as Bear got his own hefty plate. She beckoned him when he caught her eye.

Bear plopped down next to the knife thrower, across from Andreas and Amara, a young sword swallower who spoke broken English.

"Shubh prabhat," He said to her, and to the others: "Good morning."

"Good morning, killer," Andreas greeted, flashing his straight, toothpaste-commercial-worthy smile. He redirected it down under the table, where Atlanta was hiding from the rising heat in the shade. "And good morning to you, my favorite performer."

"If she ever goes missing," Whitney said around a mouthful of eggs, "start the investigation with him." The knife thrower glanced around like she was missing something, her pretty face suddenly creased with confusion. "Hey, where's Magnolia?"

Bear shrugged. "Don't know. She wasn't in bed when I woke up, so I figured she's around somewhere."

"Off with the clowns, I presume," Andreas agreed with a soft smile.

Just as he finished, the clowns pranced by on their way towards the clown alley – no Maggie amongst their ranks. Bear refused to frown or react in anyway other than another nonchalant shrug. Instead, he changed the subject.

"So, did you guys come up with any interesting new acts for the spec?"

Whitney beamed. "Oh, yeah. My throwers and I got a whole bunch of cool stuff coming up for this next show."

Andreas turned to Bear. "Is it true you're going to take Callie as an apprentice? Never thought I'd see the day."

"She told you?" Bear frowned.

"She may be finding ways to sneak it into conversation," Whitney giggled. She put a hand on Bear's shoulder. "Don't be mad at her, she's excited – and even if she bails out after a few sessions, she's braver than any of us for trying."

"I'm not mad," Bear assured with a smile. "I'm a bit concerned Roy caught wind of it before I could tell him myself, but I can handle Roy."

"But can you handle *Dee*?" Andreas said, cheeky.

"No. She might kill me. That's a risk we'll have to take."

They all laughed and dug further into their breakfast, like the opening scene to some family-oriented sitcom.

Their friendly chatter was interrupted after a few minutes by Roy himself, who paused his brisk walk a few yards away to stare directly at Bear. The Ringmaster looked exhausted, complete with a resting scowl, and he was trailed by two strangers in suits and a very annoyed looking Dee.

"Bear!" He called, waving. "Join me, my boy."

Confused, Bear furrowed his brows. He gave Andreas the rest of his bacon, earning himself a pleased squeal, and detangled himself from the table. Bidding farewell to his friends, he trailed the group with Atlanta by his side.

The adults were talking in low voices amongst themselves as they wove through the Fairgrounds. Bear scanned the backs of the strangers' bodies in an attempt to figure out who – or what – they were, and why the hell they dared step foot on their Grounds. They had the same pretentious air about them that Dave and Greg carried, but seemed more legit than some dorky Circus agents.

One by one, they filed into Roy's office at the front of his trailer. Bear chose a chair that squeaked with each nervous tap of his foot. Atlanta sat between his knees, panting in the lack of air conditioning; though her amber eyes and huge black ears were bright and alert, the rest of her body remained lax and free of any obvious aggression.

Roy sat heavy in his desk chair. The man and woman, who introduced themselves as Bill and Rhonda, settled across from him in the mismatched chairs. Dee leaned up against the wall behind Roy's shoulder, arms folded across her chest and a frown on her face. She did not seem angry – simply inconvenienced. Valid.

Taking a swig form his flask and grimacing as it went down, Roy gestured with both hands to the desk in front of him, as if presenting a flush with no cards. "Alright. Give it to me straight."

Rhonda quirked a perfectly waxed eyebrow. "Straight? Well, Roy, judging by the information you've given us to look over, I'd say you show is on its last legs."

Bear's brain caught up.

They're financial advisors. Fuck.

Bill chimed in. "Its *been* on its last legs for years. Since – and I mean this with all due respect – you took over."

"Somehow, you've managed to keep it afloat." Rhonda flipped through a stack of papers; they were alternating speaking like actors in a rehearsed play.

"But, as we all know, circuses are a failing industry and have been for decades. Hell–" Bill wiped a bead of sweat off his beak-ish nose "–we just witnessed the decline of *Ringling*."

"If Ringling's dead," Rhonda looked up from the paper. "you're all dead. Some of you just put a raincheck on the funeral."

"Dead men walking," Bill agreed.

Roy managed to remain silent the entire time, his hands folded and pressed up against his mouth, obscuring his face enough to hide any emotion. Dee, on the other hand, was beginning to look irritated. She stepped up to the desk, resting both palms flat on its surface, and leaned forward.

"What makes you so sure we're doomed like the rest of them?" The woman asked, steady and low.

Rhonda laughed, then immediately covered her mouth with her hand like she was trying to shove it back in. "Oh, you *aren't* doomed like the rest of them. You're so much *more* doomed."

Bear felt his skin getting hot with rage; if he were able to conjure fire out of thin air, his hair would be ablaze. His fists clenched into the thick fur around Atlanta's neck, and he planted his lips on the top of her head to keep himself from speaking out. He didn't know why Roy insisted on him being here, but he knew for a fact it wasn't for that.

"Why?" Dee pushed, anger and desperation cracking her voice. "We draw crowds!"

"You do," Bill said, raising two hands. "Your issue would be an easy fix, and you might have time to fix it."

"Its the animals," Rhonda said plainly. "Circuses rely very heavily on animal acts, as well as sideshow attractions – *freaks*, if you will. Your refusal to incorporate either was your downfall."

Bill sighed as if he were sorry. "Animal and human rights activists are pushing in on shows. They like you, but unfortunately they aren't giving you any money, are they?" He hesitated, then dropped his voice lower. "We heard you just welcomed a boy with severe hypertrichosis. Any plans to put him on stage?"

Roy shot up like someone put a thumbtack under his ass. He was rigid with anger, red in the face, and baring his teeth like a dog. The sudden change in attitude shocked Bear enough to flinch, but the financial advisors only a few inches away from his fury remained calm and still.

Steadying himself with a few long breaths, Roy growled: "We do not exploit here. Not people, not animals. There is no promise of money large enough to change that."

Rhonda shrugged. "Then you will lose your show, simple as that. You need animals, at the very least. Consider it. We'd hate to see you go."

With a snide grin, Roy took another drag from his flask. "You seem to be forgetting something, Bill, Rhonda. I *have* an animal. One that every recruiter – *poacher*, if you will – is sniffing after."

The advisors frowned, confused.

Roy leaned back in his chair. "I have a Bear."

In unison, the strangers turned to fully face Bear. Caught off guard, he was sitting straight up, mouth agape, hands buried in his dog's fur.

"The firebreather," Bill breathed, like he just noticed he was there. Or, he just realized who he was.

Rhonda faced Roy again. "That boy –" A finger jabbed in Bear's direction, "– is the only thing that's keeping you in business. They come for him. Then they stay for the others."

Bear didn't like that. They were making him sound like some kind of siren, luring sailors into the deadly waters. Dee seemed to agree with him: her face was twisted in anger and her body had tensed up.

Roy, on the contrary, was smirking proudly. He had won the poker match.

After the meeting with the advisors, Roy politely asked Bear to leave without saying another word. So, Bear left, reeling with a handful of unprocessed thoughts. The weight of responsibility Roy thrust upon him dragged his feet like concrete boots.

He wandered the Fairgrounds, lost, until he stumbled upon Callie sitting on the warmed metal of a carnival ride, her pale skin gleaming in the sun as she focused hard on the book in her lap.

The acrobat looked up as Bear approached, letting her sunglasses slide down to the tip of her nose. "I tried learning Korean from my mom's family before she died," Callie sighed. The cover closed with a snapping sound. "They weren't fluent in English. I wanted to learn how speak it so I could speak to them at holidays."

"How far did you get?" Bear asked, leaning his back against the ride's base next to where her feet where dangling off.

Callie huffed. "Just the basics. My dad was more concerned with 'actual academics'." The last two words were accompanied by dramatic air quotes and a sour expression. "Fucking dick."

"Yeah," Bear agreed. "Sounds like he was." He tipped his head up to look at her. "You want to go into town? I got a few things I need to grab, and I need to get out of here for a bit. We can go visit Quinn, too." Callie hesitated to answer and Bear nudged her leg gently. "We can play that last part by ear. I need shampoo."

Teeth bit down on her smile. "Let's do it. I just have to tell Roy. Its one of our things."

Bear hesitated, unsure if it was safe to go back there. He didn't plan on telling Callie about the meeting or anything said during it. Hands tied, he let Callie backtrack his steps to Roy's trailer.

When they knocked on Roy's door, it was Dee who called them in. She was standing with one of their contortionists, a twenty-year old girl with thin hair and sunken eyes. Her clothes were discarded on the floor except for her underwear, and she was standing in front of a scale. Bear had seen this before with Allie: he knew what this was about.

"We're going to town," Bear announced, not sparing the scene anymore consideration. "I need shampoo, conditioner, toothbrushes." He listed off what he could remember, mulling over each one.

"Step up," Dee instructed Allie, then to Bear asked: "Callie?"

"Company," He said, he reminded her: "I can't find Maggie."

Dee watched the numbers on the scale instead of Bear, her eyebrows brought together with worry and tongue tracing each tooth in her mouth. "Go ahead, then." She waved them off. "Don't get lost."

Bear backed out of the trailer with Callie. Atlanta was waiting for them patiently, receiving love from Whitney. Bear waved at the knife thrower and guided his two female companions towards the Fairgrounds exit. Callie was walking slowly, watching the ground all the way until they were down the road that led to the entrance.

"What was Dee doing with Allie?" She finally asked quietly.

Bear glanced at her. "Just making sure she hasn't lost any more weight."

It took an hour or so to walk deep into town, depending entirely on how fast you walked. Not on a schedule of any kind, Callie and Bear took their time. They stopped on a bridge over a creek and Bear picked up rocks near the bank. He handed them to Callie and they tossed them overhand into the rushing water, seeing who could throw the highest, furthest, who could hit the biggest rock sticking up in the middle. Callie giggled until her cheeks turned pink.

Their first real stop was a supermarket that was bustling with mid-morning shoppers, mostly elderly with the occasional young adult. Bear pulled a leash out of his belt loops, checking to make sure the service dog patches were still on it, and clipped it to Atlanta's heavy-duty collar.

"Sorry, bug," He said, ruffling her neck fur. "Rules are rules."

He wrapped the leash around his waist for hands free convenience and led the two girls through the store. They got a few strange looks; Bear noticed Callie lost her confidence half way through and stuck close to his side. He glanced down at her sympathetically and nudged her towards the self check out. He had what he was in dire need of, whatever else he wanted he could come back for alone or with Wes.

"Why does everyone stare at us like that?" Callie asked as Bear rung up what they had.

"Because I reek of gasoline and have a cool ass dog." Bear used Roy's credit card to pay, crumpling the receipt into his back pocket. "C'mon, let's go." He carried the bag with toothpaste, toothbrushes, and shampoo while Callie munched on the chips she picked out.

As soon as they were out of the store, Bear let Atlanta off her leash and they kept walking in the direction of the hospital. It was a warm spring day with no wind or humidity, just a comfortable sixty-five degrees that brought out more walkers than cars. Bear smiled politely at the occasional person they passed on the sidewalk but never got one in return, only scrunched up noses and faster walking as they tried to escape the aroma of gas.

Bear clipped Atlanta to her leash again as they approached the hospital. Callie slowed down her walking, looking increasingly more anxious the closer they got. Bear hesitated.

"We don't have to if you aren't ready," Bear said gently.

Callie puffed out her chest. "No. I should."

Bear smiled and offered her his hand. "You got this."

The hospital lobby was quiet when they stepped through the automatic doors. A mother was nursing her child in the soft chairs by the windows, an older woman was bravely carrying two cups of coffee without lids towards her husband. Bear froze, holding Atlanta's leash in one hand and Callie's in the other, and realized he had no idea where Quinn's room was.

"Should we just wander around until we find her?" Callie asked, smirking.

"No," Bear huffed. He tugged her towards the lady behind the desk near the directory, figuring she was a good enough shot.

She looked up as they approached, eyes on Atlanta. "Uh, sir–"

"She's a service dog," Bear grumbled. "Army."

Her bangs didn't suit her face at all, and her brown roots were showing as the blonde grew out. She straightened in her seat and cleared her throat. "My apologies, what can I help you with?"

"We're from the Circus," explained Bear, gesturing to Callie. "We're looking for our comrade who was admitted a few nights ago. Quinn."

"Last name?" The receptionist asked, peering up at him over the thick frames of her readers.

Bear's mind drew a blank. "Um..."

"Lacey," Callie interjected. She spoke to the receptionist but glared at Bear: *you should know that.*

"Ah, yes," The woman said. She shuffled through some paperwork, her glasses sliding down the bridge of her nose. "She should be on floor four, room 32A. There's a map by the stairs."

"Thank you."

Bear started off towards the stairs, not willing to take the elevator, figuring he'd spare the noses of anyone who made the mistake of riding with them. They made it to the second floor before Callie was panting dramatically and groaning in complaint.

"There's an elevator for a reason!" She whined, dropping Bear's hand as he continued on without her.

Bear laughed over his shoulder. "Aren't you a pro athlete?"

"Technically, my whole act is about how good at falling I am," Callie pointed out. She caught up with him on the fourth floor.

Bear looked over the map with his hands on his hips and Atlanta heeled between his legs. The floor plan was confusing, like they wanted to trip them up on purpose. He was growing more irritated by the second. Callie joined him at the shoulder, mulling over the image in front of them. She chewed on her fingernail anxiously.

Atlanta suddenly stood and started staring down a hallway with her ears pricked and her tail wagging slowly, a quiet whine emitting from her closed mouth. Bear raised an eyebrow at Callie.

"I don't know why we didn't think of this before,"
He said as they let the Shepherd lead them down the
corridor. Atlanta picked up her pace as they turned a
corner. She tried to stop abruptly but her paws slide on
the linoleum floor and she skidded a few feet past the
door for 32A. Bear pet her side roughly. "That's my girl."

A nurse stepped out of the room, drawn by the
commotion. "Can I help you?"

"We're here to see Quinn," Callie spoke up. "We're
from the Circus."

The nurse clapped her hands together in
excitement. "Oh, how wonderful! She'll be so pleased!
Come on in."

Bear dropped Atlanta's leash as the dog wiggled her
entire body in excitement through the doorway. Callie
instantly reached for Bear's hand with a death grip.
Before they even slipped past the nurse into the room,
they heard a shriek of pure happiness.

"Atlanta!" Quinn wailed. "Oh, Atlanta! I missed you
so much!"

Atlanta was up on the hospital bed, assaulting the
young girl with kisses as she wrapped her arms around
the dog's neck and held her close. Quinn didn't even
notice Bear and Callie for a good thirty seconds while
Atlanta made up for all the lost love.

"Atlanta, hey, c'mon, bug!" Bear chastised. "Let her
breathe."

The Shepherd dropped off at the command, coming
loyally back to Bear's hip. Quinn's face became somehow
brighter when she saw them. Bruises were on her cheeks
and there was a bandage over her nose, but she didn't
seem to mind them at all as Callie broke away from Bear
to race to her friend's side. The girls embraced, Bear

noting how Callie was careful around Quinn's legs. Pointless.

Bear shook out his head at the cynical thought and took a seat at the chair next to the bed. The nurse offered him some water and he accepted for Callie and Atlanta. She returned from down the hall with two plastic cups and told him to buzz if they needed anything. It took a long time for the two girls to break apart, and when they finally did, Quinn was wiping tears away from her face and smiling at Bear.

"It's good to see you, Bear!" Quinn said. She held up her wrist to show him a small, temporary tattoo that was so faded it took him a moment to figure out what it was. A cartoon flame with big eyes and a tongue sticking out. Bear couldn't focus on anything but the hospital bracelet.

"That's great, Quinn," Bear murmured gently. He nudged Atlanta towards the bed again. "Go on up girl, but be careful."

Atlanta hopped back up, curling into a black ball by Quinn's side under her arm, like a GMO'd wooly bear caterpillar. The girl nuzzled into the mass of dog with a cheeky grin, her hand tangled with Callie's against the harsh white hospital sheets. The entire room was a painfully bright shade of eggshell, and the blaring sun shone through the big window.

Bear peered out of it from the chair, scanning the town from this height like he was looking over a model village. Far off in the distance, he could see the unmistakable, towering Big Top. The harder he looked the more he could pick out, like the Ferris wheel, the rides, a small billow of smoke coming from the fire pit, the trailers like neatly placed Lego blocks. Bear's heart ached for Quinn. He couldn't imagine having to look out of a window day in and day out, watching the Circus come to life every night, knowing full well she'd never perform again.

"I'm learning how to breath fire." Callie's proud declaration stole Bear back from the window.

Quinn's blue eyes were wide. She looked equally impressed and terrified. Bear's jaw tightened with guilt, recalling the young girl's fear for the fire show. He then wondered if Callie had been lying when she said she wasn't as afraid of it as Quinn was, or if she really was driven by loyalty to her friend. All the sacrifices he made for Maggie shuffled through his head like a film reel. Love is not fear, love is conquering it.

"*Fire*?" Quinn echoed.

Callie nodded, ecstatic. "I'll be performing alongside Bear in no time!"

Bear sighed heavily, not bothering to point out that she was a long way away from ever performing in front of a crowd. Three pairs of eyes shot in his direction. Bear forced a thin-lipped smile onto his face, hoping it came across as genuine and they couldn't pick up on the dread growing in his belly like indigestion.

To cover his own ass, Bear changed the subject. "How are you holding up here, Q?"

"Fine." Quinn shrugged, toying with the sheets tucked around her waist. "I'm bored," She admitted, her cheeks a faint shade of pink. "And I want to go home."

Home, home? Or the Circus?

"I believe it," Bear whispered.

Callie sniffled, her bottom lip quivering in warning before she buckled with a sob. Quinn gasped in shock and reached for her friend as best she could, frantically trying to swipe tears away from Callie's cheeks with her thumbs.

"Callie, what's wrong?" Quinn urged, looking like she might start crying herself.

"This is all my fault!" Callie cried. Her face dropped into Quinn's pillow and her small body wracked with sobs. Voice muffled, she choked out: "I dropped you!"

"Stop that!" Grabbing Callie by the shoulders, Quinn lifted her up from the pillow. "It was just an accident! Don't tell me you've blaming yourself this whole time." When Callie didn't answer with anything other than a subdued sob, Quinn went from distressed to calm like something in her brain flipped a switch. "Callie, danger is part of the job I signed up for. I knew this could happen. Just like you, I risked it every day because its what I love to do, and because I love *you*."

A pang of emotion shot through Bear's heart, strong enough to fold him over in his chair. With his elbows on his knees and his face in his hands, he listened carefully to the girls' conversation become hush with affirmations and comforting touches. He thought about Maggie applying ice and ointment to his mouth, always waiting for him below the stage after a set, always laying awake with him when the pain would not let him sleep. Somewhere down the line, everything turned into a sacrifice.

Bear straightened his spine and found the Circus beyond the town, imaging he could see tiny bodies moving around the Fairgrounds. He barely registered Atlanta coming back to him. Her west nose nudged his arms apart so she could crawl halfway into his lap and he focused on her heavy, even breathing instead of the crippled fifteen-year-old girl a few feet away.

Quinn called out to him. "Bear?"

Turning to her, Bear said, "Yeah?"

"Do you think they'll let me come back?" The young girl asked quietly. Bear felt the color drain from his face as she continued, somehow more hush, "I mean, I know I probably won't ever perform again, but..."

"Roy can't wait to have you back," Bear interrupted. "All of us miss you so much." It occurred to him that he forgot her bouquet.

The smile on her face warmed his chest in a way the fire never did.

* * *

<u>CALLIE</u>

Callie stood across from Bear underneath the Big Top, clad in a tank top and shorts – less clothing means less of a chance it'll go up in flames, Bear advised. Roy and Dee were there too, sitting on the lower rows of bleachers with their arms crossed over their chests. Wes loitered in the trench below the stage with his elbows up on it, two torches in his hands and Atlanta sitting patiently next to his head, ready for any command.

Bear paced for a moment, scanning the area, Callie, and their onlookers. He pursed his lips, then gestured at Callie.

"Sit down," He said, lowering himself to the floor. "Criss cross."

Confused, Callie followed suit. They were about a car's length apart on the hard-packed earth; Bear looked comfortable but Callie shifted, grimacing at the ground digging into her glutes. Bear put his palms on his knees

and touched his index finger to his thumb in a standard
meditation post, nodding at Callie to continue copying
him.

"Control your breathing," Bear hummed, eyes
closed and head tilted backwards. "Calm yourself down.
Handling fire with even the slightest nerves is the
difference between charred eyebrows and total
cremation."

Callie peaked one eye open when she heard Roy
cough out a laugh. Smirking herself, she closed her eyes
again and tried to match her breathing with the slow
pace Bear's was at. It was harder than she thought, and
she couldn't find a comfortable way to sit. Frustration
was starting to nestle in her belly. Callie huffed and
opened her eyes, straightening out her legs.

"Bear," Callie whined, "this is stupid."

Bear opened his eyes with a scowl. "It's not stupid,
Callie. You're doing this because you're mad and lost,
and trust me, those aren't good emotions to let lead you.
Not in life, not in fire."

"I thought I was learning how to do a Circus act,
not getting a life lecture." Callie stood and dusted off the
front of her shorts, glaring in Bear's direction. The fire
breather's eyebrows were knit together and his mouth
was a thin, straight line.

"Hey," Wes chimed in. He was playing tug of war
with Atlanta with a stray sock. "Don't be a brat, Cal. He's
making some good points. Like how we stretch before
each show so we don't pull any muscles – Bear
meditates."

"So I don't burn down the whole Circus," Bear
finished. He clambered to his feet and walked over to

Wes, who handed him two torches and a can of kerosene. "But, if you want to dive right in, fuck it. Dive."

He lit the first torch and used it to set up the other one, handing the second one to Callie. The flame burned on the end of the metal, close to her nose, hot and crackling like her own personal bonfire. Her heart fluttered with anxiety and excitement, Bear raised an eyebrow at her, obviously sensing it. His deep brown eyes said what his mouth didn't.

Told you so.

"We'll start with a simple kill," Bear began. "Also known as extinguishing the flame with your mouth." Simple enough, Callie had seen him do this a million times. Bear tilted his head back, "Make sure your head is straight and open your mouth as wide as you can."

Slowly, he lowered the torch into his mouth. The flame licked up the handle towards his fingers but his mouth closed in a perfect *O* shape around the wick. He held it there for a moment, his broad chest expanding with a breath, his frayed brows tugged together.

Then, like a child with a lollipop, Bear pulled the torch out of his mouth, coughing as smoke filtered out of his nose and mouth. He gestured to Callie. "Go on."

Callie looked down at the fire in her hand and immediately understood why Bear wanted her to mediate first. She was seconds away from potentially burning her face off. Or from proving Bear wrong. Best or worst-case scenario, no middle ground. Glancing over at the bleachers, she saw Dee watching through her hands and Roy taking a swig out of his flask. Wes was pouring a bottle of water out on a towel.

Inhale, exhale, Callie centered her breathing like she was about to take a dive off of her ledge. She tried to imagine the feeling of tangling in the curtains and swinging through the air with Quinn. Four pairs of eyes were boring into her skull.

Hoping no one could notice her trembling, Callie tilted her head back and started bringing the torch towards her open mouth. Just like with Bear's, the flames started traveling upwards towards her bare hand and she panicked, ripping it downwards with a yelp.

"You have to do it quickly," Bear said. "Before your hand gets burnt."

Callie turned her wide eyes on him. "But my mouth gets burnt instead?"

Bear said nothing in return, just quirked his upper lip to show off his array of blisters. Callie stuck out her bottom lip and repeated the first steps. This time, she got the wick close enough to her mouth that the skin from her chin to her nose started to burn in unbearable pain and her flight response activated again. She yanked the torch back so hard the flame went out and she was just standing there, panting and tearing up.

"Fuck," Callie gasped, trying to catch her breath.

"It's okay," Bear was at her side, gently taking the instrument from her and hooking it up in his belt loop along with the other. "Do you see the importance in meditation now?"

"Yeah, I get it."

Wes hopped up on the stage and made his way over to them. "Can I see the fire ball?" He asked Bear, giddy like a child.

Bear grinned from ear to ear. "Yeah, hand me the kerosene."

Instructing them all to duck down into the trench, Bear took a gulp of kerosene like Roy taking a hit form his flask. Callie grimaced just imagining the awful taste, but Bear seemed unphased. With his cheeks puffed out like a chipmunk he lit a torch and held it up with his head at a forty-five-degree angle. He released the fuel out onto the open like a sitcom spit take and a huge burst of fire exploded across the length of the stage.

Callie shrieked in excitement and felt Wes clap his hands together. It really did make him look like a dragon.

Before the flame died down, Atlanta, who had been sitting quietly at their feet, jumped up like someone zapped her in the ass. Just barely tall enough to place her two front paws up on the stage, she began barking madly, trying to lift herself up onto the platform.

Confused, Wes tried calming her down, all efforts for naught. "Atlanta, what the hell, girl?"

Focused on Atlanta's sudden outburst, they all stopped watching Bear. Dee was the only one who had the piece of mind to turn her attention back to the fire breather. Callie watched her face go from confused to mortified in a split second. Atlanta finally managed to haul her body onto the stage at the same time Dee yelped in horror.

Bear was stumbling, lit torch dropped on the ground and rolling dangerously close to the kerosene bottle. He was coughing, and even from a few meters away, Callie could make out the unmistakable splatters of blood.

Roy and Dee were scrambling out of the bleachers as Wes threw himself back up over the wall, but it was Atlanta who made it to her owner first. She shot low to the ground in an army crawl with perfect timing and position for Bear to collapse backwards. His head hit her body instead of the stage floor.

"Son of a bitch!" Wes threw the wet cloth over the torch before kneeling down next to Bear's head, feeling his pulse with two fingers. "He's alive, Roy what do we do?"

Roy hovered over Bear's limp body for a second, staring down at it with a face of pure hysteria and grief. Callie remembered the last time she'd seen him towering over one of his fallen children. Bear couldn't have collapsed more than a few feet away from where Quinn's spine shattered.

The Ringleader scooped Bear up princess-style like he weighed nothing, and in the way the light hit his face, Callie could see flowing tears.

"Dee, get the truck."

The woman nodded, stunned into silence, and sprinted out of the Big Top. Atlanta was barking frantically still, circling Roy's feet and trying to jump up and look at her owner.

"Callie," Roy called softly. "Calista, honey, come here." Callie took the long way to the stairs up to the stage, coming to Roy's side, trying not to look at Bear's face. Roy sniffed and tipped his head at Wes. "You two, take care of Atlanta, okay? We're going to bring him to the hospital. Tell everyone what happened and where we went." He was addressing Wes mostly, who looked equally stricken but was probably functioning better than Callie was. "You good?"

Wes nodded. "Is he..."

"He'll be fine," Roy assured. He smiled sadly. "It's Bear."

Headlights shown through the fabric of the Big Top and Dee laid on the horn once. Roy carried Bear out like a sleeping child and Wes, Callie, and Atlanta followed to see him load the fire breather gently into the back seat before crawling in after him. The pick up truck was old and rattled something fierce while running, but it was the most convenient vehicle for fast travel.

Atlanta jumped and whined, struggling against Wes' grip on her collar. Drool dribbled out of her snapping jaws, her long body moving like a serpent. Andreas had to replace Wes in holding her back as the Shepherd watched her owner be hauled off without her. To Callie, it felt a lot like watching herself in the third person the night Quinn fell.

Silence settled over the Fairgrounds. It was the loudest silence. Even Atlanta ceased her desperate whines and howls, watching the taillights disappear down the road with pricked ears and the intense eyes of a herding breed. It was like they were all partaking in a vigil, but Bear couldn't be dead. Whitney was the one who spoke first.

She huffed and rolled her eyes, stabbing the point of one of her knives into the top of a picnic table. "Maggie don't even know."

"Oh god." Wes was still on one knee from when he had been restraining Atlanta. "Maggie."

As if the name reminded her of her grief, Atlanta cried again, pathetic and weak, her body losing all fight against Andreas' chest. The dog collapsed like someone sniped her; her body limp as the man holding her gently lowered her to the ground. Atlanta was, for the first time, decommissioned.

Callie went down with her, legs giving up and sinking her to the ground next to Wes. She bent over, forehead to the night-cooled grass, and let sadness engulf her and replace the shock. No one moved to comfort her.

Not even Atlanta.

WHEN IT COUNTS

<u>MAGNOLIA</u>

New Hampshire turned into Vermont; Vermont turned into upper New York State. Adele drove a brand-new Audi with crisp leather seats and a tree air freshener that was labeled "new car smell". They drove mostly in silence with the occasional snippet of small talk. Adele seemed incredibly interested in Circus life, but was respectful enough to only toe that boundary. Maggie found it hard to explain exactly what she contributed to it, anyway.

I-90 W went on forever. Adele didn't need a GPS: she drove the roads to the prison like she was driving to her mother's house. It irritated Maggie in a way that reminded her of a mosquito she couldn't swat away. She checked her phone again for any contact from anyone at the Circus. The only thing on her lock screen was Candy Crush letting her know she had full lives again.

Fuck yeah.

"So, why a clown?" Adele's question came out of nowhere, completely ruining the euphoria from Maggie's Candy Crush high. The judge shot her a sideways glance with a friendly smile. "Just out of curiosity. Is it an easier position, or just something you were passionate about?"

Maggie thought about it for a second. It was a legitimate question. Out of everything she could've become, including a renowned performer like Wes or Bear, Maggie chose to be nothing more than a clown. No one questioned her, because you don't do that at the Circus, so she never had to explain herself to anyone but herself. She wondered if she could find a way to articulate it that didn't sound downright pathetic.

"I guess," Maggie began, "I just spent a long time being judged by how pretty my face is," She cringed at how self-absorbed that sounded, "that it felt really nice to be able to hide behind a face I got to create myself."

Adele nodded and murmured: "Safety blanket."

"Something like that," Maggie agreed, hoping the conversation would fade off after that.

"Your father knows," Adele continued. "He's seen you on TV."

Maggie frowned. Between promotional commercials and homemade videos, she didn't doubt that, but it made this meeting somehow more daunting knowing he'd know everything about her and she would hardly recognize him. On the bright side, it took away the pressure of having to admit it. It also took away any opportunity to *lie* about her profession and life. Win some, lose some. Thanks, internet.

They were driving through what appeared to be a neighborhood and then opened into a vast field. Barbed wire fences announced their destination and Maggie wrinkled her nose, finding a sense of dark humor that she was excited to share with Bear when she returned.

"Those houses must be cheap as hell," Maggie snorted. She hoped Adele caught the upturned note of humor in her voice.

With a dashing wink that shocked Maggie, Adele shot back: "The locks on their doors sure as hell aren't."

As they pulled into the parking lot, a man in a security uniform approached the car. Adele rolled down the window and he peered in, nodding upon seeing who it was. They exchanged pleasantries and she pulled into an empty parking lot near the front. She put the car in park and turned to examine Maggie with pursed lips.

"They're going to search you. Anything you should leave in the car?"

Maggie thought about it, then pulled out her knife out of her boot and the cigarettes out of her breast pocket. Adele nodded, opening the glove compartment for her to hide them in. Maggie was instructed to take her beanie off, too. Once her appearance was good enough for Adele, they stepped out of the car into the deceiving sunshine. It was chilly out.

Immediately upon entry into the lobby, they were
patted down. Two Shepherds accompanied the guards,
sniffing for contraband their owners couldn't feel out.
They were dark sable in color, the bigger one nearly
black with grey hairs forming on his muzzle. He sniffed
her hand, tail tip wagging just slightly. The handler
raised an eyebrow at her.

"I have a Shepherd," Maggie explained, smiling.
"Looks almost just like him, but she's all black and about
half his size."

"Yeah?" The woman said, backing up.

"Yeah. Retired military."

Impressed eyebrows shot up.

They were handed paperwork to fill out next, which
took them about twenty minutes. Maggie had some
trouble answering some of the questions they asked her,
but Adele was patient with helping her. The clipboard
she was writing on had annoying little divots and chips
that kept catching her pen. Anxiety heightened every
emotion and she eventually slammed the pen down,
suddenly at her wits end. Adele put a calming hand on
her wrist and took the board and pen away, turning in
their paperwork as is.

Guards searched them again before they actually
went in, this time with iron scanners. The dogs were still
hovering close by and Maggie yearned to find comfort in
petting one, even though she knew it was strictly
prohibited. She missed Atlanta.

A man in uniform led them down a straight
corridor with mirrors on one side. Peaking into them,
Maggie could see numerous visitations happening. Most
were just one on one, but there was one woman seated
with two children on her lap, an elderly looking couple

talking to what appeared to be their son, and a pair of two young looking teenagers. In the furthest corner, a man sat alone, looking down at his tattooed hands.

Maggie froze. Adele bumped into her back, caught off guard by her sudden stop. Maggie's heart started to race and her stomach turned over, her knees going weak. The guard looked at her with equal confusion in concern, and Adele put a comforting hand on her shoulder.

"Magnolia," The older woman said, soft and easy. "Do you need a minute?"

Maggie nodded, not trusting her voice just yet. It was all becoming very real very quickly. She hadn't even psyched herself up on the car ride over, figuring she'd be less intimidated if she just settled on winging it. Horrible plan. One of her worst. She was thankful, at least, for Adele's presence to be both a buffer and a guide on Maggie's super fun, interactive tour of traumatic childhood events.

"You should allow cigarettes in here," Maggie said to the guard without thinking, still breathing heavily. The man coughed out a laugh as Adele shook her head. Maggie squared her shoulders, trying to mimic what Bear probably did before each show. "Let's do this."

The sealed room was filled with overlapping, quiet chatter. No one bothered looking up from each other as Adele led Maggie through the room, leaving the guard behind at the door. Their footsteps padded on the tiled floor and Maggie's father snapped out of his trance as they approached. Maggie hesitated a few feet away from the metal table he sat at, giving her brain one last opportunity to wake up before she dove the rest of the way in.

Her father's face was exactly how she remembered it, if not slightly more aged. His dark brown skin had almost no wrinkles on it except for around his mouth that were visible as he frowned, and his almost-black eyes were void of any emotion Maggie could pick up on. He kept his hair in a short cut, she remembered him with dreads, but she saw herself in the shape of his nose, lips, and jaw. Her bright green eyes were solely her mother's, unfortunately.

"Magnolia." His voice was a rolling rumble, smooth and rich like balsamic. "You look wonderful."

"You do, too, Dad," Maggie responded. Adele had already sat down and was looking pointedly at her to sit herself down. Maggie lowered herself slowly, already displeased by the coldness of the seat seeping through her clothing. She tried her best to force a genuine smile on her face, insecure without the extra assistance of clown make up. "Its really good to see you."

"Likewise," Damien Mendoza said. He nodded to Adele. "Thank you for doing this."

Adele smiled warmly. "Of course. She's a pleasure."

Maggie blushed, shaking her head. She had ignored most of Adele's advances for conversation and when she did speak, it was mostly with an attitude. Good to know the judge was either wonderful at lying or used to people giving her their bad side. In her profession, it could be a mix of both.

"So," Maggie's father said, leaning back. "The Circus, huh? Got that tired of living with your mother?"

There was no note of sarcasm to the way he said it, only a small sliver of curiosity and a smaller incline of sympathy. "Something like that," Maggie answered.

"It's... different than a lot of people think. There's more to it than what they let us show."

One eyebrow quirked up. "Yeah? Enlighten me."

"Well..." Maggie trailed off. There were a lot of places to start. "Most of the performers are runaways, except for a handful that were born and raised in the Circus. A lot of them are under the age of twenty. None of them have anywhere else to go. My best friend is an Army vet that joined with his retired bomb sniffing dog, one of our contortionists is recovering from anorexia. Our grounds workers usually filter in from towns we stop at looking for work, they don't usually last very long but the ones who do are usually running from something, too. Every act is something they developed or taught themselves before they even knew the Circus existed. There's an energy there. A strong sense of camaraderie that overrides everything else."

She had to stop to take a breath and because she had become acutely aware of how much she was talking. Damien was watching her curiously, taking in every word. Adele looked like she was enjoying the spill, too: it was far more than anything Maggie confessed on the car ride. No one interrupted or spoke, so Maggie took that as a cue to continue.

"When things went increasingly south with Mom, I just... had to leave." Maggie fiddled with the cuffs of her jacket. There was a stain of red paint from when she painted a portrait of Bear one summer's evening. "I stumbled across it a few towns over from home and it seemed like a good way to waste a night. My friends were going, anyway. I ended up meeting Bear and the more I talked to him, the more appealing the lifestyle sounded. He was young and full of life still and spoke so highly of what he believed in that he convinced me to believe in it, too, without even trying. An accidental con man."

"Who's Bear?" Damien asked.

"The Army vet. He was medically discharged due to an accident that left him with a bad ear." Maggie recounted the stories Bear had told her about his time overseas. "He taught himself how to breathe fire when he was seventeen."

"You joined for him?"

Maggie shook her head. That didn't sound right. Sure, Bear was the final push she needed, but it wasn't his fault or his doing. At that point, living in a tent under a bridge would've been a better gig than staying at home with her bitter mother.

"No, I joined for *me*. I *stayed* for Bear."

Damien nodded. "Your mother was always crazy, you know. My Pop always warned me not to marry a white woman." He laughed dryly and tapped his knuckles against the metal table. He examined the skin like he expected the light impact to split it. "I'm glad something good came outta it though. Second you were born, she hated you. I could tell, 'cause you were beautiful even as a newborn. I remember my brother sayin', 'man, ain't newborns supposed to be ugly?' You weren't."

Maggie felt tears welling up in her eyes. Her mother's brother thought she was beautiful, too. He couldn't resist it, he said, and that's how they ended up here. Maggie always knew her mother held some petulant jealousy towards her. Her skin was pale, her blonde hair was thin and straw-like, her lips were thin and her green eyes were sunken under eyebrows she had to fill in with make up. Magnolia was like a level up of all of her traits: deep tan skin, thick and wavy hair, full lips and brows that never needed plucking.

Who the hell hates their daughter for being beautiful?

"She blamed me for the murder, you know," Maggie whispered. The tears were flowing freely now, not streaking any paint for the first time in forever. "That's why I had to leave. She said every time she looked at me, she saw her brother's beaten face."

"Yeah," Damien sighed. "She visited me once a few months after I got here. She said she was mad at me for acting the way I did but was even more mad at herself for raising a whore. I reminded her that you were eleven, but that didn't matter to her." For the first time since she sat down, Maggie's father looked her dead in the eye. "I made sure she knew I loved doing it, and that if I had the opportunity, I'd do it again in a heartbeat. Hell, I even told her I'd find a way to do it to her if she ever laid a finger on you."

"She never did," Maggie assured, wiping away the tears that were starting to drip off of her chin like water torture.

Her father flashed straight, white teeth. "Hell, no she didn't. 'Cause she knew I was dead serious."

Maggie laughed into her palm, amused at the idea of her mother scared straight by what anyone else would assume to be an empty threat. The last seven years of her life spent under the reign of that woman exhausted Maggie's heart and mind nearly to the point of no return. Bear freed her, in a way: convinced her to jump from the nest with only paper wings. In some romanticized alternate universe, Damien and Bear would get along well, swap stories over a cigar and some Hennessy.

"So, Magnolia," Damien continued. "What do you *actually* want to do?" When Maggie couldn't respond, too confused by the nature of the question, her father huffed and rolled his eyes. "When you grow out of this Circus phase, what's next?"

"I..." Maggie's response hung unspoken in the air above the table like a rainless cloud. "I don't know. I never really..."

"It's okay if it isn't a phase. You just spoke about it like it was."

Did she? Was it? She said herself that she had only stuck around this long for Bear, who certainly wasn't going anywhere. Put under this new light, Maggie realized she could count on one hand the amount of things she's done for herself since joining the Circus. Getting the guts to come visit her father was one of them. She wasn't unhappy, nor did she feel trapped or used: sacrificing so much for Bear came like a second nature, like a purpose she was born for.

Bear wasn't a phase. Maggie refused to pin him as some project of hers, a heroic attempt at fixing a broken person or preventing them from disappearing all together. Some shitty coping mechanism in which she nursed someone else back from their traumatic past as a way to avoid ever coming to terms with her own. Maybe that's what it was deep down, maybe that's how they came to care so deeply for one another – but her love for Bear was not artificial, nor was it a study in escapism. It was the only thing that made her feel real.

But Bear belonged under red and white tarps and spotlights, chasing the validation from strangers he never got from loved ones. He lived his life so loud that everything else beyond the moment was just an indistinguishable jumble of memories quiet enough to drown out. Each drop of gasoline chipped away slowly at his body and mind, molding him with a process that would take thousands of years, for sudden rainstorms could not change the course of a river.

Maggie took a deep breath, still trying to figure out how to answer her father in a way that he could follow and understand. "I don't think I would've lasted very long by myself," Maggie admitted. "I never felt the sense of family growing up that a lot of my friends did. I could've survived on my own, but I had begun to crave a sense of belonging."

Damien nodded solemnly. "I wasn't around."

Maggie smiled, face wet with tears. "You were when it counted. And Mom was around all the time, and that didn't make her a good parent."

Her father leaned forward, forearms on the table and hands clasped together. "Let me ask you a question, kiddo." Maggie nodded, taking a moment to wipe her tears on her scratchy denim sleeve. "Assuming you found it at the Circus, do you still feel that sense of belonging?"

"I don't know," Maggie said honestly, the reality of that fact settling in for real as she finally said it out loud. "Some of the things I've seen there, Daddy..." She thought about Quinn falling, the sound of her bones crumbling on the ground, amplified by the silence in the crowd. "You don't un-see them."

It occurred to her that she was talking about horrific events to a man who bludgeoned a man's skull in with a cheerleading trophy. In a game of one upping, her father would wipe the floor with her.

"But you can escape them."

Just as she had escaped her mother. Maggie was tired of running. She wanted somewhere to call home, and her heart wasn't ready to accept that the Circus wasn't it.

* * *

<u>BEAR</u>

He could hear voices just out of audible reach. He tried to open his eyes but his lids felt heavy and sticky. When he finally managed to peel them open, a harsh, invasive light caused him to snap them shut in a mere second. Bear groaned, trying to move his hand over his brow to shade his eyes. He felt a slight tug and stopped. The voices ceased, too, and he could feel eyes on him.

"Barrett?"

Fuck. You.

He didn't even recognize the voice, which just made the fact that they used his full name somehow more obnoxious. Driven by irritation, Bear defied the brightness and opened his eyes.

A doctor in a lab coat and a nurse in scrubs were staring at him, their heads cocked to the side. Bear took in the rest of his surroundings: the tug he'd felt on his arm was an IV, the annoying light was simply the harshness of the white hospital walls and sheets, and the jumbled voices were because his good ear had been angled downwards to press into the pillow. A hospital gown replaced his sweaty show clothes. He also noted that he was about to vomit.

The puke was mostly clear and runny as he spit it up over the edge of the bed, right next to the nurse's ugly tennis shoes. She tried for naught to hide her disgusted grimace for the sake of professionalism. Bear saw right through her and let her know with a cheeky grin.

As she knelt to clean it up, the doctor went over his clipboard, coming to stand by Bear's head. "Nice to officially meet you. I'm Doctor Hall. What do you remember, Barrett?"

"That I hate being called that."

The doctor froze, frowning. "Bear, right? The men who brought you mentioned that."

You're on a fucking roll, Doc.

"Dee's a woman," Bear hissed through clenched teeth. Hall looked genuinely confused and not at all apologetic about the misgendering.

"Well." He held the clipboard with both hands down by his crotch. "At least you remember that much. Anything else?"

"Just that I fucked up a fireball and passed out during practice." Bear lifted his arm attached to the IV. "And all of *this* is unnecessary."

Hall stared at him for a moment before turning on his heels and plopping down in the rolling chair on the other side of the room. He glided over with his feet like a misbehaving child, stopping in front of Bear's bed – on his bad ear side.

"Bear," He began, "Are you aware of fire breather's pneumonia?" Hall leaned forward in his seat, as if for dramatic soap drama effect. "It's a rare disease caused by the inhalation or aspiration of fatty substances, or a large quantity of petroleum-based product."

"Acute exogenous lipoid pneumonia," Bear clarified, grinning. "What, are you reading off the Wikipedia page?"

"Pretty much. So, you're aware of it?"

"I am. I'm not an idiot. I do my research."

"Okay, genius – are you aware it's currently killing you at a surprisingly rapid pace?"

Bear hesitated. Of course, he knew that. The coughing and vomiting, the blood, the fatigue, the restless sleep or vivid nightmares, the passing out, the purple lips: he'd be an idiot to skim over the obvious. Was he in denial, or better yet convinced he could out run it? Apparently. And apparently, he was not doing a very good job at all.

He missed Atlanta.

"Yeah," Bear murmured. "I knew that."

Sympathy softened Hall's features. "You have to stop. You're a dead man walking."

Shaking his head, Bear asked: "Are Dee and Roy still here?"

"No. You've been here all night, they had to go back."

"When can I leave?"

The doctor was slow to answer. "I suppose whenever. I'd like to monitor you a few more hours at least. It's barely noon. Are you hungry?"

Bear's stomach made a low rumbling sound before his mouth could answer. The nurse, hiding out in the corner, zipped off at the point of the doc's finger.

While they waited for the food, Bear got the normal check up routine. Blood pressure, stethoscope, a look into his eyes, ears, and mouth. Hall made a sound in his throat when he shone the light down Bear's. The blisters must've looked particularly ugly, or the poor middle-aged man had yet to deal with a fire breather in his medical career before Bear. He lowered the instrument away from Bear's open mouth with a heavy sigh, a free hand moving to pinch the bridge of his nose.

"Your teeth are surprisingly clean," Hall settled to say as the nurse returned with a tray of food.

"I brush them a lot." Bear shot him a cocky smirk.

The nurse, a moderately attractive but probably-got-bullied-in-school-looking girl, brought over a plate sectioned neatly with green beans, grilled chicken, a side salad, an apple, a small bowl of soup, and two glasses, one with water and one with orange juice. Bear's eyebrows shot up, surprisingly impressed by the quantity and quality of the hospital food. It wasn't Dee's homemade meals, but it was something to appease his rumbling stomach.

"I wasn't sure what you like," The nurse said, blushing slightly.

Bear set aside the orange juice and the soup with a polite smile as he pointed at his throat. "No hots or citrus. I got a million paper cuts up in there."

He managed to make her giggle, and she still was when she exited the room to check on other patients. Doctor Hall stayed in the room while Bear ate. Bear watched him file through paper work, occasionally doting something down or erasing half a page. Absentmindedly, Bear wiggled his toes, and then froze.

"Am I near the other Circus performer? Quinn?" He asked.

Hall glanced up. "Yeah, she's down the hall. Any idea if I'm going to be getting any more of you in here? I didn't realize the Circus coming to town would provide us this much business."

"Usually we take care of our own."

"Why are you here then?"

Bear didn't answer. If Maggie had been there, he wouldn't be here. She would've known what to do and how to handle it. He frowned at the thought.

Bear sat up a little more and peered out of the window, searching far beyond the town. There was the Circus in the distance, the Big Top tall and mighty in the field. It looked so pathetic at this hour of the day, like an abandoned playground, void of all its purpose. Void of its fire breather.

He had to go home.

* * *

<u>MAGNOLIA</u>

It had become so late that Adele asked if she would be comfortable spending the night at her house so they didn't have to make the long drive twice in a day. Maggie agreed, emotionally and physically exhausted anyway.

The judge lived two hours away from the prison, in the opposite direction of the Circus, in a modest looking house in the middle of a neighborhood right off the highway. Inside, the decor was antique and homey, and there was a faint smell of cinnamon that welcomed them as they stepped through the front door. Adele led her up a back staircase that was wooden and creaky with each step to a bedroom with A-frame ceilings and one dim lamp in the corner.

While Maggie sat on the edge of the stiff mattress to peel off her heavy boots, Adele went off down the hallway. She could hear the woman rummaging through a closet or a dresser, murmuring to herself while Maggie tried to fend off sleep. Adele returned with a pile of clothes neatly folded across her palms.

"They were my daughter's. They're clean."

"Thank you," Maggie said, taking the PJs gratefully.

"Of course." Adele hovered for another moment. "Sleep as long as you need. I'm proud of you for doing this."

Maggie smiled. "Thank you," She repeated, too exhausted to formulate any more of a response. She was proud of herself, too.

"Goodnight, Magnolia."

"Goodnight."

Maggie changed into the soft cotton matching pajama robotically and flopped onto the bed. This would be her first night sleeping alone in a long time, and it would've been a daunting reality to face if she wasn't already slipping away into unconsciousness. She thought about Bear sleeping alone in the trailer – except he wouldn't be alone, Atlanta would be spread out beside him, and they'd wake to the familiar sounds of the Fairgrounds right outside their window.

Maggie figured the panic would set in tomorrow, so she'd wait until then to process the events of the last few hours. For now, she just imagined she was curled up next to Bear and their dog, surrounded by the faint aroma of gasoline and fried food.

She slept for eighteen hours.

MARTYR

<u>BEAR</u>

Wes was waiting outside on the sidewalk in a patching of sunlight, nursing the last of a cigarette with his wavy blond hair pushed back from his face with a headband. It was bizarre seeing him in an environment that wasn't the Circus.

His tall, lean body looked out of place in a turtleneck and jeans. Dark sunglasses covered a greater part of his handsome face, and one eyebrow cocked over the rim as Bear approached. Having been discharged in exactly what he came in wearing, Bear had to stick himself back in his show clothes that reeked of gasoline, sweat, and were decorated with dust and splatters of blood.

Bear was greeted, much to his surprise, with an enthusiastic, but mindful, hug. For a moment, he didn't know what to do when Wes met him half way and threw his arms around him, pulling him in close and exhaling deeply. Bear stiffened briefly, slowly melting into the embrace, returning the hug and making it tighter and more drawn out.

"You scared the shit out of me," Wes muttered from where his face was buried in Bear's neck. His breath was hot against his skin. "You fucking asshole."

Bear couldn't help but laugh as they broke apart; Wes was chuckling too. The trapeze artist dropped his cigarette butt on the ground and stomped it out with his heavy boots before patting himself down in search of another. The pack was empty when he fished it out. Wes kissed his teeth in irritation.

"We can stop for more on the way back," Bear assured as they set off away from the hospital.

"I feel like we were all so close to quitting before all of this," Wes said, shaking his head in discontentment. "Fucking cancer sticks – like we don't put our bodies through enough."

Bear gestured to the hospital bracelet still on his wrist. "We can survive putting much worse things in our bodies."

They walked through town, taking their time enjoying the warm weather and gentle breeze. As they walked past town hall, they noticed a bulletin board covered in fliers for the Circus, and they stopped at

132

looked at flashy pictures of themselves staring straight back.

Wes stepped up to it, standing in front of an eye-level poster of himself and Judas, flying through midair, Judas' legs wrapped around a swing as he hung upside down to catch his brother. Right next to it, Bear was blowing out a breath of flame that took up more of the paper than his body, and there was a tiny black dot in between his legs with Atlanta's three-point stack.

There were other, smaller, posters of various other performers, but Bear and Wes stood out the most. The barkers obviously had a science to their barking.

"Shits weird," Wes murmured, stepping back from the wall. "They do a good job at making us look like something we aren't."

"Say what you want about yourself." Bear nudged Wes with his shoulder and winked. "I *am* that badass."

Wes smirked. "Douche-bag."

They found their way to a 7/11 where a group of preteens were loitering outside on their bikes, eating fruity candy and sucking down sugary sodas. Wes and Bear were recognized even from a distance and they were beckoned over with excited waves and high-pitched shouts. Bear exchanged a look with Wes, who was already rolling his eyes as they strode over to their little fan club.

The boys hassled them for cigarettes and alcohol and Wes and Bear humored them with exaggerated Circus horror stories. Wes clambered onto Bear's shoulders to show off how tall Andreas was, igniting shrieking laughter, pointing fingers, and loud applause fueled them as they showed off. Performers at heart.

The youngest one, a boy with ginger hair and a face more freckles than anything else, popped a lollipop of out of mouth and pointed it at Bear. "I saws you in the hospital when I was visiting my Ma." He was squinting as he said it, probably a candidate for glasses later in life.

Bear crouched to let Wes off his shoulders. "I was visiting someone." He hoped they wouldn't point out the hospital band.

A kid with blue stained lips and the most expensive looking bike butted in. "The girl who fell on your opening night, right? She dead? Someone said her spine shattered and stuck out of her mouth." The last bit made his friends gasp in a mixture of disgusted and impressed.

Wes' biceps visibly clenched. "She didn't die, hence us visiting her. And nothing came out of any mouths. She's fine."

Bear could tell the twin was getting irritated quickly, his mood plummeting as they continued questioning about Quinn and her condition. Leave it to middle school kids to ruin the fun. Grabbing Wes by the arm, he tugged gently towards the store.

"Leave it, Wes." Bear kept his voice quiet as he waved goodbye to the kids.

Wes went straight to the cashier to get the cigarettes while Bear casually browsed the aisles. Making sure the clerk was completely distracted by Wes, he pocketed a package of Reese's and grabbed two bottles of water to pay for. They were rung up together and paid in crumpled bills and loose change that they had to dig out of multiple pockets and count out on sweaty palms. Before they left, the man behind the counter stopped them.

"Y'all in that Circus that's posted up round the way, right? I recognize ya faces from all them fliers."

"Yes, sir," Bear responded.

He eyed them up and down. "Ya do good work?"

"According to some." Wes had puffed out his chest proudly.

The man simply rolled his eyes and turned back to the newspaper he had been reading. Bear led the way back out into the late afternoon sun, thankful to find the teenagers gone and the parking lot empty except for a woman pumping gas into her mini van.

Bear presented Wes the candy as they walked along the main roads back to the Fairgrounds. The sun was dipping below the trees and the air was beginning to chill, and apart from the occasional passing car or chirping cricket on the side of the road, its quiet. Over their heads, the dying sun silhouetted the harsh skyline of a jagged pine tree forest, the sky turning orange beyond its deep purple and blues. Its peaceful and an unknown feeling of serenity so far removed from their normal.

It was pleasant for now, but Bear knew he couldn't live like this forever. He missed their hectic, loud, colorful home. Wes seemed to feel the same, as he pushed his sunglasses back up onto his head as their purpose became obsolete and he became more fidgety.

And then the trapeze artist's walking speed became suddenly erratic. He slowed, then sped up, then stopped abruptly. Bear stuttered, unsure of what to do himself, confused as he was ripped out of his own thoughts by his companion's distress.

"Hey," Bear said, placing a hand on Wes' chest to still him. "Hey, you good?"

Head hanging, Wes started a sentence a couple times but failed to get the first words out, slumping his shoulders. "Man, I – I think Judas wants out."

Bear blinked, trying to catch his brain up. "Out?"

"Of the Circus, Bear."

Oh.

"Shit, man," Bear kept his hand on Wes, tightening it into a fist that balled up the front of his shirt. "Why?"

Wes shrugged and resumed walking, forcing Bear to release his grip and fall into pace with him again. "Ever since Quinn, he's been acting weird. He's not into it anymore... I thought... after our parents..." He trailed off.

A heavy silence fell over them again. It was nearly dark now, and a single star was brave enough to defy the blank, dark slate of night sky, twinkling by its lonesome, like the only fly caught on a glue trap. Or like a single Circus performer alone in the middle of a mighty stage. Roy always said it didn't matter if you performed with a group or by yourself: you were never truly on your own.

A fucking romantic, that man was. And a hopeless one at that.

Bear sighed into the evening. "Sometimes," he said, careful about choosing his next words. Wes was lighting his third cigarette. "I think that's why Maggie left. Like she had enough and didn't have the heart to tell me."

Wes frowned. "Bear, Roy said she was coming back."

"I know. But I think she's close to done, too."

Passing the cigarette to Bear, Wes laughed in a way that said he didn't find a damn thing funny. "We'll probably be the last damn people left on that stage."

"Yeah," Bear agreed. "Unless I drop dead soon."

Wes' face contorted like someone put something foul smelling underneath his nose. "Don't talk like that. You won't."

"I might, according to the doctors."

"Well, shit Bear. What do they know?" Wes was getting angry again, his hand that wasn't holding the butt went carding through his hair anxiously.

"Probably more than we do." Bear tapped his temple with his pointer finger and clicked his tongue. "Medical degree."

"Fucking bullshit, man."

The Fairgrounds were coming into view at the top of the road. Twinkling lights glowed like lightning bugs ahead of them, guiding them the final yards home. Bear's heart rushed with adrenaline and his tired legs found a little bit of fight left to close the distance, already imagining his warm bed and familiar sounds of Circus life. Completely transfixed, he hardly noticed Wes slow to a stop once again until he was a way ahead.

Bear felt Wes' eyes boring into the back of his head. He stopped and turned, waiting for an explanation, too exhausted to ask for it.

"Doctors won't know when its right for you to stop," Wes said. "Only you will."

"No, I won't," Bear said, simply. "Because I'll never stop."

That wasn't the right answer nor the right mindset, but Wes relaxed. And in that moment, Bear knew what he had become to Wes: a martyr. Someone else who was prepared to die for all of this – and maybe Wes became the same thing for him.

They had a history of butting heads, but that's what happens when you're too similar.

Judas and Maggie, along with the rest of the performers, were the lucky ones, the ones who could imagine a life beyond this. One day they'd grow out of their show clothes and replace them with collared shirts and white picket fences, and the Circus would just be a source of stories for their kids and grandkids. Told around a campfire, or while they lulled a child to sleep, or in passing conversation in the office: that's all Bear would be to many of them.

A fairy tale about a dragon.

He never considered Wes might be the only person left that truly understood it, and no doubt Wes was thinking the same about Bear. The poor kid had put all of his faith in his twin brother, who was stood next to him while they watched their parents plummet to their deaths.

Now he was standing out here under a fresh cloak of darkness with someone who wasn't even raised in the Circus – someone who swooped in and stole his rightfully deserved fame and glory.

If someone came in and did that to Bear, he'd hate them, too.

Bear beckoned Wes onward. He waited until he was caught up to keep walking, praying his legs would even make it the long haul to the back of the Fairgrounds where his trailer was.

It was early in the night so the Grounds, while closed to the public, were still alive with music and lights and one or two working rides to entertain the nocturnal circus performers. Bear could see smoke rising in the distance and smell the tantalizing scent of dinner cooking as he stepped through the gates, closing them with a loud clang behind them.

There was one, sharp, excited bark as a warning and then Atlanta was streaking towards them, her black coat a mere blob of shadow as it came careening out of the rows of kiosks. Bear couldn't help the joyful laugh that escaped him or the way his knees buckled as she jumped into his arms. He stumbled backwards, careful not to drop her as she squirmed and whined in his arms, licking his neck and shoulders and scratching him with flailing paws. Bear knelt to place Atlanta back down on the ground, staying at her level so she could continue her onslaught of licks and playful nipping.

"Bear!" Callie followed the Shepherd, also running at a full tilt. Bear managed to stand in time for the young girl to throw herself at him as well, her small arms just barely managing to wrap entirely around his frame. Bear hugged her back, placing a gentle kiss on the top of her head and inhaling the familiar aroma of fried food and *Circus* that clung to her. Callie pulled back to look at him, bright eyes and beaming smile. "You're okay!"

"Never better," Bear hummed, ruffling her hair.

The rest of the performers were starting to notice his return, breaking away from their games or food to run up and greet him. Roy and Dee were some of the last to appear.

They looked disheveled but were smiling brightly when they embraced him in a group hug, placing loving kisses on his cheeks and head. Dee brushed his hair away from his face, cupping his cheek and shaking her head in disbelief.

"You little shit," She said, breathless with relief. "When is enough going to be enough?"

Bear smiled. "I'll let you know when I figure it out."

Dee and Roy both huffed, displeased, grins on their faces. Roy patted him on the back, shoving him towards where dinner was cooking. Bear went simply because he was too tired to argue, his stomach growling as it considered a meal that wasn't ice chips. He wouldn't be able to sleep at this point anyway. He sat as a picnic table with Atlanta between his legs and Callie and Wes on either side of him. Both Ringleaders joined across from them and slid a plate of pasta salad and grilled chicken under Bear's nose.

Bear wolfed it down in seconds, desperate to rid himself of the hunger and lack of sleep headache he was developing. He could feel the other table occupants watching him closely, except for Wes who was also stuffing food in his mouth. Finally, Bear caved and placed both hands palms down on the table as in an invitation to begin speaking.

Roy started. "What'd they say?"

Bear narrowed his eyes, trying to read his Ringleader for any sign of emotion in those cold, grey eyes. "Exactly what you've all been saying," Bear said with a shrug. "It's only going to get worse if I don't stop."

"Stop completely?" Dee asked, "Or just cut back?"

"Stop completely."

A pregnant pause. Wes was scanning the Fairgrounds, no doubt for an identical face, but Judas was nowhere to be found. Maggie wasn't, either.

"Well, what are you going to do?" Roy's voice was quiet, weathered. Once a smoker but long time quit, he still maintained the undeniable cigarette drawl and grate to his words, exaggerated by exhaustion, age, and stress.

Bear said nothing, and that was an answer enough. Dee shot up out of her seat when she realized they'd reached the end of the conversation, her facial features heavy with distress as she shook her head at Bear. She stormed off and Roy watched her go, exhaling a long breath. His eyes were sad when he turned back to Bear.

"I can't stop you," Roy said. He scratched the grey scruff on his chin. Was he thinking about his declaration to the financial advisors? "But I can hope you find the strength to stop yourself." He stood, slower than Dee had, and pulled a flask out of the front pocket of his jeans. Taking a swig, Roy waved a farewell. "Get some sleep, kids. I love you."

Bear, Callie, and Wes all echoed him, and then they were alone at the table, the only performers sitting in a corner while the rest of their comrades played out the night with laughter and games. It was all Bear needed just to watch them, their raw joy and freedom lifting some weight off his shoulders and taking some fatigue with it.

Wes addressed Callie after a couple minutes of silence. "Where's Judas?"

Callie blinked, unaware of the true meaning behind the question. "He turned in early, he said he had a good book he wanted to start reading."

"Maggie?" Bear asked.

"Nothing." Callie sounded sorry. Bear rubbed her back.

"She'll be back," He said.

Callie nodded, nuzzling under his arm and resting her head against his shoulder. Bear used his free hand to wrap around the back of Wes' neck to pull him in against his other side so they were all squished together under the bright lights of the Fairgrounds.

* * *

<u>MAGNOLIA</u>

Adele's car turned a sharp corner, waking Maggie from a dreamless sleep. Her neck was sore from the odd angle in which she had been leaning against the window, and when she twisted around, she found an iced coffee and a Dunkin Donuts bag in the center console. Adele looked over at Maggie's movement and greeted her with a pleasant chirp.

"Good morning slash evening! Donut in the bag, I hope I got your coffee order right."

Maggie took a long sip and moaned in happiness. "Perfect."

She settled back down in the seat, munching on the glazed donut and watching the New Hampshire landscape speed by. Growing up in New York City, Maggie had always forgotten this key-shaped state even existed, much less did she ever appreciate how beautiful it was. There was constant talk every fall from kids whose parents would drag them out to New England for the stunning foliage, and some more well-off classmates boasted about their lake houses or mountain cabins they frequented in the summer. The pictures they returned with were stunning, but did not do the state any justice.

The setting sun was bathing the rolling hills in brilliant light, turning the grass a stunning shade of pastel peach. Fields of wildflowers stretched far beyond the highway, interrupted by the occasional golf course or horse pasture in the distance. Further out, Maggie could

142

see the jagged, harsh angles of the White Mountains reaching into the sky, towering over the land like noble kings. Strangely enough, they called to her.

"Have you ever been to the top of Mount Washington?" Maggie asked Adele, wondering if one of the peaks she could see was the infamous mountain.

"Yes, a few times," Adele responded. "We drove up the auto road, and let me tell you girl, it does not get any less nerve wracking the more times you do it!"

"Nerve wracking?" Maggie echoed, trying to imagine a perilous road.

The woman beside her nodded enthusiastically as she recalled the memory. "Two-way traffic on a dirt road barely the width of one car, no guardrails and a steep drop off a cliff on your right. But my God, is it worth every heart palpitation."

Maggie laughed nervously at just the thought. "Wow, I had no idea it was that intense. I'd love to do it, though."

It took a few more hours until familiar landmarks started to appear as they neared where the Circus was set up, and Maggie straightened in her seat in anticipation. She was excited to see Bear again and be surrounded by her family after such a confusing couple of days, and she knew she had a lot of explaining to do.

The car bumped up the old dirt path, past the flattened-out patches used for parking along the side of the road. Now that it had progressed into nighttime, the arching entrance and dazzling Circus sign were illuminated as Adele put the car in park a few yards away from the gate. Maggie tried to peer beyond into the Fairgrounds for any sign of life, but could only hear excited chatter and the occasional chorus of laughter.

Adele smiled. "Well, you have my number," She said. "Call me when you want to visit him again. We can arrange something."

"Will do," Maggie said, although she wasn't sure if she would. "Thank you."

"Thank *you.*"

Maggie stepped out of the car, her legs stiff from sitting for so long, still in the clothes she left in. She needed a shower. Adele waved from inside the car as she turned and drove back down the road. Maggie waved back, waiting at the gates until she was completely out of view, and the quiet evening befell her.

The gates were unlocked to her surprise. She managed to open and close them without a lot of noise, but she had walked right into a crowd that had formed a circle around something or someone. Andreas, towering a few feet over the rest of the heads, noticed her with wide eyes. Everyone followed his gaze to see her, equally shocked, and Maggie could see that they had been watching a small black box that Allie's head promptly popped out of.

Maggie froze under their confused eyes. Not the warm welcome she was expecting at all.

"You're back," Whitney said, more of a statement than an exclamation. Her eyes glossed over Maggie's condition. "Where'd you go?"

"Not important," Maggie answered, hoping they'd agree.

Allie had clambered out of the box and stood with her hands on her hips, speaking deadpan. "Bear had to go to the hospital."

Maggie's heart dropped like a rock, and all of a sudden it felt like the planet was spinning faster than normal. This was it. Every single nightmare that woke her, every single vivid image that kept her from sleeping in the first place, had come to life on the one god damn day she left. The terror in her chest must've been reflected on her face because Whitney quickly butted back in.

"He's okay," The knife thrower said. "He was only there for a few hours. Collapsed during a practice. Wes brought him home; I think they're having dinner with Roy and Dee."

Maggie nodded, unable to speak, and set off towards the food tents, trying not to choke on a sob that was bubbling up her throat. She turned a corner around a vendor and stopped dead, taking in the scene that welcomed her.

Bear, Wes, Callie, and Paris were sitting at a picnic table, Bear and Wes on one side and Callie and Paris on the other and a deck of cards between them. Wes slapped down a card and shouted, "Uno!", earning himself groans of complaint from Bear and Callie. They were all smiling and laughing and didn't even notice Maggie until she called out.

"Bear!" It was almost a whimper.

Heads snapped in her direction and Atlanta's black muzzle poked out from under the table. Bear dropped his cards instantly and darted towards her, scooping her up in his arms and nearly suffocating her. Maggie released the shaky sob she had been holding in and hugged him back, straining herself to hold on as tightly as she could. The scent of gasoline was faint and replaced by something more sterile. Hospital sterile.

She pulled back to cup his face with both hands, scanning each blister and scar, trying to spot any new ones. "Are you okay?" Maggie breathed.

"Fuck that," Bear said, grabbing her wrist where it rested against his cheek. Maggie spotted the bracelet. "Are you?"

Maggie nodded. "Yeah, I'm okay."

Atlanta's wet nose nudged against her thigh and Maggie laughed, breaking away from Bear to kneel down and embrace the dog. Bear followed her to the ground, wrapping them both up in his arms and pressing his lips into Maggie's hair. Maggie forgot about prisons, her uncle, the long car rides. She was here, and Bear was alive, and that was all she needed.

MOVING MOUNTAINS

<u>CALLIE</u>

A single, loud and purposeful knock on her trailer door startled Callie fully awake. She had been drifting for a few hours now, listening to the gentle snores coming from Paris at the other end of her trailer.

(He had begun to occupy Quinn's empty bunk, something Callie suggested herself. It was lonely and drafty without someone to share it with, and Paris was a good roommate: clean, organized, quiet, and respectful.)

The knock made the boy stir, too, but not fully wake. Callie waited, wondering if she had imagined it, but then it was followed by a second, more aggressive knock. She shot up, throwing the covers off of her and peering through the curtain. It was pitch black out, but Bear's red hair was bright enough to pick out through the shadows.

Yawning, Callie opened the door with a scowl. Maggie, Bear, and Atlanta were all standing in front of her with cheerful smiles.

"Whatever you want," Callie hissed, "better be worth your lives."

"Want to go for a hike?" Maggie asked, whispering. Her eyes were bright with excitement and she, along with Bear, was wearing hiking boots and light backpacks.

Bear butted in. "You can sleep in the car on the way there, come on. Get P, too."

"I'm in." Paris' sleepy voice from behind Callie surprised her. She turned on him, he was wrapped up in a blanket and rubbing his eyes with the heels of his hands. He looked at Callie when he lowered them. "What? I've never been hiking before."

"It'll be awesome," Maggie assured. "Get dressed."

With Maggie's guidance, Callie and Paris got dressed in appropriate clothes. Bear waited outside the trailer, chewing on an unlit cigarette and humming one of the Circus tunes. As they stepped out to join him, Callie and Paris sharing the blanket, the fire breather was taking the keys to the truck from a very sleepy looking Roy.

Bear and Maggie hopped in the front, Bear behind the wheel and Atlanta by Maggie's feet. Callie and Paris huddled in the back, still yawning off the last of their sleepy haze. The seats were faded upholstery, and aided by the moonlight, Callie saw dark stains of splattered blood right before Paris sat down on them, unbeknownst to the little reminder of Bear's scare below him.

Roy was waiting by the gates to open them, waving them off into the early morning with a sleepy smile. Callie turned to watch the entrance shut behind them. She was wide awake now, beginning to buzz with anticipation as the truck bumped down the dirt road to the paved side streets. Maggie was looking down at her phone, absentmindedly chewing on a thumbnail while Bear swung the truck out left onto the road without stopping.

"What'd we settle on?" Maggie asked.

"Welch and Dickey," Bear answered.

"Might be tough for those two."

Bear's eyes flashed with challenge in the rear-view mirror. "They'll be fine."

There was one long, winding highway that stretched from the top of New Hampshire to the bottom, Maggie said. Callie watched towns turn into pastures that turned into mountains as Bear zipped further into the darkness, following the North Star. After an hour of driving Bear pulled off of an exit. The familiar, taunting sigh to a Dunkin Donuts shone lonesome in the darkness.

"Is there a Dunkins every square mile in this state?"
Callie asked, her belly rumbling for a chocolate glazed
donut.

Paris, who grew up in Massachusetts, giggled into
the blanket. "Yeah, pretty much."

They drove down winding back roads, through
neighbor hoods and along a bend around a large, still
pond. Maggie rolled down her window as Bear slowed to
nearly a stop. Through the night, Callie could recognize
the sound of peeping frogs. Bear sped back up, a few
minutes later they passed a deep brown, large, wooden
sign that said "White Mountain National Forest" in bold
yellow letters.

The paved road took a sharp uphill turn, the trees
closer than they were on the main road. It opened up
into an empty parking lot with a map on the far end of it.
Bear parked as close to the trail head as he could and
stepped out into the chilly morning. Atlanta and Maggie
hopped out next, Callie and Paris following more
reluctantly, limbs stiff from sleep and sitting so long.

"Reviews say to hike Welch first, then Dickey.
Which means turning..." Maggie twisted around, trying
to figure out her directions in the darkness.

"Right." Bear pointed to the sign with the trail
names accompanied by little yellow arrows. He pulled
two headlamps out of his bag, handing one off to Maggie.

The clown rolled her eyes and started off down the
path with Atlanta trotting a few paces ahead. Bear waited
for Callie and Paris, walking slowly at their sides. It was
only a few meters into the woods that they came to a
stream bubbling across the trail. Maggie and Atlanta
crossed first, jumping from rock to rock until they
reached the other side. Bear helped Callie across and

then Paris, taking up the rear to make sure no one slipped.

Callie walked behind with Bear while Paris skipped ahead to join Maggie. It was eerie in the forest but somehow Callie didn't feel anxious. It was peaceful, quiet, and Atlanta's calm disposition made her feel a lot better. Through the trees, the moonlight illuminated a towering cliff, bending like the arch of a sleeping giant's back, spindly trees sticking up like the quills of a porcupine.

Bear followed her gaze. "We'll be on that ridge."

"Really?" Callie found it hard to believe, but it gave her a needed push onwards.

Within forty-five minutes, they broke out of the trees and back under the moonlight, picking up into a jog across an open rock face, following yellow trail markers on the ground. Atlanta skidded to a halt ahead of them, her front paws halfway off a sudden dip down into a valley. The view was hard to appreciate in the dark, but Callie could see towering mountains right ahead of them, seemingly so close that she could reach out and touch them.

Bear glanced up at the sky. "Let's keep going. Got to beat the sun."

The trail, which had been pretty moderate up to the first view, turned into a sheer rock face. Maggie stood with her hands on her hips, watching Atlanta bound up with ease and disappear into a patch of forest over a hump. Her curious black head peaked back over the edge, as if to say, "*What's taking you guys so long?*"

"Damn dog," Bear huffed, and led the way up the rocks, using his hands to aid him.

Callie was almost out of breath by the time they reached the first ledge. They were starting to be able to see over the mountains and trees as they kept climbing, occasionally breaking to glance over their shoulder and judge their process. The night was beginning to fade, a thin line of light peaking bravely over the furthest hills. Maggie passed around water bottles and trail mix as they sat down on some rocks right where the trail finally plateaued again.

Bear sat next to Callie, sharing a water bottle and a handful of trail mix with her. He scowled lightheartedly when she picked out all of the M&Ms to shove selfishly into her mouth before he could get any himself. Callie stuck her tongue out at him.

Sat on the ground, Paris was watching Maggie with a frown on his face. The clown pretended not to notice, although the stiffness in her body and the way she angled it slightly away from him told Callie that she knew he was staring at her. She was just trying to avoid what came next.

"Where did you go?" The boy asked. No one had bothered questioning her, not when she came back, not in the following hours. Callie figured if anyone was going to risk bringing it up, the person she had the newest relationship with would be the best bet.

Maggie's perfect posture slouched on an exhale. She looked at Bear with an emotion in her eyes that Callie couldn't identify, but Callie guessed that they were expecting the same thing out of the fire breather. But Bear, against Callie's expectations, did not tell Paris to forget about it or leave it alone, or say that Maggie didn't have to tell them. He sat there, stoic, like a poor, sorry man who made the mistake of looking at Medusa.

Maggie tugged her bottom lip into her mouth. "I got contacted by the judge that worked on my father's case. She invited me to go visit him."

"In prison?" Callie blurted, unable to stop herself. Immediately she slammed a hand over her mouth.

"Yeah, in prison." Maggie didn't even spare Callie a glance. She was trying to gauge Bear's reaction. They all were.

Bear's face never changed, he kept that emotionless mask on, but his eyes gave everything away. They went from cold and unmoving, to swimming with confusion, to fiery with hurt.

"Why didn't you just tell me?" Bear asked, quiet and, if Callie dug a little deeper, insulted.

Maggie almost went to reach for him but pulled her hands back. "Because I was afraid, I thought I was going to lose my nerve, and the less people to know that I couldn't go through with it..."

"I wouldn't have judged you for that," Bear cut in. "I *don't* judge you for any of it."

"I know," Maggie whispered. "I was just scared."

"It's okay to be scared. And it's okay to not tell me everything." Bear tossed Atlanta a pretzel. He sighed and finally smiled. From Callie's angle, it looked forced. "I get it."

Maggie didn't respond. She looked guilty, like she didn't believe Bear's sentiment, but she didn't argue. Callie wondered if she thought the darkness was hiding her wet eyes.

Then Bear lifted his head. "I've taken Callie as an apprentice."

Maggie's jaw dropped in shock, and then not even the shadows could disguise how her face went flush with anger. "You *what*?"

A jolt of electricity shot through Bear's body. He went rigid like someone flipped a switch. Callie could feel his muscles contracting where they were pressed together on the small rock; Atlanta began to whine in warning, pressing closer to her owner and licking his hands.

"She wants to learn," Despite his stiff posture, Bear's tone was cool and collected: *what are you going to do about it?* "Who better – who *else* – to teach her?"

"How about no one?" Maggie hissed back. The unfamiliar hostility between the two made Atlanta's ears fold back. "Because, I don't know, it's killing you and could eventually kill her? Have you lost your mind? Or are you just finally willing to admit you care more about this Circus that anyone or anything else?"

"You ran off!" Bear blurted. "You were gone, and I can make my own decisions for what I think is best."

Maggie laughed; it was bitter, stinging Callie deep in her belly. "You think this is best, Bear? You and Wes, man. You're both fucking delusional."

"How come I can accept you disappearing out of thin air and leaving everyone worried for a full night," Bear said, "but you can't accept this?"

"Because this is hurting you!" Maggie said, exasperated.

Bear stood up, sending Atlanta reeling back in shock. "I went to the *hospital.* I was the closest I've ever actually been to dying, and *you weren't there.*" He spit the last three words out with petulant venom.

The pair fell silent.

Atlanta was staring up at Bear, whining, nudging his hand to get his attention. The fire breather tore his eyes away from Maggie's watery expression to kneel down with his face buried in his dog's shoulder.

Callie glanced over at Paris, who had his head hanging and foot tapping nervously. The mountain was eerily quiet until, eventually, Maggie spoke.

"I'm worried about you," She whispered, waiting until Bear was looking at her to continue. "And I know that you hate that I am, and I do have faith in you and your abilities, but that doesn't mean I don't worry about you."

"We all are," Paris softly added, not raising his head. Bear looked at the kid, confused, but returned his attention to Maggie.

"I'm sorry," Bear murmured. "I don't blame you; you just scared me."

Maggie laughed. "Well, it's about time, right? You scare me every day."

Surprised by her lighthearted chuckle, Bear fumbled for a second before mirroring her tired smile. "Yeah, alright. We're even."

"Far from even yet."

Behind them, the cliff side Callie saw from the woods was looming nearer. Despite the aching in her legs and lungs, her body buzzed with energy, urging her to continue. Atlanta was pacing around them, ears pricked into the darkness, eager to get moving as well. The group exchanged glances and nodded, packing up the water and continuing along the open rock face. They bounded up more rocks and then Callie gasped, realizing they were on the hump of the first mountain.

"Wow," She gasped, turning to admire the 360-degree view. Down the other side and up another cliff, the second summit towered higher even.

The White Mountains rolled in every direction around them, like a blanket with wrinkles in it. The ranges moved with one another, a perfect unity of valleys and rivers. Light was starting to illuminate the individual bumps and curves, turning them from undistinguishable blobs of shadow to something more unique from one another. Callie could pick out each tree on the nearest ones. They stood in silence, as unmoving as the mountains themselves, admiring the view. Even Atlanta sat solemnly at Bear's feet, watching where he watched.

"This is Welch," Maggie announced. "I want to get to Dickey before the sun rises."

"Onward then!" Bear called, already making his way down the other side of the hump with Atlanta.

It was a short walk down one mountain and up the next, through a canopy of low trees and slick rocks. The trail markings became few and far between and difficult to spot. Atlanta ended up being their guide, finding her way through the dark forest with her nose to the ground, walking slow enough so they could still spot her black coat through the shadows.

Callie grumbled with complaint when they broke out of the trees and faced yet another steep rock scramble. "I'm getting tired of these cliffs."

Bear was already at the top with Atlanta. "This is the last one! I'm at the summit, come on."

With Paris and Maggie on either side of her, Callie heaved herself up the last few yards. She turned towards the east, her breath catching in her throat as she took the view in.

Below them, Welch stood closer than the rest of the mountains. The sunrise was in full effect, an exquisite mixture of pinks, purples, blues, oranges, and yellows, like a wayward artist ran along the horizon line with a paintbrush. The bold golden sun was determined to make its statement against the canvas of colors, rising over the peaks and casting everything below it in dazzling aurum light.

Bear stood at the very edge of the summit, Atlanta between his legs, the wind blowing his hair and cigarette smoke to the left, in the same direction the clouds were moving. Callie stayed back a few meters, huddled up with Paris and Maggie against the invasive mountain gusts, watching as the fire breather slowly raised his arms to a 'T', palms to the sky, as if desperate to float up into it.

From this far back, with the mountain ranges rolling like ocean waves beyond him, Bear looked, for the first time in Callie's eyes, tiny. Even when he was alone on that stage underneath a towering red and white ceiling, surrounded by rows and rows of bleachers with dozens of eyes on him, Bear had the ability to make himself big.

He was insignificant here. Is that why he brought them here?

Or was it something else entirely. Was it for the way the incline made their lungs ache, reminding them that they are in fact living beings, and not just souls occupying a borrowed body? Every burn and blister, every scar and tattoo, every white blood cell fighting against the sickness plaguing his body belonged to Bear – could he feel that, here? Did he struggle to feel attached to those things just as Callie found it impossible to believe these chalk-dried hands and aching muscles belonged to her?

Maggie broke off from their huddle and joined Bear at the edge, gently taking both of his hands in hers, lowering them so she could wrap her arms around his shoulders and embrace him. He returned the hug ten-fold, burying his face in her neck, holding so tightly her feet came off the ground. Although not able to see either of their faces, Callie knew they were smiling and crying all at once.

A mutual apology, mutual reassurance.

Callie couldn't help but wonder if Maggie would go see her father again. With Bear's blessing, she might. Was there really closure in that? Maggie did so much to race so far ahead, only to slow her pace to let her past catch up.

Eight months ago, Callie ran to the Circus because she couldn't stand to be home after her mother died. It all felt like her fault: the broken marriage, the scattered siblings, the alcoholism and debt that followed. Maggie joined on a stroke of rebellion, an escape from a prison. Paris was brought there like an old sofa being dumped at a landfill: Paris was considered a freak, and freaks belong at the Circus.

And Bear – Bear who refused to become lost in a statistic. Bear who would not let himself blow up, unnamed, on a battlefield; Bear who would not let his life slip away in a hospital bed. Bear who would be known, who would be plastered upon posters, even in death.

They were not *freaks*, and neither was Paris.

They were just lost. And now they were found.

THURSDAY

<u>BEAR</u>

Backed by some newfound confidence from their hike, Callie met Bear under the Big Top the next morning with a puffed-out chest and a strut in her step. Bear was playing tug with Atlanta with an old tattered rope, his muscles bugling out from his thin black tank top. Maggie, Wes, Roy, Dee, and Paris were all sitting up in the bleachers, leaning forward with anticipation.

Bear only brought a can of gasoline that had about two inches left, three torches, and a bottle of water to share between them. He was center stage, coughing into his elbow as he lowered himself to sit on the ground. Callie sat across from him without arguing this time, looking far more willing and less defiant than she had last time.

Crossing his legs, Bear nodded to Callie. "Breathe."

The young girl closed her eyes, face stoic, and took long, deep breaths. Bear's lungs struggled to do the same, each inhale becoming more difficult and each exhale burning a little more than the one before it. He felt like he was trying to breathe through a straw while someone sat on his chest. Peaking one eye open, Bear saw Maggie staring at him from the bleachers, a frown posted on her pretty face. Callie was still meditating in obedience, her back straight and each breath coming in perfectly timed succession to the prior.

Bear sighed in quiet frustration, wishing his head would stop pounding and his lungs would open up. Callie blinked open her brown eyes, curious, to see Bear slouched over and breathing heavily.

"Feel relaxed?" He rasped; hands flat against the hard ground, he pushed himself to his feet.

Callie followed suit and stood, still eyeing him strangely. "Yeah. Super relaxed."

"Perfect." Bear moved towards the torches and kerosene. His vision went in and out of focus but he shook it off. Not the time for another episode.

He got each torch ready, feeling the heavy weight of Maggie's green eyes boring into his back. A natural born giver, Maggie gave and gave until she nothing else left to give – but she would not give her blessing to Bear, not for this. It was a lesson she was trying to teach him, no doubt. He had never been susceptible to those.

Rocking on the balls of her feet, Callie waited for Bear near the center of the ring, looking as if she was trying to maintain her childlike eagerness. Bear sighed inwardly, slightly disappointed to see that her time meditating did nothing to calm her down. Instead it appeared to amp her up even more, like revving an engine before slamming on the gas. Except, in this case, it was gas over an open flame, inches away from her face.

No pressure.

"Calm yourself, Callie," Bear instructed. "I can see you vibrating from here."

"It's anxiety," Callie lied. She didn't sound anxious at all. There was a youthful pitch to her voice that frightened Bear more than anything.

To negate her point, Bear reminded her: "Anxiety can be worse than excitement, you know."

As if he had shown a bright light at her face whilst she was sitting at a questioning table, Callie froze, caught in the act. She steadied her feet and straightened her back, tossing her head as if she were a chastised filly. Her head returned to its stationary position with a more focused, serious expression on her face, and only then did Bear hand her an unlit torch.

"For now," He began, stepping back. "Just put the wick in your mouth; get a feel for the size and shape." By happenstance, Bear glanced in the direction of Wes, who was mouthing *that's what she said* from his seat in the bleachers. Bear rolled his eyes and flipped him the bird.

Callie didn't appear to notice the exchange; she was hard focused on the torch, spinning it around by the handle in her dainty hands. It looked much bigger compared to when Bear held it. Somehow, this situation was becoming less and less ideal, and Bear didn't think that was possible.

With two hands behind his back like a general surveying his troops, Bear watched Callie experiment with the torch. She brought it towards her open mouth cautiously like it was already on fire. Briefly, Bear wondered if her jaw could open wide enough to fit the broad, rounded square wick. It did, to his surprise and dismay. The whole scene felt wildly inappropriate, worsening still when she gagged and pulled it out of her mouth in horror. Bear scrunched up his nose.

Short on breath, Callie gasped, "I'm supposed to do that while its *on fire*?"

Bear choked on a laugh despite himself. "Yeah. That's kind of the basis of eating fire."

"Right." Callie sounded quiet and almost ashamed of herself.

"You don't have to do this, you know." Bear tried to keep his tone light, struggling to keep out a note of hopefulness or, if misunderstood, challenge. "There's a reason fire acts have such a high wash out rate. You either wise up, and choose something else or you get your face burnt up and your lips melted together."

His young companion's face twisted in disgust at the vivid image. "Which category do you fall under?"

"I think I'm nearing total lip solidification." Bear grinned crookedly, his smile favoring the left side of his face, as always. Realizing he was fighting a losing battle, he gestured with his own unlit torch towards the bottle of kerosene sitting patiently. "You ready?"

Callie nodded, eyebrows knit together in concentration. Bear took Callie's torch from her and then lit each one, careful to hold them far out as the initial fireballs shot up into impressive, but hopefully short-lived, existence.

"If you can master putting the flame out with your mouth," Bear said, "we'll move on to tongue transfers." He passed the torch back to her, making note of the nervous flash in her wide, brown eyes.

"What are tongue transfers?"

"With one torch, you transfer the flame onto your tongue, and then pick it back up with a second, unlit torch." Bear grabbed himself another torch and performed a simple version of the act he had long since mastered. The acrobat in front of him looked incredulous. Once he trusted his voice to speak again, he looked pointedly at Callie's wick just burning away. "Go on, then. Put it out."

Bear didn't know when or why he decided to become such a hard ass of a teacher, but he figured at this point, with this girl, it was the best he could be. He knew what she was going through and the risk of feeding into her rebellion was too high.

Callie looked at the flame in her hand with uncertainty, flashing Bear a wide-eyed plea: "Can you show me again?"

He showed her the move once more, coughing out a puff of smoke to punctuate it. She still looked unsure but she didn't hesitate any longer. Neck back, tongue out, mouth open, Callie brought the flame towards her soft face with more confidence than she had the last time. Regardless, she still yanked it away last minute, panting like she had just run a marathon.

Bear felt a surge of irritation spike through his nerves. It was misplaced, which made him more annoyed with himself – how dare he be irked that Callie was reacting in the very way he prayed she would. In a moment of epiphany that rolled his stomach slowly like he had become suddenly sea sick, Bear realized he was projecting. He could not train Callie with the same hard hand he had trained himself with.

More desperate now, Bear repeated, "You don't have to do this."

Callie glared daggers. "I'm doing it," She growled.

"Okay. Just remember: don't breathe in until you remove the torch."

The torch approached her mouth once again, this time with more purpose. Bear watched, subconsciously picking at a blister until he felt it pop and leak pus near the corner of his mouth, not even noticing it around the stinging taste of gasoline still residing on his tongue.

Callie took one last deep inhale with the flame safely away from her mouth, then closed the distance. Bear's eyebrows shot up, equally shocked and impressed as her lips formed the perfect *O* shape around the wick of the torch, cutting off all oxygen from the fire. There was the split second of hesitation before Callie whipped it out of her mouth and promptly emptied her stomach contents out on the stage floor by her bare feet.

Bear was too proud to notice the vomit, his hands flying up in the air in excitement. "Atta girl!" All previous worries forgotten about, he snatched the torch away from her before she could drop it.

He was already picturing it: him and Callie, a duo of utmost skill, performing for huge crowds. The money would rain down on them, the Big Top would shudder with the calls of their names.

A flipped switched in Bear's mind. This could work.

He rubbed her back sympathetically as she remained bent over, spitting out like a dog that swallowed a bee. Scattered applause came from the bleachers but barely carried over thanks to the poor acoustics in the Big Top. Bear and Callie stayed in their own little world; he helped her straighten up, wiping the tears from her cheeks and commanding Atlanta to fetch them the bottle of water.

The Shepherd trotted over with it proudly, disposing of it in Bear's hand. Like a mother, Bear tipped it upwards so Callie could drink hands free, still rubbing her back in big circles. She gargled and spat most of the water like mouthwash, but she finished off the rest of it with heaving, desperate gulps.

"See, not that bad, right?" Bear laughed, using his black tank top to dry off her chin and cheeks.

Callie smiled weakly, her voice hoarse and already damaged. "Yeah. Easy peasy."

The others had trailed off towards the food tent, listening to Callie chatter with excitement as they tried to feel it with her. Bear saw the looks of disapproval on their faces when they past him, though: it was hard to look Roy and Maggie in the eye. Wes had given him a pat on the shoulder, one gentle squeeze, and said: "They'll come around."

Bear doubted it.

He stood alone underneath the Big Top as the vacated it, promising he'd be there soon. With robotic movements, he cleaned up the torches and the kerosene, dumped his drinking water on Callie's vomit, mopped up the floor with his towels. He hooked his torches up to his belt loop and stored the kerosene away in the back behind the curtains.

Atlanta watched him, stoic. Those bat ears stayed pricked, occasionally angling towards him if he walked away, but she remained still and silent. Bear found it more difficult to deal with her silence than anyone else's.

Kneeling to her eye level, Bear traced a finger along the length of Atlanta's thick muzzle. Her whiskers twitched and she sneezed.

"Are you mad at me, too?" Bear asked her, staring into her brown eyes, trying to find a hint of the human emotion. "I'm doing what I can," He pressed. "I'm trying to please everyone, Atlanta."

The Shepherd closed the distance between them, her large head resting against the crook of his neck. Bear wrapped his arms around her body. For minutes they rested there, matching their breathing, until Bear couldn't stand the taste of gasoline in his mouth anymore.

"Come on." He rose to his feet. Atlanta grabbed the pack he brought, and at his German command she dropped it in his hand. Bear rummaged through it until he found the brand-new toothbrush and tub of toothpaste.

Behind the Big Top, there were troths of water set out for people to wash off makeup or the reek of the day's work. Bear sunk to the ground in front of one like a bag of rocks. He lathered the bristles of his brush with flavorless toothpaste and went to work, his dog sitting over his shoulder like a watchful statue.

Bear leaned over the water, brushing his teeth with ferocity. He scrubbed his tongue, almost down his throat, until he was gagging and vomiting into the grass.

What dribble down his chin afterward was a foaming mixture of toothpaste, spit, and bright red blood; he caught some in his hand, watching it travel in the tiny crevices of his palm lines. The toothbrush bristles were flattened and a deep shade of maroon.

Atlanta's tail wagged against the grass, a swishing sound that doubled as a warning. Bear turned around, the movement causing his head to swim and his vision to blacken for a few moments.

When he could see again, Bear saw Judas slowly lowering himself down next to him, a steadying hand reaching out to cup the back of his neck. Disoriented, Bear saw Wes first; and then his brain recognized short hair and an expression softer than the other twin was capable of.

"Bear," Judas said, "are you okay?"

"I'm fine," Bear gasped out, not even sounding convincing to himself. His lungs were protesting each breath, begging for a break that he could not give to them. "Just brushing my teeth."

"To the gum?" Judas was looking at the blood still flowing from his mouth.

Bear wiped it on the back of his hand. "More or less."

"Here." The aerialist passed him a water bottle. His tone hardened. "Drink."

Too tired to do anything but comply without argument, Bear chugged the water until it was empty. His mouth had finished bleeding by the end and he opened his eyes to see Judas scratching behind Atlanta's ears absentmindedly.

"Better?" Judas asked as Bear crumpled the plastic up.

"Yeah, thank you."

Judas watched him carefully, but curiously. Bear rearranged so he was off of his hands and knees and sitting up, head tipped back towards the sky, breathing heavily. He knew what was coming, the question was inevitable, and so he just waited for it.

"So, you're training Callie?"

Ding, ding, ding.

Bear tilted his bloody chin down. "Yeah. She just ate fire for the first time."

Judas nodded. "Wes just told me – he's proud of you. Both of you."

There it was, the disapproval in his eyes. It flashed briefly, like a bird flying by a window, a fleeting hint. Bear understood; it was not for him. It was for Wes.

"I think he's living vicariously through me," Bear said. "You know, with you here he won't ever need to take an apprentice – at least not for a while."

Judas bestowed him a small smile. "He likes you. I know he can be a jealous dickhead, but he was just used to being the best before you came around. You weren't necessarily part of his success plan."

"Roy's, on the other hand..." Bear trailed off with a laugh.

His smile turned sad; Judas agreed. "Yeah, you were like striking gold to him." The twin looked at him. "You know there's more though, right, Bear?"

Frowning, Bear echoed: "More?"

"Than this." Judas gestured towards the bloody toothbrush still resting in a puddle of translucent vomit. "And I'm sure you don't need one more person telling you this, but I'm worried about you, Bear. You don't look so hot lately."

"You don't think I'm handsome?" Bear gasped, throwing a hand dramatically to his chest. Judas looked confused for a moment before breaking out into a giggling fit, his cheeks rosy and flushed.

"You're very handsome," Judas said after he regained himself. With not much effort, he smacked Bear's shoulder. "Jackass. You know what I meant."

Bear nodded, the movement making his head swirl again. Using Judas' arm for support, he managed to clamber to his feet right as Maggie and Wes turned the corner, each holding a cone of cotton candy. Their smiling faces turned into worried ones when they saw the blood, but Bear quickly waved them off.

"Just brushing," He said nonchalantly.

"Everything clean?" Maggie asked, stepping up to him. They were chest to chest, Maggie about a head shorter than Bear so she had to go on her tip-toes to align their faces. When her nose was in front of his mouth, he parted his lips and exhaled just enough for her to get a quick whiff.

"Can you smell the gasoline?" He whispered as she dropped back down to flat feet.

"Yes," Maggie said, honest and quiet.

Bear wrapped his arm around her shoulders, planted a quick kiss to the top of her head, and called Atlanta to his side. "Everyone's just going to have to deal with it then, huh?"

Wes grinned his shit-eating grin that told Bear he was on his side. "C'mon, let's get something other than fire in that belly." To punctuate his point, he slapped Bear lightly on the abs. "It's Thursday!"

* * *

MAGNOLIA

Thursday nights were special at the Circus. It was their last down night before the weekend shows to practice, perfect any new quirks, or get crossed by the fire pit.

Roy drove the truck through the Fairgrounds, fist heavy on the horn, announcing the arrival of alcohol and bags of fast food. The older performers raided the six packs and bottles of wine out of the bed of the truck while the younger teenagers fought for the McDonalds fries.

Maggie sat on Bear's lap in a camp chair by the fire pit, sucking on the end of a joint while the fire breather rolled up another one on her thigh. Judas sat on a blanket with Atlanta by their feet while his twin brother rummaged through the alcohol pickings. Wes returned to them with a bottle of Jack Daniels and two nips of Fireball. He plopped down next to Judas, taking the joint from Maggie's outstretched hand.

Scanning the large group of performers loitering by the fire, Maggie found Callie and Paris sitting at a picnic table with Dee, smiling as they stuffed their faces with hamburgers and chicken nuggets. Even Mavis found some energy to join the festivities, sitting safely in her own secluded area with Roy, chatting and sharing a milkshake. Maggie sighed contently and nuzzled into Bear's shoulder.

She tried not to let herself get too comfortable, too used to the peace. This would all be over in twenty-four hours, all the carefree happiness and youthful energy. By Saturday morning, they'd all be back to nursing wounds or sleeping away migraines, barely able to crawl out of bed for breakfast. Bear would be brushing his mouth bloody, the trapeze artists and Strong Men would be applying muscle soothing lotion on their entire bodies, knife throwers would be wrapping each other's wrists in homemade braces.

Instead, Maggie tried to focus on Bear's arm tight around her waist, the shit-eating grin on his face as he shot back and forth with Wes, and Atlanta sprawled out on her back as Judas rubbed her belly. She found herself spacing out in the direction of the Ferris wheel where it stood tall and desolate, a circular metal skeleton against the dark sky. The others must have caught her staring, because their conversation faded to a halt and they followed her gaze.

Wes sniffed and stood, wobbling on unsteady legs for a moment. "Let's slip out," He said with a grin.

They all followed suit, quietly as to not alert anyone they didn't want accompanying them. Moments like these belonged to just the four of them, plus Atlanta, as they always had for many years. Through the shadows cast by kiosks, they walked single file like ants towards the Ferris wheel. Bear knelt for Wes to put Atlanta up on his shoulders, Maggie stuffed the bottle of alcohol into her jacket pocket, and Judas led the way up through the beams. Maggie could've climbed it with her eyes closed, as familiar with the structure as she was with riding a bike.

The tallest cab was never the same, as it was stopped differently every night. Judas opened the door and clambered in, reaching down to offer Maggie a hand. They slid over to the furthest side so Atlanta could hop off of Bear's shoulders, and the two last boys could heave themselves in after her. They rocked back and forth with the momentum.

"I used to be terrified of it shaking like this," Judas laughed, echoing what Maggie had just been thinking.

Wes nodded at Maggie; she pulled his alcohol out and handed it across the cab to him and Bear who were sitting practically on top of each other. Bear's head was tilted back and his breathing was slow and shallow, Atlanta curled up by his feet. Wes was downing the Jack Daniels by himself, his offers to the rest of them all politely declined. Judas was silent, looking out beyond the Fairgrounds to the mountains in the distance.

"Do you guys ever wonder," The boy began, quietly, "what else there is?"

Bear answered without opening his eyes or lifting his head. "I've seen what else there is. It isn't fun, Jude."

"You only saw the bad parts, Bear," Judas countered. "There's got to be good parts, too."

"There are," Maggie agreed. "Somewhere out there."

"This—" Wes gestured widely with his arm, almost smacking Bear in the face in the process. "— is the good part. Look at us! No job, no responsibilities, no rules to follow; we're living everyone's dream lives right now."

Judas glared at his brother. "How can you even say that after Quinn? After our parents? What twisted reality do you live in that *this* is your standard for the 'good parts'?"

"They knew the risks!" Wes hissed. "We do this because we made the conscious choice to make the sacrifice. Everyone here knows what they're putting on the line."

"I didn't get to choose!" Judas blurted out. "I was born into this! I didn't get to decide, this is all we know."

Silence.

Wes was breathing heavily, jaw clenched. Bear was finally sitting up, fully aware, one eyebrow cocked up in anticipation. Filling the sudden cease in conversation was the gentle creak of the Ferris wheel cabs moving in the breeze, and the faint chatter around the fire pit below them. Wes polished off the last of his drink, scrunching his nose at the bitter burning that melted down his throat.

The twins were at a crossroads, a Western-style standoff that was a long time coming. Maggie found some sick sort of comfort in getting verbal confirmation that she wasn't the only one beginning to tire of the emotional toll of the Circus. Judas was right, though.

Unlike Maggie, who had simply fallen in love with the idea of a freedom different from anything she'd ever experience, Judas was born into this life and never got a chance to step outside of it. He had to see a constant flow of troubled kids stumble into his home, bags under their eyes and tears on their cheeks, seeking out an escape from the very life he was yearning for.

The grass was always fucking greener.

"So, what?" Wes eventually said. "This is your swan song? Twenty-two years of our parents' efforts, and you're bailing?"

His twin brother sighed in defeat. "You don't get it, Wes. My whole life, I've been doing this for mom and dad, and now for you. For once I want to do something for *me*."

Maggie flinched because the desperate plea was nearly identical to the guts she spilled to her father.

From the outside looking in, the twins' relationship appeared completely different from Maggie and Bear's – but the root of it was the same. Sacrifice in the name of love.

She felt eyes on her. Chocolate brown perfectly sandwiched between nearly-burnt off eyebrows and above heavy grey bags, Bear was gauging her knee-jerk reaction to Judas' declaration. Maggie would not turn to look at him, terrified that her own eyes would give away her heart, as he said they did often. At the fire breather's feet, Atlanta whined.

Bear bent down, petting his dog around her collar and kissing her on top of the head, right between her pointy black ears. "What are you going to do?" He asked Judas, keeping his tone light. Wes was still brooding, a lit cigarette between his teeth as he stared blankly down at the fire.

Judas glanced warily at his brother. "I don't know. I was thinking of going back to San Fransisco."

That made sense. Maggie remembered the last time there were there, back in January, Judas fell head over heels for a local girl. He fit in well with the scene, too, and had spent a lot of free time going out with the girl's friend group. He spoke about returning a lot but no one ever thought much of it – it was a game they played. Bear's heart yearned for the mountains of Colorado, Wes felt a connection to Michigan, and Maggie loved Tennessee.

But Judas wasn't speaking wistfully. He said it with earnest and determination.

"You already have plane tickets, don't you?" Maggie asked.

Judas sighed. "Pepper and I have been arranging it for a while now. I leave tomorrow."

A stunned silence was the only response he got; even Maggie was taken aback. "Were you just going to leave without telling anyone?" Maggie whispered, her heart shattering more by the passing second.

"You did."

"I came back!"

"You're not even going to stay for one last show?" Bear asked, incredulous.

Wes stood out of nowhere, shoving past Bear and out of the cab. Maggie leaned over to watch him shimmy his way back down the Ferris wheel without looking back up. When she turned back to the remaining boys, Bear was shaking his head at Judas, muscular arms folded across his chest.

"I get it, man," Bear said. "Or, I'm trying to - but leaving like this? That doesn't sit right with me."

"I was going to find a better time before this," Judas insisted, only now beginning to look guilty. "But Quinn happened, and then Maggie disappeared, and then you... I just didn't want to be another piece of bad news."

"I don't think this is much better, brother."

Judas didn't respond. His blue eyes traced the peeling paint within the cab like the answers he searched for might be ingrained in the colorful patterns. Maggie didn't have to tell him that he wouldn't find what he was looking for. The trapeze twin waited for a few more minutes until he realized no one had anything else to say to him either way. Bear and Maggie weren't in the business of changing minds, especially one so made up.

Judas stood, whispering a quiet goodnight, and slithered down the emergency access ladder after his brother.

And then it was just Maggie, Bear, and Atlanta, sitting like a lonely ellipsis at the end of a trailing sentence. Three peas in a rocking, metal pod at the top of a Ferris wheel. Atlanta whined, her front paws up on the cab so she could peer over the edge and search for her departed friends.

Bear sighed heavily. "I do get it, wanting to leave, but leaving like that just feels..."

"Dirty," Maggie finished for him, wondering if that was even the right word for it. Another word rang in her subconscious: hypocrite.

But she had come back, and perhaps Judas would, too. Maybe he'd get to San Francisco and spend a week or two and realize he missed the Circus something fierce, and nothing could compare to the late nights and Ferris wheels and fried Oreos. Or maybe he'd sit by a rain-wet window with a mug of tea and a blanket spread over legs that didn't ache or bruise, reading a good book, humming the chords to a Fairgrounds song that was only a distant memory.

Maggie hoped he'd find what he was looking for out there, that he'd find those good parts he talked about. She hoped he'd bring some back for her one day, too.

NOTHING ELSE MATTERS

<u>BEAR</u>

Bear watched him walk into the Big Top, but Wes was nowhere to be seen when he slipped underneath the canopy himself.

The stage was bare. A vast and expansive space, illuminated by a single spotlight that hung directly over it. Shroud in darkness, the bleachers looked more like a wall that was closing in on every side. Claustrophobic for some, enticing for Bear.

A whooshing sound caught his attention, followed by a gust of air that carried an object a few feet from the top of his head. On instinct, Bear ducked, although whatever it was had long since flown away. He straightened. It was no object – it was Wes, swinging like a pendulum around the stage on one of the hoop-shaped trapeze swings.

Content just to watch, Bear followed him with his body, spinning until he got dizzy and had to stop. He wasn't even sure if Wes knew he was there – he gave no indication either way.

Until he stopped, somehow on a dime. The swing rocked gently in an imaginary breeze, Wes' legs looped around it, hanging upside down, and right in front of Bear's face. Their noses were almost touching. Bear held his breath, stunned, transfixed. Blue eyes stared into his brown ones, searching, watching.

"What do you want?" Wes asked, breaking the mirage.

"To check on you," Bear rasped, unsure of why his voice wasn't working properly.

Wes huffed and was suddenly swinging again. Out of Bear's line of sight, he was missing for a minute and a half before reappearing at the top of a set of bleachers, blending in with the shadows. If Bear hadn't been searching so desperately for him, like a man searched for water in the desert, he would've missed him.

He stood in the center of the stage, ducking when something whizzed by his ear. "The fuck was that?" Bear snapped, and a circus peanut skipped like a stone across the hard ground, disappearing underneath one of the curtains.

"Trying to see if I can hit the target." Wes' voice was slurred. Bear turned and saw the knife throwers wheel posted up at the far end of the tent, a good yard or two away from where Wes' peanut landed.

"You suck at this."

"I'm a trapeze artist, not a thrower."

"Yeah, stick to that." Bear took a step closer. "Can I come up?"

Wes shrugged, not denying his company, so Bear began the steep climb up to the top row. He rarely saw the stage from this angel, the vast spread of it took his breath away. They all must've looked so tiny down there: ants in a desert. Somewhere along the way Bear had convinced himself that he appeared mighty to the dozens of eyes that judged him every night.

The burden of insignificance felt heavier up here.

There was an entire row of seats that Bear could've chosen, but he chose to sit so close to Wes that their thighs and shoulders pressed together. He noticed a bottle of Jameson that was dwindling in contents.

"You're never going to hit that thing if you keep drinking," He pointed out, keeping his tone light.

"Good point."

Wes split the bag of peanuts between them, the shells spilling out of Bear's cupped palms. They sat in silence for a long time, just throwing peanuts as hard as they could, never coming close to hitting their goal. It got more comedic every time and Bear was pretty sure they eventually stopped trying. On Bear's last peanut, the last one in the bag, he hit the target spot on with a dull crack.

"Shit," Bear said, eyes wide. "I wasn't even trying."

The smile and humor had melted off of Wes' face like hot wax, leaving behind a scowl. Bear frowned at the rapid change in emotion.

"I'm sorry," He said, and he really was. "I wish I had more to say."

"I just don't get it," Wes whispered, staring dead ahead at the far side of the tent where the red and white stripes were darkened by shadows. "I always heard identical twins have that weird connection, and we were born and raised the same way, witnessed the same life... how'd we stray down such different paths while under the same roof?"

Bear shrugged. He couldn't remember much about his siblings besides his older sister. His two brothers were in and out of the house and even older than his sister, so by the time they all went up in flames, they were basically strangers to Bear. Strangers that took his lunch money for weed on more than one occasion.

"I don't know, man." Bear brushed peanut dust off of his black pants. "Can't expect everyone to see the world the same way you do. Even if y'all shared the womb."

Wes finally looked at Bear, somewhat quizzically, as if he had just now noticed he was there. They were so close to one another that Bear could smell the alcohol on his breath and see the cloudy coverage over his eyes.

There was a tenderness to Wes that was out of character for a boy who built up so many walls, content to only share this side of himself with a twin brother who, in his eyes, had just spat on their entire lives.

Even if Bear were eloquent enough to come up with the right words to say, his efforts would be for naught.

Judas was the only thing that could provide any shred of comfort.

Even then, that comfort would be fragile. Even if Judas walked under the Big Top in front of them, declaring that he changed his mind, whatever trust the brothers had built up was already shattered. It broke Bear's heart and terrified him. His had tried to ignore it, tried to pick out the good from the bad, but not even he could ignore the obvious signs anymore: Maggie was on the same path of realization Judas had traveled.

Bear took a deep breath and after a pregnant pause, he said, "You know, I'm not going anywhere, Wes." The boy next to him snapped his head up from where it had been hanging in defeat from his slim shoulders. Bear offered him a weak but reassuring smile. "I know I'm not Judas, and I can never be to you what he was – but you aren't alone. You and I, we see this place in the same light, I think. And if that's all you need from someone... well you can have it from me."

Wes choked on a breathless "Thank you."

Nodding, Bear added on a second thought: "Can you do me one favor, though?" Wes nodded, for some reason unable to speak. "Try to convince Callie to do trapeze with you this weekend. She isn't ready to perform with fire and I'm afraid..."

"Yeah," Wes said on an exhale. "I'll handle it."

It was Bear's turn to say thank you. The silence that settled over them was filled by the mulling sounds of laughter outside the Big Top, becoming few and far between as performers and workers began turning in for the night.

For a while, this was what Bear and Wes had. Sitting alone somewhere together, with Judas and

Atlanta, talking amongst themselves while larger groups gathered without them. A bottle of scotch shared between them, a deck of cards, stale M&Ms or discarded carnival food – a recipe for a belly ache. They preferred it this way, and it was enough for them.

Until a girl with tears on her cheek and a fire in her belly stumbled across the Circus one day and told Bear she needed to know there was more to life than what she had experienced. That night, something clicked in Bear that he never felt before. He couldn't put a name to it, couldn't hope to feel it ever again. The first time he saw Magnolia smile, nothing else mattered.

He thought about her asleep in bed, cuddled up next to Atlanta. Nothing else mattered.

Bear stood and picked up the bottle of whiskey. A small grunt escaped Wes as he shoved the bottle back against his chest.

"Don't do anything stupid," Bear grunted, overcome with a wave of exhaustion. "I think we've had enough drama this week to last us the rest of the summer."

"Agreed."

Bear ruffled Wes' hair. "Goodnight. Try and sleep, even if it's just by downing all of that and passing out up here."

Wes laughed, his cheeks rosy. "Goodnight." Bear made it half way down the bleachers before Wes called out to him. "Bear, wait." Glancing up, Bear waited patiently, blinking at Wes who was just staring at him. "I..." Their eyes met somewhere in the middle and Bear could hear the beating of his own heart louder than he ever had. Wes' shoulders slumped and the moment was gone. "Never mind. Goodnight."

With no energy left to read into it or argue, Bear
waved him off and slipped out of the Big Top. There were
still a few loiterers flitting around the Fairgrounds,
mostly carnies who were cleaning up bits of trash left
behind by partying performers.

Bear coughed into his elbow as he passed them; he
pulled it away from his face to see splatters of blood on
his skin. It didn't go unnoticed by Cody, who was
scrapping together the last of a runaway pile of napkins.
The carnie raised one unimpressed eyebrow, his lips
loosely holding an unlit cigarette.

"I wonder if they'd ever let you donate blood," Cody
mused. Bear rolled his eyes and kept walking. "Or if
there's a limit to how much gasoline there can be in your
bloodstream before you get denied."

Not bothering to point out the scientific flaws in his
teasing, Bear ignored him. He waited until he was right
outside his trailer to wipe the blood off of his arm using
his t-shirt, holding back the urge to break into another
coughing fit. He lost the battle, his chest folding in on
itself as his lungs heaved and contracted, spitting out
more and more blood until his head swam.

"Fuck," Bear rasped, his mouth wet with phlegm
and blood. Tiny bolds of pain shot through his throat as
each blistered popped at once. The grass got gifted a
lovely puddle of pus, more blood, and alcohol as Bear
vomited his entire stomach's contents for the second
time that night. He stumbled until his back hit against
the wall of the camper and he slid down it, knees
buckling.

The door swung open and Atlanta sailed out,
bounding over to Bear and climbing into his lap. She
lapped at his mouth and chin to rid his face of the left-

over bile, an act of comfort and service. Maggie followed her out with a towel and a cup of ice. Bear took the ice from her so she could sit next to him, her arm hooked in his, and her head on his shoulder as he tilted his neck back against the wall.

Breathing evenly was a struggle that got easier once he timed it to the rise and fall of Atlanta's chest pressed firmly against his. Bear did his best not to cry – he'd lose his breath again. Maggie sang a song under her breath, a gentle lullaby that eased Bear down from his panic. The red rubber band was still on his wrist and he snapped it against his skin, trying to get his brain to focus on a pain elsewhere from his lungs.

Long minutes passed before Maggie spoke up. "Are you okay?"

"I don't know, Mags."

"You *will* be okay."

"I don't know, Mags."

Maggie pulled away from his shoulder to look him in the eye, those green irises swimming with emotion. She reached out to cup his chin in her small hands, the smile on her face soft and beautiful like the smell of bread baking. Seemingly without thinking about it, she pressed her lips to his, chaste and without any force or passion.

They remained like that for a fleeting moment, connected at the mouths: scarred and ugly against smooth and soft. How he tricked a girl so beautiful and kind into giving a shit about him was beyond Bear's grasp of understanding. But that was the thing about Magnolia: she did not need to be tricked or convinced into caring about people. She simply did because that's how her heart was designed.

"Could you taste the gasoline?" Bear asked when she pulled back.

"Barely. Mostly just blood."

Nodding, Bear pressed his forehead against hers, breathing in her warmth and comforting vanilla smell. Maggie combed her fingers through his hair to push the long strands out of his face, and resumed her humming.

"Someday," Maggie whispered into the shared air between them, "people will write stories about you, and everyone will know how extraordinary you are."

Bear wanted to believe her. So, he did.

The next morning, on a Friday, Judas packed for the airport just as the sun broke over the horizon.

Wes was nowhere to be found, although no one put in much of an effort to find him. Bear didn't even bother; if Wes wanted to go about this like a child throwing a temper tantrum, Bear wasn't going to be the babysitter to pick up after him.

Most of the performers were either still asleep in their beds, or blinking bleary in the sunlight, grimacing with hangovers. Their goodbyes were half-assed – not because they didn't care about Judas, but because they were too confused and sick to understand the gravity of the situation.

An expertly planned escape. Bear had to give that to him, at least. It was dirty to not wait until all of his friends were well enough to say proper goodbyes; Judas was looking for a way to leave without making anyone else mad at him. Bear couldn't help wondering who was going to get the brunt of all of that when everyone came to.

Callie was wrapping her arms around Judas' slim waist when Bear snapped out of it. The twin was so much smaller than his brother, so much softer.

When water shapes rocks, it goes one of two ways: it smooths them over into sleek mini mountain ranges, somewhere you could feel safe to sit upon. Or, it cut jagged cliffs, sharp edges, nowhere safe for another person to claim.

The twins were shaped by water, each in their own way – one a riverbed, one a waterfall.

Bear was sure Judas knew that, though. He stepped up to the trapeze artist when it was his turn, and held out a hand. Judas looked at it for a moment before grabbed it, shaking it once. They locked eyes and Bear felt like he was staring into Wes' for a second, they were so identical. But like when Judas found him by the water troth, Bear knew it wasn't Wes, because Wes was not made of softness.

And neither was Bear.

For this reason, Bear tugged Judas in for a hug. The embrace was awkward, improvised, and the boy ate it up. He clung to Bear like he might drift away like a balloon if he didn't, and all Bear could do was return the tightness.

"You smell like the Circus," Judas whispered, right in his ear, so only Bear could hear it.

"Gasoline, too?"

"Yeah. A fuckton of gasoline."

They broke apart, laughing, and Magnolia replaced Bear in Judas' arms. He was close enough to hear them exchanging hushed goodbyes, though he couldn't make out exactly what was said. It didn't matter, those words weren't for him.

Maggie stepped back enough to hold Judas' cheeks in her small hands, just as she did with Bear so often. It was her way to get a point across, to make you look her in the eye and understand her, hear every word she threw at you.

"Keep in touch, okay?" She was saying, pinching his cheeks for added effect.

Judas giggled, blushing. "Yes, of course." Quieter, he added, "Will you be okay?"

"I'll be fine," Maggie promised.

Bear frowned before he realized he was going to. He suddenly had the feeling he had missed something. Before he could continue to question it, Wes appeared.

The boy looked like a castaway just recently returned to shore. His eyes were sunken in, his skin was ghostly, and his lips were dry and thin, set in a straight line on his handsome face. Those dead blue eyes found Bear first, refusing to even cast his brother a glance.

Bear felt a fiery jolt of anger towards Wes, and not in the usual way when they got in a dick-sizing contest about their acts. This was a new kind of irritation, like one might feel for a dog who won't come when called, or a toddler who refused to take a bath. Clenching his fists, Bear had to curb the urge to grab Wes by the collar and drag him over.

Thankfully, he didn't have to hold back for much longer. When Wes realized Bear wasn't going to make any kind of friendly move towards him, the trapeze artist deflated and approached his brother.

In Bear's mind, Judas was always the more cowardly of the twins, and Wes was the one who would round them up into a devious or reckless plan. Now, their roles were reversed: Wes was cowering in on himself and Judas stood firm and confident, his chin raised to counter how his brother's head was lowered.

"So, this is it?" Wes asked.

"Yeah, Wes," Judas sniffed. "I'm not changing my mind. Not yet, at least."

"And if you do," Bear jumped at the sound of Roy's voice behind him, not even realizing he had come to join them. "we will always be here. Well," The Ringleader laughed, "not *here*, specifically, but you know what I mean."

"I do." Judas smiled. "Thank you."

He turned to his brother, arms out: an invitation, or a plea? Whatever it was, Wes embraced him with vigor. They hugged for a long time, longer than anyone else, and whatever they whispered between one another drifted away with the wind.

Atlanta trotted up to them. She nudged Judas thigh, looking for attention of her own. The brothers knelt down to pet her and she peppered their faces with kisses, tail wagging and ears back. When she pulled back and Bear got a proper look at Judas' face, he realized he was crying.

"I think I'll miss you most of all," Judas told the Shepherd, planting a big kiss in between her ears.

"There's dogs in San Francisco, you know," Maggie joked. She leaned her head against Bear's shoulder, their arms looped together.

Judas continued to stare longingly into Atlanta's eyes. "Dogs, sure – but not her." She gave him one more sloppy kiss. "She's one of a kind."

Bear, Maggie, Roy, and Wes circled around Judas in a group hug, squeezing him until his feet came off the grass. There were assorted giggles, mostly from Judas himself, just as a taxi pulled up to the Fairground gates.

"Alright, kid," Roy said, patting him on the back. "This is it. You ready?"

Judas looked equally nervous and excited; his blue eyes were blown wide but his smile reached his ears. "Yeah. I'm ready."

Wes turned and disappeared back into the grounds before he could see his brother go. The look of hurt on Judas' face was almost unbearable. Roy ushered him towards the cab with Maggie's help and Atlanta trotting along, always available to help.

At the cab door, Maggie and Roy each gave Judas one more quick hug, and as Maggie stepped back to wipe her wet eyes, Judas called out to Bear.

"Hey, Bear!"

"Yeah?"

Judas had one arm resting on the door. "Don't die, okay?"

Forcing a smile, Bear said: "I promise I'll try not to." He refused to say *I won't* because he refused to have his last words to Judas be a lie.

Shoulder to shoulder, they watched the driver take away their friend. Roy took a sip from his flask and offered it to Bear and Maggie, who graciously accepted. The whiskey burned down Bear's throat, similar but not as intense as the gasoline. Back and forth the flask went until it was dry.

Maggie sniffed. They had been watching the empty road for a long time now.

"Someone should probably check on Wes, right?" She asked, not committed to the task, but still concerned.

Shaking his head, Roy pocketed his flask. "When he's ready, he'll reach out."

Bear wasn't so sure. He stood there with Maggie when Roy turned and left without another word. Bear watched Maggie, and Maggie watched the curve in the road that stole Judas from them, as if she could change his mind by sheer force of will.

"Come on," Bear said gently, tugging her back towards their trailer. "Everything's going to be okay."

"Promise?"

Nodding, Bear wrapped his arms around her frame, breathing her in. What he wanted to say was: *'yes, I promise – I'll spend the rest of my life proving it to you, and I'll make your tea every morning and try to get it right, and I'll pick wildflowers to stick in your hair and I'll learn to play your favorite songs on the guitar. I'll make this worth it, just please stay with me, stay with me and be happy'*.

But all he said was:

"Promise."

SAVE THEM ALL

<u>MAGNOLIA</u>

Maggie sat out on the step of their trailer, watching the sun slowly climb up the sky behind the Ferris wheel. She was exhausted, having barely managed to scrape together a few hours of sleep, her mind still reeling from Judas' departure.

Her cigarette was reaching the end of its purpose, hardly more than a nub between her fingers, begging to be stomped out. The heel of her boot ground it out against the wooden stairs. It was satisfying to imagine the tobacco as her own worries being snubbed out under her foot.

Behind her, the door opened and Bear stepped out, holding a mug of steaming tea. He sat next to her, handing it off with a soft smile. Atlanta squeezed between them, prancing around the Fairgrounds into the far woods to do her business. Warm blooded, Bear was in shorts and a tank top despite the chilly morning. Maggie shivered under her layers just looking at him.

"Are you going to go?" Bear asked, wrapping an arm around her and pulling her closer into his warmth.

Adele was waiting for her in the Denny's parking lot. She arranged with Maggie on Thursday morning. If Maggie went to see her father again, she'd miss tonight's show and make it back just in time for Saturday's.

"I don't know," Maggie answered honestly. She rested her head on Bear's shoulder, eyes closed, listening to the birds singing good morning.

"I'll be okay if you go," Bear promised, as if he could read her mind.

"I know."

Bear kissed her forehead. The tea warmed Maggie's throat down into her belly. She finished off the last few sips just as Atlanta came trotting back, pouncing on grasshoppers that leapt into her path. Bear took the mug from her and yawned, calling Atlanta to his side as he stood.

"I'm going back to sleep," He told Maggie. "I'll see you tomorrow?"

Maggie smiled. "Yeah. I guess you will."

"Cool. Be safe. Love you, kiddo."

Atlanta gave Maggie a kiss goodbye, dragging a snail trail of dog slobber from her chin to her forehead. "Love you, too," Maggie laughed. She watched them both slip back into the trailer to catch more sleep, a bit longingly.

But Bear was right. She could trust him to take care of himself after pushing his limits the last time, and she shouldn't pass up any opportunities to see her father. So, she cracked her back and stretched, yawning into the morning. The time on her phone assured that she still had plenty of time to make it there, especially if she jogged.

It hurt less to leave them behind this time. Unlike the time she snuck out like a shameful child, now Maggie left with purpose in her step and her chin raised high. Only the most committed of the workers were awake at this hour to see her approached the gates, and it was Cody who stopped her before she could slip out.

"You're actually doing it?" He asked, peering up at her under sandy blond bangs. His hands were already stained with grease and he spoke around the butt end of a cigarette. The carnie had been working on the electrical cords that powered the fairy lights on the entrance. "Color me impressed."

"You didn't think I would?" Maggie felt a hot flash of defensiveness flood her face with pink blush.

Cody shook his head within a billow of smoke. "Nah. I knew you would. I just wouldn't have been able to."

Maggie smiled. "Would you have wanted to?"

A moment of hesitation, and then Cody chuckled and turned back to his project. "No. I put to much effort into getting away from all of that drama. The way I see it," He said, squinting against the bright morning sun. "If I got a foot in the past and a foot in the present, I got no feet left to help me towards the future."

Without thinking about it, Maggie glanced down at her own feet, clad in worn down Doc Martens. "Yeah, I get it." And she did. She really wished she didn't, though. It felt like dragging slabs of concrete when she continued walking.

Maggie was late in arriving to the meeting spot because she didn't have the energy to run. Her mind plagued her with thoughts of Judas, somewhere on the Golden Coast, and Quinn locked away in a hospital room like a princess in a tower. Standing back from the view of Adele's car mirrors, Maggie hesitated at the very far corner of the parking lot, like a force field had suddenly appeared in front of her.

In an act of second nature Maggie reached down to trail her fingers over the tips of Atlanta's ears. When she felt nothing but empty space, her heart plummeted to her stomach.

What *was* she doing here? Or hoping to accomplish by continuing to take a shovel to the grave of her long-buried childhood? Her escape to the Circus had been exactly that: an escape. Like an animal finally chewing its way through a chain, Maggie had freed herself from a life she knew she didn't want to live anymore. Yet here she was, continuing to dwell on it.

Her father deserved a place in her life, but the sad truth was that he wasn't going anywhere. She took the plunge already, sought him out against her heart's better judgement, and vomited her buried memories onto the surface of a round, metal table. It had been easier to spill in front of two total strangers than she ever let it be to speak to Bear.

She didn't let herself think about it anymore; Maggie pulled her phone out and found Adele's unsaved number in her recent texts. A quick exchange of meeting place and time were the last ones sent until Maggie typed out, *'Can't do it. Sorry'* and hit send. Hidden within the shadows of a thick hedge, she watched Adele's lights come on. The Audi pulled out of the parking lot and sped away, all while Maggie buried her face in her father's denim jacket and sobbed.

With tears still flowing freely down her cheeks, Maggie let her feet lead her to her next destination. She stumbled like a drunk through town, a sight for sore eyes on such a bright and sunny Friday morning. Briefly it occurred to her that not one of the many cars driving past her thought it best to stop and check on a girl who was obviously in some sort of distress. She was thankful for that. If anyone bothered, she'd probably threaten to rip their throat out without even thinking about it.

Her toe caught in a deep crack in the sidewalk and Maggie stumbled forward, catching herself on a sigh. She blinked in surprise when she read the bold white words. Somehow, her feet had led her to the hospital.

It was a square, beige building with large bay windows, standing strong and bold against the sky, casting upon the streets below it a large shadow that Maggie had stumbled into. Quinn was in there somewhere looking wistfully out into the sunshine, heavy with the knowledge that she'd never prance in it again.

Maggie didn't expect to see Roy in the hospital lobby when she shuffled through the automatic doors, but there he was in all of his unshaven, mismatched outfit, probably on his third cup of coffee glory. He was sitting in one of the arm chairs by the window, foot tapping nervously against the carpet. Maggie walked up to him with dragging feet, unnoticed until she was right in front of his nose.

Roy's blue eyes widened with shock when Maggie sat down in the chair next to him, offering nothing but a shy smile. "I thought–"

"I couldn't," Maggie interrupted. It was easier to admit that she thought.

"Why are you here?"

"I haven't visited Quinn yet," Maggie said, twisting to try and squint towards the directory. "What room is she in?"

"She's gone," Roy deadpanned.

Maggie's exhausted brain couldn't process Roy's response fast enough. Gone? Gone could mean a lot of things. She could already be back at the Circus being doted upon by her loving companions. Gone could mean her hospital bed accidentally rolled down the hallway and the nurses were still trying to track it down. Or that monitor flat-lined out of nowhere and they couldn't get to her fast enough. Maggie's heart started to palpitate as her mind raced out of her control.

"Gone?" She managed to choke out, echoing Roy's vague declaration.

Roy nodded solemnly. "Her grandparents came today. They arranged with her mother to bring her home with them until her mother can come out of rehab. They want to take care of her there. Her grandmother was a rehabilitation nurse, I guess, so it worked out perfectly."

Perfectly. What an odd choice of words.

"Callie...?"

"I tried to get them to wait so I could bring her to say goodbye." Roy buried his face in his hands, his broad shoulders shaking with a wavering sigh. "But they had a return flight to make."

Just a few hours ago, Maggie believed she cried the last of her tears. But here she was, chewing on a bloody fingernail to subdue the pathetic sobs she was trying to hold back. Quinn's return to the Circus meant a lot to everyone waiting back there. And now Roy would have to return to them and deliver the bad news no one had expected. They had known from the start that death was a possibility, perhaps the default their minds went to first, but this was out of left field, even for a realist like Maggie.

"You know," Roy began, staring down at his palms. His hands were dry and littered with tiny scars like tally marks, each one a different story of hard work and dedication. "In the wake of my father's death, the fate of the Circus was unstable. My oldest brothers and sisters wanted nothing to do with it – and not just because of the work load or commitment, but because of the reputation. When you say 'Circus', those around you get those images in their heads of PT Barnum, of animal abuse and exploitation of disabilities or human 'mutation'." He put that last word in air quotes, punctuated with a grimace.

Maggie nodded. She was guilty of such prejudices before joining. When her friends invited her to join them that night, she put up some ethical front of not supporting such a toxic industry. Of course, when her they assured there were no animals involved, she immediately agreed. If she had known then what she knew now about the people behind the face make up, Maggie wondered if she would've felt any different.

Roy continued with a disgruntled sigh. "I knew Dee for a long time before this. She came to us, as you know, as a bearded lady. The rampant transphobia followed her even to the Circus. When no one else would step up, I knew I had to. I was overseas in Europe when I got the call, working my dream job as a travel guide in London. For Dee, I came back. Together we scrapped everything – we had a vision we wanted to build upon. We lost a lot of good performers in the transition, but it was so worth it every time some kid told me this place saved them."

Was he thinking about Bear? Roy had owned the Circus for many years before this generation of performers came around, but Maggie and everyone else knew that Bear was the epitome of everything Roy wanted to create. Bear was the vision. Bear was Roy's pride and joy, a son he wasn't related to, a perfect example of what he was able to accomplish. Is that why he wasn't putting forth more effort into urging Bear to stop? Maggie suppressed a bitter, dry laugh. Even the most selfless couldn't resist the temptation to be selfish.

"You've done a good job," She assured, because truthfully, he had. She didn't know Roy had given up a dream job just to come be a Ringleader in a dying Circus. And here she was, thinking she was the one making the ultimate sacrifices. "We're thankful. All of us, more than you'll ever know."

"Not a good enough job, apparently." Roy returned to looking longingly out of the window, as if searching the sky for the plane that carried Quinn far, far away. "I guess I can't save them all."

Maggie's heart tightened in her chest; that was not a guilt this wonderful man should be burdened with. "But look how many you *have* saved."

Roy turned to her, blue eyes wet with tears that wouldn't overflow. "Oh, Magnolia," He said with a slight shake of his head. "I know I've done wrong by you. And I do know, deep down, that someone has to stop Bear. I hoped he would learn himself, because I, too, was once so consumed by the insurmountable need to be better than the rest. But it only made me worse." The Ringleader leaned forward in the chair, hands clasped together. "Bear is bold. He commands the attention of everyone in the room – and deserves it. People will witness him, or wish they had. He isn't stupid, he's fully aware of what this is doing to him, which is why he is so hesitant to train Callie down the same road. He's *magnificent*, that boy."

"And he will die where he stands," Maggie said bleakly.

Roy locked eyes with her, and nodded. "And his body will rot where it falls."

* * *

<u>CALLIE</u>

It was past noon when Roy finally returned to the Circus, Maggie in tow. The sound of the truck rumbling up the road was heard minutes before it actually spluttered through the entrance. Maggie hopped out of the passenger side first, being greeted by Atlanta within moments of her feet being on the ground. She made it over to Bear in a light jog, throwing her arms around his neck and embracing him. Roy was still in the car, his hands in a vice grip around the wheel and his forehead pressed against it in between them.

"Is Roy okay?" Wes asked Maggie, who was still preoccupied with hugging Bear.

The two broke apart at the question, Bear casting a nervous glance in Roy's direction over the top of Maggie's head. Maggie bit her lip nervously and tugged on Bear's forearm.

"Maybe you should go talk to him," She said.

Wes put a hand on Bear's chest to prevent him from taking another step forward. "Hey, no. He went to visit Quinn. Whatever he has to say, he can say to all of us."

Bear was glaring at Wes, forcefully shoving his arm to the side. Callie sucked in an anxious breath when the boys went nose to nose, Bear's muscles flexing in his sudden rage. They said nothing, just remained chest to chest, breathing in the air the other exhaled out, eyes locked together. A car door slamming shut broke them apart, and Callie could breathe again.

Roy was walking over with a scowl directed towards Wes and Bear, who were now sulking like chastised children. "Big Top. Now. All of you," Roy demanded without stopping, making a beeline for the massive tent that towered over the rest.

Like moths to a flame, his performers followed loyally and without question. They all filed through, not bothering to take a seat in the bleachers, but instead they formed a jagged semi-circle around Roy who stood center stage. Callie stuck close to Bear, who knelt down to wrap an arm around Atlanta's neck. Wes stood at his

other side and Maggie had somehow ended up next to
Roy, whispering something in his ear.

The Ringleader nodded solemnly to her and Callie
could make out his mouth thanking her. Maggie stepped
back into the half circle, squeezing in next to Cody.

Roy took a deep breath. "As most of you know, I
just went to go check on Quinn, and I have some news."

"Good or bad?" Cody called out.

"Whatever you make it, son," Roy responded,
keeping the emotion out of his voice. Callie's heart didn't
know what to do: palpitate with excitement, or worry?
Roy waited for the confused murmurs to die down.
"Unbeknownst to me, and Quinn herself, the hospital
had arranged with her grandparents to bring her home,
where she will be cared for by her grandmother, who is a
retired nurse. She was already gone when I got there."

A heavy silence fell upon them like a heavy hand.
Maggie was the only one who didn't look taken aback;
she was staring at Bear who was silent, his cheek pressed
against his dog's muzzle, both pairs of brown eyes tilted
upwards. Then Callie realized Maggie wasn't staring at
Bear, she and everyone else under the Big Top was
staring at *her*. The reality of the news hit her like a
freight train.

Quinn was gone. Stolen from out from under their
noses like a piece of candy in a cupboard.

Before Callie could react outside of her own mind,
Wes stormed out, muttering some string of swears. Bear
stood and looked like he was going to go after him, and
last second decided not to. Instead, he turned cautiously
towards Callie.

"Are you okay?" He asked, and his tone was a rare
form of gentle. Callie saw those blisters up close again,

the reek of gasoline flowing over her as she became
acutely aware of the burning in her own throat. She
thought about the daily efforts Maggie put in to making
sure Bear didn't choke on his own pus or permanently
scar his mouth.

Could any one of them really commit to doing ten
times that amount of work for Quinn, when they had
their own, more manageable injuries to nurse?

Nodding, Callie choked out: "Yeah." It was easier to
speak than she thought. "Nothing I can do about it,
right? And if she's going to be anywhere, might as well be
living with someone who can take care of her properly.
No sense in lugging her around with us when none of us
have the training to make her comfortable."

Bear frowned, but nodded. As if to punctuate
Callie's point, his fingers drifted to the cracking
lacerations around his lips. He understood, or knew
better than to argue when his very existence proved
every word.

Roy looked relieved and proud all at once. "You're
right, Calista. We'll miss her, but they did promise they'd
bring her to visit when we were close."

"We're still her family," Dee added. "Right?" A
chorus of agreement rose around her. "And tonight, we
begin our weekend of shows, the first since we lost
Quinn, so let's show these people what we got, okay?"

A louder, more powerful rise in shouting followed.
The performers were beginning to get amped up, fueled
by Dee's speech. Callie didn't even notice Wes had
returned; he had his arms full of alcohol bottles that he
dumped on the ground in the center of the stage. Roy
rolled his eyes but stepped back, gesturing to the crowd.

Cody stepped up first, grabbing the nearest handle without checking the label, and his carnies followed.

"Don't get drunk!" Roy warned, pointedly staring at Cody and Wes. "We're live in seven hours."

Whitney turned on her speaker to the opening notes of a Frank Sinatra song. Callie settled down on a blanket that Allie spread out, watching the adults pour each other drinks into red solo cups for one another. Bear bypassed that all together, instead reaching for a very tired looking Maggie who was necking a bottle of Jameson whiskey. Callie had never seen Magnolia drink; she would nurse a joint every once in a while, but she was never one to chug a drink.

Bear gently took the bottle out of her hands, passing it off to Dee. Maggie was crying, looking utterly defeated in so many ways, and Callie couldn't even think of why.

Above their heads, Callie saw Wes and a few acrobats setting up the tight ropes and curtains. Led by the trapeze artist, they began dancing above their heads, their bodies twisting in the air to the gentle tunes of 60s love songs. Callie wanted to join them, but she was also hesitant.

She hadn't watched an acrobat show from the audience in a long time. Atlanta trotted over to the blanket and curled up next to Callie, chin on her knee.

The opening notes of *"The Way You Look Tonight"* crackled through the old radio and Bear, holding Maggie close to his broad chest, began to sway her around the stage. Callie could just barely here him humming the lyrics into her ear, his cheek pressed to the top of her head. It took a few moments for Maggie's crying to subside enough for Bear to start seriously spinning her around, and with each movement of their bodies, her smile grew more dazzling.

It was hard for Callie to believe that this was the same tent that nearly took Quinn's life; that the ground Bear was so carefully dipping Maggie towards was the same ground that shattered spines and cracked open skulls. This tent – this *Circus* – was a paradox within itself. It sheltered love and the fragile souls that built it, but it also kept buried the harrowing truth of this life from the prying eyes of its patrons. Some people found beauty in that. Others, such as poor Judas, were simply unable to cope, even if they were raised within it.

It took a special kind of person to truly belong here.

Callie wished Quinn or Judas could've been one of those people – or Maggie for that matter, who was destined to be the next goodbye, should she manage to tear herself away from Bear. She watched the pair dance like no one was watching them, content to exist within their own bubble. Bear was wiping Maggie's cheeks dry of tears and Maggie looked up at him like he was the sun in which the planet revolved around. Maybe she didn't belong here, but she certainly belonged with Bear.

Atlanta nuzzled Callie to ask for a belly rub, breaking the trance. Callie giggled, petting the Shepherd and planting kisses up and down her head. She was so preoccupied with burying her nose into the comforting scent of dog that she didn't notice Roy's shadow cast over them until he politely cleared his throat.

"Can I sit?" He asked, gesturing to the blanket.

"Of course." Callie shuffled over to give him some more room.

Roy lowered himself, grimacing slightly as his knees bent. He waved at Allie and Whitney, who paused their conversation to wave back with bright smiles. Callie sat quietly, allowing Roy to take his time to speak first. The man had his chin tilted upwards to watch his acrobats, the ghost of a smile on his greying chin, the crow's feet around the corner of his eyes prominent against the dark circles beneath them. Roy certainly wasn't old, just barely reaching his fifties, but for the first time, Callie noticed how aged he was. Like an ancient pine.

When he spoke, his voice was still rough from years of chain-smoking. "I'm proud of you." It was a simple statement with no bold declaration, he didn't even turn away from the acrobats to look at her when he said it. He did tear his eyes from them to continue. "You've grown a lot in this past week. More so than you should have, but I'm proud of you. It takes a lot of courage to be here."

"Thank you," Callie said and she buried her face into Atlanta's neck fur to soak up any tears that tried to escape. She didn't feel like crying, but it was a precautionary measure.

Roy had switched his attention over to Bear and Maggie, who were still dancing even though Sinatra was booted out by Paul Anka.

"Those two..." He trailed off, shaking his head. "I don't know what the hell to do with them."

Callie shrugged and fiddled with Atlanta's collar. "Nothing. They'll find their way." She twisted the collar around, searching for an ID tag, but there was none. Bear wasn't worried about Atlanta running away.

"Yeah," Roy smiled at her softly. "They will." He leaned over and placed a kiss on her forehead, then stood and wandering back over to Dee.

With Atlanta on her heels, Callie slipped out from the Big Top into the warm spring afternoon. The sun was directly above her head at the highest point in the sky, and a few carnies had escaped the commotion under the tent as well and were working to set up for the open. Cody was amongst them to Callie's surprise; she hadn't noticed him leave. He had traded the alcohol bottle for a water bottle and was leading a group of barkers towards the front gates, reading off a clipboard.

She was too preoccupied with watching the carnies work that she didn't hear Paris approaching until his shoulder brushed hers and jumped. Callie scowled as he laughed.

"Sorry," The boy said. "I didn't mean to scare you."

"You didn't," Callie sniffed, her arms folded across her chest. They locked eyes for a brief moment before bursting into a fit of giggles.

"I wish I got to meet Quinn," Paris whispered after a moment of quiet had settled over them. "She seems like such a wonderful person. Everyone cares so much about her."

"Everyone cares so much about everyone," Callie corrected him with a smile. "Even you, even though you just got here."

"Really?" Paris didn't sound so sure. Callie imagined he was blushing under the hair on his face. "No one's ever cared about me..."

Callie sniffed. "Well, get used to it, kid. You're stuck with us now."

Paris giggled again, tucking his chin against his chest. "You guys aren't that bad."

"Damn straight, we aren't," Callie laughed with him. Atlanta barked, excited, her tail wagging for attention. "Plus, being here is better than being out there."

"Yeah," Paris agreed quietly. "Are you worried about Quinn?"

Shrugging, Callie said, "I'm not sure. I think she'll be okay. She kind of treated this place like a summer camp, you know? Come winter, she was going to go home for a few months anyway."

"Are you worried about Bear?"

Callie felt like lying. "No. He's smart. If it's time for him to stop, he'll stop."

Engrossed in their conversation, neither Callie nor Paris noticed Mavis shamble out of her tent. The psychic made her way to a massive poster of Bear's face, bright oranges and reds, and sank to her knees in front of it, crying and praying.

WHEN IT RAINS

<u>BEAR</u>

It was May 11th, the day after Bear's thirteen birthday.

His father was a raging drunk, his mother had been checked out since giving birth to her first child twenty-seven years ago. Birthdays were scrappy celebrations, usually forgotten about until they woke with hangovers mid-morning. That day, though, Bear was surprised to find both of his parents awake when he tip-toed downstairs an hour after the sun rose.

With zero grace and some semblance of aggression, Bear's father dropped a twenty-dollar bill in his open palm and said: "Go nuts."

Their radiator had been broken for a while. Summer was around the corner, but Bear's parents' room was in the basement and it was cold and dingy down there year-round. Over the winter and into the spring, they settled on using a space heater that spluttered and rattled throughout the night. He didn't know a shred about fixing a radiator, but he had naive hope that showing up to a hardware store with a crisp twenty would get him *something*.

He didn't have a bike like the other kids in the neighborhood, so he had to walk into town. It was an hour there and an hour back, and he set off around ten in the morning. Across the train tracks, past the skatepark, over the footbridge, down Main Street: he walked the same way to get to the library.

Bear made it to the top of Main Street before a convoy of three fire engines and multiple police cruisers went screaming past him towards the direction he came, sirens blaring. Something told him to follow them. Sometimes he wished he hadn't, but deep down he knew the outcome would've been the same either way.

It was the space heater that finally did it, they said. The outlet sparked and the motor caught on fire, and there was enough alcohol down there, spilled about the floor, that it spread instantly. The whole house went up and there was no way to escape out of the basement.

Bear made it back to his street just in time to see the entire thing collapse in on itself. He was close enough to feel the heat of the flames against his cheeks and have ashes land in his dirty blonde hair. Police officers held him back even though he didn't plan on running any nearer. Shell-shocked, Bear sunk to the ground and watched his entire life and family become swallowed by licking, orange flame.

After that, he was sent to various boys' homes. Each one was more violent than the last but thankfully, Bear had years of experience taking his father's belt that the housemen's strikes were nothing but a light spanking to him.

In his junior year of high school, he lived within a home that had a therapist that came to visit every so often to check on the residents. It was one of the nicer establishments he stayed in. He was stuck there after a run around with a particularly tough reform school he was sent to on account of a minor crime he couldn't even remember anymore.

The therapist, a woman in her mid-forties who looked aged beyond those years, had kind, tired eyes and a smile that went tight-lipped when she saw Bear. Her lips were always smeared with a slightly purple lipstick that didn't do her complexation any favors. Bear was her side project. She wanted to be the one that fixed him, the person who got all the credit for breaking him down and opening him up.

He went along with this game she didn't realize they were playing because he wanted the attention. There was something about having someone's complete focus that awakened a new lust for life within Bear. Growing up with as many siblings as he did, raised by himself instead of his neglectful parents, he never got such attentiveness. Jen Peterson – yes, that was her name – wanted to know everything about Bear's life up until the second he met her.

Bear let her hear the stories of his past, but he really wanted her to listen to his dreams for the future.

It was her that showed him the fire breathers.

She had been watching a movie the night before, she said, when she saw a commercial for a traveling circus. It was ridiculous to her. Unable to fathom why anyone would want to swing via silk or walk across a tight rope, she did give credit to one act that appeared interesting, though reckless: the fire show.

With no access to the internet, Bear taught himself how to breathe fire in the earliest morning hours. He burnt his eyebrows off, seared the corners of his mouth, and gave himself third degree burn on the left side of his face.

None of that compared to the power he felt he had come to possess. Orphaned, fending for himself within the foster care system, sent from home to home with zero say in the matter, Bear had finally found something he could control.

And he became *hungry*. Ravenous, even, for a sense of purpose and prestige. Tired of being a name on a list that went for miles, determined not to be another statistic of an orphaned, abused child – Bear set out on a mission: if he belonged nowhere, he'd burn his way to his own *somewhere*.

Those first scars were still there. He bore them with pride.

* * *

<u>BEAR</u>

The sun had not yet set.

Bear sat on the cold linoleum floor of Dee and Roy's trailer with his knees to his chest, his eyes bleak and empty and staring dead ahead at the blank wall in front of him. He counted the textured bumps; he had to keep restarting when he hit thirteen. Why couldn't he make it past thirteen?

Dee's long, skilled fingers worked on his hair, parting and braiding and tugging every now and then to keep him in the present moment. Her knees framed either side of his broad shoulders to keep him in place, and Atlanta sat in front of him like the Sphinx, ears forward and eyes sharp and alert. She was watching for a cue. Bear would not provide her any.

His lungs ached. It felt like he was trying to breathe with a body on his chest; when he inhaled through his nose, it wasn't enough air at once and it burned of gasoline, but when he tried to breathe through his mouth, the blisters in his throat sent shooting pains throughout his entire body. He was fighting against his body's urge to cough, afraid of splattering his hands with blood before the show even began.

Tears began blurring the edges of his vision and Atlanta whined low and long. Dee pulled his hair again.

"Stay with me, little bear." Her voice was gentle and grounding. Bear made a point to count how many words she spoke to him. "You are here," Dee said, "and you are so magnificent."

Thirteen words.

Bear couldn't stop the shuddering breath that escaped him and the way his body went rigid, one leg kicked out, barely missing Atlanta's nose. He pulled it back in and tried to shake out his head to get rid of the ringing in his bad ear, but Dee kept strong hands on his hair, preventing too much dramatic movement. Atlanta was nudging his hands away from his face before he could even process he had started picking at his blisters. She was aggressive in the way she did this. He complied so she'd stop nipping at the sensitive skin around his fingers.

Dee was patient for him to settle, and then she spoke again. "I still remember the first time I ever saw you." She went back to braiding his long hair, slow and with the care and attentiveness of a mother with her newborn. "You were a pathetic little thing – angry, too. I hardly believed you had just come from the Army. It was in the middle of downpour that you showed Roy what you could do with fire. I've never seen that look on his face before, and haven't since. I doubt I ever will again. But what I remember more than anything is how afraid I was that the rain would put you out. Not the flames you worked with, but *you*, because you were a little spark yourself, just the beginning of what would become a blazing wild fire."

Bear let each word soak over him. He remembered that day vividly: the determination to prove himself, the pure desperation to find somewhere he belonged, somewhere he could put a roof over Atlanta's head. He remembered the torrential rain, and the soggy earth at his feet, and the way he filled a puddle with his own vomit. Why had they been so impressed with him?

"I see what you've become," Dee continued. "I watched you grow and become the most extraordinary display of human spirit. It's funny, though, Bear. I still worry about you when it rains." There was a heavy pause where Bear took in that last part, the guilt of knowing what he was doing to those around him aching more than his collapsing lungs. Dee's voice broke when she asked: "Why do you do it?"

He said the first thing that came to mind, his most honest truth. "History tends to swallow ordinary people."

Dee stood and moved around him to kneel in front of him so she could look him in the eye when she said, "You are anything but ordinary, Bear. I think you've proven that a thousand times over."

Bear shook his head without restraint now. "*My* history is trying to swallow me," He whispered. He could feel the flames licking towards his face, he could see the roof cave in, and if he focused hard enough, he could hear the screams for help. His torches felt heavy in his belt loop, and he yearned for the can of kerosene just beyond the door. "I have to swallow it first."

Every flame, every spark.

"Darling boy," Dee cupped his face. "Hasn't anyone warned you that you can't fight fire with fire?"

"I'm starting to realize that."

He had no other weapons. He thought about Callie, who was complaining this morning about a blister in her throat. The responsibility was on him for that, and whatever injuries and hardships followed. It would've been so easy to ignore her pleas and just let the impulsive urge blow over.

It was more evident than ever. Bear fucked up.

"I spent a lot of my life miserable because being my true self would compromise too many relationships," Dee went on to say. "And then when I finally felt a semblance of comfort, I became a sideshow act." She snorted and hung her head, as if embarrassed. "I figured it was worth it to play along, so long as they were calling me a woman. Roy took over and put a stop to it, which I am forever thankful, because I don't think I would've ever found the strength to stand up for myself. Point is, Barrett, you shouldn't have to sacrifice who you are for what the Circus wants you to be. You come here to belong as your truest self."

Dee was the only person in the world, besides Maggie, who could get away with calling Bear by his full name - and she knew it. It emphasized her entire point. Bear couldn't compare his insatiable lust for the flame to her struggle with society's hateful transphobia, but it was true that the Circus created a sort of middle ground. What was supposed to save them, was nearly killing them. Dee fought it. Bear was reaching the point of no return.

"How do you fight it?" Bear asked her, desperately quiet. He snapped the rubber band aggressively against his skin, counting each and every contact point and stopping at thirteen.

Dee smiled like an August morning and warm tea and acoustic songs. "You just do, my little fireball."

There was a quiet knock on the door. Dee stood and opened it, revealing Maggie in full attire and make up, peaking in at Bear on the floor. Her face went from nonchalant to concerned in an instant, the face paint unable to hide it, but Bear raised both hands in surrender before she could speak.

"I'm okay," He assured. Why couldn't he stop lying to her?

But then her face relaxed again and she smiled a shy smile, rocking back and forth on the balls of her feet in excitement, and he remembered why he'd never admit he was anything but fine. Bear clambered to his feet with the help of Atlanta's sturdy body, his legs asleep from sitting so long. Maggie handed him his black bandana when he got to her; he ignored it to scoop her up off the threshold and toss her over his shoulder, using what little strength he had left to make her giggle.

Bear turned back to Dee before leaving. "Thank you."

"You're welcome." Dee still sounded sad. Bear hoped Maggie wasn't picking up on it. "Be safe, kids."

The horizon was painted by orange and yellow brush strokes as the sun dipped below the tree line. The temperature remained comfortably warm under the early night sky and patrons were bold enough to leave their sweaters at home as they gathered beneath the twinkling lights. Many led with their noses, drifting towards the food kiosks where food was rolled in flour and submerged in bubbling oil, while some sought out the rides first, chasing a momentary thrill.

Bear dropped Maggie off his shoulder so she could twirl and dance with Atlanta as the dog weaved between her moving legs, tongue out and tail wagging.

A sharp whistle from a hot dog vendor caught her attention and she trotted towards him, no doubt sporting her best attempt at puppy dog eyes. Bear okayed the man to toss her a frank and she bounded about happier than ever. Children and adults alike reached their hands out to invite her over and she ate the attention up just as passionately as she ate up the hot dog.

Maggie did, too, when she could be disguised under her alter ego. She followed Atlanta up to their chosen victims and she teased those with clown phobias and impressed those who asked for tricks or magic. Atlanta jumped through her arms and balanced on her back, and Bear stood a few paces away, focusing on them to avoid reaching for the blisters on his lips.

He couldn't shake the feeling that someone was watching him, so he glanced around until he saw Mavis standing at the entrance flap of her tent, ignoring the line of people forming. She blinked once, slowly, before turning and disappearing into the darkness of her cave.

Bear followed, seemingly without realizing it.

Inside Mavis' tent, the air was thick the scent of rosemary and something underlying. Was it gasoline? Bear narrowed through the shadows.

Mavis was a ghostly apparition at her table, admitting a low humming of a song Bear didn't recognize. He approached her cautiously, half expecting Maggie and Atlanta to barge through the tent, but they didn't. So, Bear slid into the chair across from her.

"How are you feeling, Mavis?" Bear asked, careful to keep his tone friendly and patronizing.

"How are *you* feeling, Barrett?"

"Bear, please."

Mavis touched a face-down tarot card with thin, pale fingers. "You have been given many names. Good for you for standing strong with the one you've chosen for yourself."

Bear didn't respond. He was waiting for her to continue speaking. Thankfully, she didn't leave him hanging for long.

"There's an old Chinese proverb about wishing your son into a dragon to bring upon him good fortune and wealth." Mavis slide a script across the table at him.

Holding it delicately, Bear traced his fingers over the Chinese lettering, down the spine of a red-ink dragon.

Mavis said, "If they could see you now."

"I'm not rich," Bear said, handing it back to her, "nor am I in good fortune or wealth. I live in a trailer and wear the same three outfits every day."

He intended to come off as lighthearted, but Mavis' neutral expression went bitter with anger.

"You want to be?"

Bear shrugged. "That's why I joined the Circus."

Mavis leaned forward. "All of those people out there are going to come in here and ask me if I can see how they're going to die. I don't have that power, Bear, no one does. Not even you."

There was no way in arguing that, so why did Bear feel the insistent need to do so?

A few weeks back, he might've tried to. He once believed that so long as he could control fire, he could control every aspect of his life. Fire had governed it long enough.

He knows now the flaws in that logic. If he could change the course of life to fit his own masterplan, Quinn and Judas would still be fooling around outside on the midway. San Francisco and who-knows-where were not in the outline.

Bear could not allow himself to believe in a higher power. After his family died, he tried his best. He turned to various churches, various pastors, a cult or two – none of them made him feel as understood as fire breathing did. Or maybe it wasn't the fire at all – perhaps it was just the Circus.

Either way, Bear didn't like the idea that someone had a plan for him. If that were the case, it was a bullshit plan.

Mavis could read minds.

"No one has reins on life, Bear," The clairvoyant said. The harshness in her voice melted into something kinder. "You must stop living in fear of the unknown. Embrace it."

Stepping back into the fresh air of the Fairgrounds, Bear noticed Wes loitering by the base of the Ferris wheel, smoking a cigarette.

Bear crossed the way to him, careful to avoid children who ran without destination, unaware of their surroundings. The Ferris wheel was turning at its leisure pace as it carried squealing teenagers up, up, up to the bright and lonesome stars. Bear didn't bother trying to count them when he joined Wes; he knew he'd lose count at thirteen.

"Sometimes I think that dog belongs here more than I do," Wes said, handing off the cigarette to Bear. He followed his line of sight to where Atlanta was performing tricks for a group of bystanders with Maggie and some of the other clowns.

Bear inhaled the nicotine, secretly kicking himself for picking the habit back up. "I always do. I'm glad I could give her a better life."

"You think it's better?"

"Than the war?" Bear passed the butt back, letting the smoke sit in his lungs for a moment before exhaling towards the sky. "Without a doubt."

Wes exhaled on a dry chuckle. "I forget about that."

"Lucky you."

"You know," Wes murmured, ignoring a family that was chattering and pointing in their direction, "I grew up thinking I'd be the glue that held this place together. That crowds would come to see *me*, not some kid who wasn't even raised here."

Bear frowned. "I'm sorry."

"Don't be." The trapeze artist shook out his blond hair. "That's not a pressure I'd want to be under. You're stronger than you know, being able to bear it. No pun intended."

"It's heavy," Bear whispered. "Every time I look at them, I'm terrified of seeing disapproval in their eyes. I walk on eggshells, Wes. When I almost died, the first thought I had was, *I hope I haven't let them down.*"

"You could never let them down. You could never let me down."

"I could," Insisted Bear, staring intently into Wes' cold blue eyes. "If I die, this entire operation could fail within weeks. That sends everyone back into the lives they had to escape. I'm literally the only thing preventing them from that."

"You aren't," Wes hissed. "I don't know who's plowing it into your brain that this is your sole responsibility – Roy, your own damn self – but that isn't true, Bear. No one's looking at you like that. You keep this place afloat, yes, but if it sinks, you sure as hell aren't the iceberg."

Bear stared at him, fighting the urge to break down and cry. Wes looked a lot like Judas in that moment – his resolve was gone, his eyes fraught with emotion. There was a distance he wanted to close, but he wasn't sure what it was, or how to close it.

"Believe me," Wes pressed. "Please."

"Okay," Bear agreed because he wanted to stop talking, not because he believed him.

They finished the cigarette in comfortable silence. Bear kept his head tilted up to watch the Ferris wheel spin, allowing his body to relax to the nicotine and rhythmic motion above him. His nerves were still going off but he accepted that they wouldn't be fully soothed until he could get around the flames.

Performers were starting to drift away from the crowds that they'd drawn on the midway and towards the Big Top: the epicenter of it all, the sun in which they revolved around. In the gentle breeze, the tarps ballooned and sunk in, like the subconscious breathing of someone sound asleep. Bear tried to match his own breathing to the tent, until Maggie and Atlanta scampered over to them, beckoning.

Wes kicked off the Ferris wheel and shimmied around in his cat suit, grimacing slightly as he shook himself out. Bear eyed him with a raised brow.

"What, are you gaining weight? Tights getting tighter?"

"Fuck you," Wes grumbled. He twisted around, trying to see himself at every angle. "Am I?"

"No!" Maggie assured, smacking Bear on the shoulder for joking about it. "You look fine."

Wes was still glaring down at his body while the rest of them kept on ahead. He swore again and jogged to catch up, using two hands on each side of Bear's shoulders to heave himself onto his back without warning. Bear stumbled forwards, laughing and trying to shake him off like a steer in a rodeo. Wes held strong with arms wrapped around his neck and his feet dragging on the ground to slow him down. Maggie rolled her eyes.

"We're going to be late, you guys!" She said, quickening her pace while Wes and Bear wrestled on the ground. "You're going to get hurt before the show even starts."

Bear had managed to pin Wes down, a task more challenging than he anticipated. "We *are* the show. Can't start it without us." Wes took Bear's boast as a sign of distraction and wiggled his way out.

Atlanta barked, bowing playfully or prancing around the scuffle, bringing the attention of confused bystanders. Bear reached for his dog to pull towards him, gently pinning her to the ground so she felt included. Wes came to her rescue with a full body slam into Bear's shoulder, hollering, "Save yourself, Atlanta!" as Bear threw him off like he was nothing more than a lady bug that landed on his shirt.

"You two are going to be the death of me," Maggie laughed, helping Wes up. Bear rolled around with Atlanta for a second more before accepting Wes' outstretched hand of truce. "Look at you." Maggie shoved past the trapeze artist to fiddle with the loose strands of hair that escaped Bear's braid and headband. "You look like we just pulled you out of the grave. You're covered in dirt."

"Better dirt than ash," Bear pointed out, bending down to place a kiss on her painted red nose.

"That logic is flawed!" Maggie cried after him as he skipped away.

Bear slowed down enough for his companions to join him on either side, Atlanta trotting in the front with her head high and her tail low. They ducked down into the shadows beyond the bustling center of the Grounds, keeping their heads bowed so they could sneak around the Big Top without being seen.

At one point, Maggie stopped, stooping down to pick up and dust off a no smoking sign that had been tipped over. She sat it up right near the main entrance of the Big Top with a proud look on her pretty face.

"Okay, this is where I leave you," Maggie said. "Good luck, boys. Give 'em hell."

"Plan on it." Wes gave her a quick peck on the cheek.

"We'll knock their socks off," Bear agreed, scooping the Clown up in a big hug. "Then this whole place will smell like stinky feet."

"Ew!" Giggled Maggie as she tried to squirm out of his embrace. "You're gross! Go!"

They waved goodbye to her, wishing her luck and telling her to have fun. They took a moment to watch her dance off, twisting and twirling happily, submerged in her character. It was comforting, familiar sight that took a bit of the edge off of Bear's nerves.

Wes nudged his arm, and Bear realized he had been staring. "You ready?"

Bear checked for Atlanta. She was sitting loyally at his feet, looking up at him with intense focus. He nodded at her. She licked his hand. Bear counted the whiskers he could see on her face, made it to fourteen, and felt the sense of power that had been missing all night flood his bone marrow.

He barely believed it himself, but Bear said, "Yeah. We're ready."

THE DEATH OF
THE DRAGON

BEAR

There was something thundering about the crowd tonight. Bear could feel their energy from behind the stage: it rumbled beyond his ears, shook the ground he stood on, electrified the fast-paced blood in his veins. Wes could feel it, too. He stood so close to Bear that their shoulders were pressed together and Bear could feel the vibrations of the trapeze artist's anticipation. Atlanta sat at Bear's feet, still as a statue, eerily calm. An ebony coated anchor.

Taking a moment, Bear knelt beside his dog and buried his face in her neck. He inhaled her scent, focused on her rhythmic breathing, the soft texture of her fur, the steady sound of her heartbeat. Everything else faded away. Whether they were deployed overseas or backstage at a traveling Circus, she was the center of the Earth. He tightened his grip on her, giving one last squeeze to say, *I'm okay*, then stood and passed back up against Wes.

Light dragonflies skimming over the surface of a pond, Wes's finger tips drifted over Bear's lightly. They became tangled together, sweaty palm to sweaty palm, the bones of their knuckles grinding together from the strength of their grip. The tremors coming from Wes ceased and the boy took a deep breath, sighing on the exhale. Bear tugged at their hands.

We got this.

The sea of performers behind them parted to reveal Callie weaving her way around bodies to get to them. Her long, straight, black hair was braided back in two French braids against her skull, reaching just below her shoulder blades. She wore light make up, nothing like what the clowns caked on, but it made her look far older than just over sixteen. She stood on Bear's other side, shooting them both a determined smile.

We got this.

Roy maneuvered his way to the front, his jacket's long cape trailing behind him like a roll out red carpet. Dee followed close behind, her tight curls pushed back from her forehead with a black headband, clad in a dress that hugged every flowing curve. Roy began to speak, keeping his eyes stuck on Bear the entire time.

"My children." He waited until the chatter died down. "It has been a long week since Quinn. I have seen how you've been preparing for this. I can sense the passion and energy in this room – it fuels me just as much as it fuels you." Roy smiled, almost sadly. He still stared at Bear. "And what do we always say?"

All around him, the chorus rose up: "The show will go on!"

In booming, powerful voices, leaking with determination and emotion. Bear kept his jaw wired shut, hoping his silence would be drowned out by the uproar. His chest was still tight, his breathing still irregular, his eyes still locked with Roy's. At some point in the frenzy, Wes' hand slipped from Bear's grip and his fingers clenched into two fists, trying to place himself elsewhere. On top of a mountain at dawn, Maggie in his arms, alive and smiling from ear to ear without the illusion of red make up.

The curtain dropped.

* * *

<u>MAGNOLIA</u>

The clowns were overtaking the Fairgrounds like never before. They were determined to pull out all the stops tonight on a crowd three times larger than any anticipated. It was hard to even navigate around without bumping into someone, and Maggie gave up all hope of sticking with a buddy long ago. Alone, she loitered close to the Big Top by the game booths, chatting up the

226

operators. She kept one ear on fluctuating noise level coming from the tent, trying to determine which act was up based on the crowd's reactions.

Cody, who was in charge of a dart throwing game tonight, split his attention between her and the kids leaning over trying to pop the balloons. The May evening was humid and most workers had their arms bare; Cody wasn't an exception. He opted for just a tank top instead of his classic windbreaker, just like Maggie wore far less layers than she usually did for her costume. She felt a pang of sympathy for those stuck under the heat-trapping Big Top come the fire show.

Something hit the back of her head.

Maggie turned, prepared to snap at some shithead preteen, on innocent looking Cody shoving almonds into his mouth. He winked at her, amused by her visible annoyance, and tossed another almond in her direction, this time almost managing to shoot it down her cleavage.

"Cody," Maggie warned, "I won't feel bad about turning you into a pickled punk."

The carnie bowed. "Would be my absolute honor to be stuffed by you, princess."

"Stop." Finding the discarded almond amongst the frills of her neck piece, Maggie threw it back at Cody, who giggled and ducked behind the booth. Maggie laughed and leaned over to see him taking cover under one of the largest prizes, a plush elephant. Above their heads, a kid finally managed to pop a balloon.

Maggie turned back to examine the Fairgrounds while Cody helped the young girl pick out a prize. A loud, excited cheer from the crowd within the Big Top caught her attention. The ground below her rumbled like the waves of an earthquake; The Strongmen were up, lifting, dropping, throwing, spinning. Cody returned to her, still popping almonds into his mouth, leaning forward on his elbows.

"You're worried," He said, eyebrows furrowed together.

"Always am," Maggie replied, smiling softly. "Its an anxiety-inducing industry we're in."

Cody glanced over at the players, making sure everything was going smoothly and no one was cheating, and then he asked: "Why *are* you in this industry?"

Maggie blinked, taken aback. "What?"

"I don't know, Mags. It just doesn't seem like you belong here." He raised both hands up. "And I mean that in the best, most respectful way possible. You got gifts, girl, and you're wasting them here."

"Why are *you* here, Cody?"

He wasn't unimpressive himself. Maggie had seen his talents in construction, wood carving, guitar playing – and time after time he demonstrated wonderful leader skills. The carnies and barkers naturally fell behind him, even though he was younger than some of them at just barely twenty-three.

Cody shrugged and pushed his long, sandy blond hair back from his face. Born on the outskirts of Malibu, he never outgrew his California surfer boy roots.

"This place kept me off the rock," Cody said. "Away from heroine, too. It gives me purpose every day, I get to do work I'm proud of, even if just for some silly ass traveling Circus." He smiled, his finger tracing the grain in the wood that had snuck through the peeling, old layer of white paint, like he was making note of which project to pick up next. "It certainly isn't something to brag about at a high school reunion, but I really got nothing else. At least for now. And when the time comes that I'm able to move on, I'm not sure I'll want to."

Maggie listened carefully, wishing with all of her heart that she felt the same level of gratitude for the Circus. Cody had joined the same summer she did, just a few weeks after her. She remembered her was skin and bones, sunken eyes and irritable moods – he stumbled into the Circus one night asking if anyone dealt. Roy offered him a job that same night, and spent a week nursing a stranger through quitting cold turkey.

They had all seen people leave the Circus: chasing after one-night stands from the town, returning home after a reconciliation with parents, finally admitting to themselves that rehab was the best option. People moved on, grew up and had families, not everyone wanted to be a lifer. Some didn't even make it through their first summer. Eventually their names were forgotten, their acts were taken over by newcomers, and they became just another blurry face that used to sit around the fire.

Maggie was destined to become one of those faces. She accepted that a long time ago.

She sighed, toying at her tutu. "I don't know, Cody," She said. She thought about her father, how he daydreamed about all of his missed opportunities. "I know I can't stay here forever, but how can I leave?"

"*Him*," Cody clarified. "You could leave the Circus tonight; your heart doesn't belong to it. Bear keeps you here."

Tears welling up in her eyes, Maggie nodded instead of speaking, because she knew if she did, she'd break down. Another kid popped a balloon, then a second, then a third. Cody pulled away to cheer for them, pointing to the highest row of prizes. Maggie smiled at the pure joy on the face of the child as he selected a large, stuffed banana.

She heard the barking first.

For a second, Maggie's brain couldn't process it. Atlanta was barking somewhere under the Big Top, but not in the excited way she did when Bear was preparing to start their show. This was a warning bark: solid, sharp, and turning more frantic by the second.

At some game a few kiosks down, someone one the biggest prize and a carnie set off a ringing bell. Maggie glanced up in the direction of the commotion; she saw the smoke rising above a string of fairy lights.

And then, only after what felt like both a split second and an hour, in which Maggie's reflexes tried to catch up, a distraught scream rose above the ambiance of the Fairgrounds: "Fire!"

* * *

<u>BEAR</u>

Andreas was bowing for a standing ovation while a dozen carnies worked to clear the area of his weights and props. What he could lift in one hand, it took multiple just to move a few feet out of the way. Allie and a few other contortionists were up next. Bear lifted his head, trying to see beyond the curtain up to the perches where Wes and Callie were waiting for their cue, hidden in the shadows.

Behind him, Dee was sitting with Paris, sharing a box of popcorn and laughing at something he was showing her on his phone. Atlanta was completely still in between Bear's legs in her Sphinx position, watching the carnies working with her head tilted to one side.

The crowd was buzzing waiting for the next show, and more and more people were starting to filter in and out. Bear narrowed his eyes. Someone was lighting a cigarette, leaving with a crowd out of a back exit.

"Hey, when do you guys go?" Paris' inquiry surprised Bear into blinking, and then the man was gone.

"Soon," Bear answered, shaking his head. "Contortionists, then Callie and Wes get a slot to themselves, then Atlanta and I go in there and finish it up."

"Awesome!" The boy said around a mouthful of popcorn. Bear smiled, despite the anxiety still turning his stomach over. Paris had only been here a week and the noticeable change in his attitude warmed Bear's heart.

An applause told him the contortionists were starting. Much like Allie herself, her parents were all teenage girls with small frames who came from gymnastics backgrounds. The youngest was a thirteen-year-old whose guardian, her nineteen-year-old brother, was a carnie.

Roy made it halfway through his introduction when Atlanta suddenly stood, legs stiff and ears pricked, opening her mouth to taste the air. Bear stepped around her, confused. The Shepherd's hackles raised as she began to whine. She started circling, smelling the ground and crying.

Dee stood up. "Is she o–"

Atlanta barked high pitched, staring at Bear like he was supposed to know something. Her barks stated to come in rapid succession, distressed and frenzied. Roy turned around, interrupted by the chaos behind the curtain that he couldn't see. The crowd went quiet. Bear tried desperately to quiet her down, speaking in a low, calm voice to her, but his dog only got more terrified. She weaved through his legs and at one point, bit down hard on his tank top, tugging him backwards.

"Atlanta!" Bear hissed, annoyed.

The familiar, strangely comforting scent of smoke filled his mouth when he spoke. His brain went haywire. That wasn't his fire.

The scream of warning came from the crowd just seconds before the back side of the Big Top, just a few yards away from Bear, Dee, and Paris, went up in flames. Bear swore and ducked, grabbing Dee and Paris by the collars and shoving them towards the stage. He shooed Atlanta after them as black smoke filled the area, swallowing the can of kerosene he had brought for the show.

Fucker.

Bear dropped to his stomach, army crawling through the billows to grab the gas before the flames could reach it. He rolled out from under the curtain, coughing, feeling Atlanta's teeth on his shirt as she helped drag him out of the smoke. Most of the guests were already filed out, but the performers were still stuck on the stage with the back exits blocked by the fire, left to do nothing but wait their turn.

"What the fuck were you doing?" Dee growled, storming up to Bear where he laid sprawled on his back. "Why didn't you follow us?"

Glaring, Bear gestured with the gasoline in his fist. "Sorry, I thought going up in a giant fireball might be too dramatic."

He clambered to his feet with Atlanta's help and looked around. The flames were quickly eating away at the Big Top's fabric and ash rained down on them like large, grey and orange snowflakes. A cry for help came from above them and Bear's heart dropped. Callie and Wes.

Ignoring Dee's shout of anger, Bear tore off in the direction of the ladders leading up to the platforms. He started climbing the one that Callie was on, ignoring how hot the metal was getting as the fire drew closer. The young girl was clinging to the ladder half way up, too terrified to go down further. She sobbed as Bear reached her.

"It's too hot!" Callie cried. "I lost Wes!"

"Its okay," Bear spoke as calm as he could manage. "Drop, Cal. I'll catch you. I promise."

Callie's brown eyes blew wide with terror at his suggestion and she shook her head rapidly. There was a loud cracking sound and a beam dropped just feet away from their noses. The Big Top was collapsing.

"Callie!" Bear roared, his eyes stinging and his throat burning. "Remember, your whole act is about how good at falling you are!" He repeated her own joke back to her, somehow managing to smile. The young acrobat was shaking with terror with her eyes clenched shut. It was like she didn't even hear him. Bear's heartbeat was picking up. They were running out of time. "Callie, honey," He begged. "Drop."

And she did, right into Bear's outstretched left arm.

He caught her with a grunt, nearly sliding down the ladder as his sweaty free hand fought for a grip. "Good girl," He panted. "Now climb onto my back."

With the skill and agility of someone in her profession, Callie maneuvered like a koala onto Bear's back like a backpack, gripping tightly and burying her face in his neck. Only when he was sure she was in the best position possible, Bear started slowly lowering them down the ladder. More beams and pieces of flaming curtain were falling around them. Bear focused on his limbs and his breathing until both feet were on the ground.

Callie slipped off his back but stuck close to his side. Bear ripped his tank top off and then wrapped it around Callie's face to protect it from the smoke. He peered through the smoke, seeing that the costumers had all exited the Big Top and the performers were starting to run out. Mustering the last of his strength, Bear stooped, picking Callie up by the midsection and throwing her over his shoulder. Roy was waiting for him, standing in the center of the stage, watching his Circus burn down around him. As Bear got closer, he could see the tear's streaking down his face.

"Everything..." Roy trailed off.

"I saw a man lighting a cigarette under here," Bear said, voice rough from the smoke. "C'mon, go."

They were the last ones to leave the Big Top, stumbling out into the Fairgrounds cover in soot and coughing like mad. Bear gently lowered Callie to the ground, removing the make shift mask from her face. Desperately, he scanned the ground, trying to spot a familiar head of blond hair.

Wes was running straight for them. "Are you okay?" The twin asked, his hands cupping Bear's cheeks.

Bear nodded, leaning their foreheads together. "I wasn't sure if you made it out."

They rested there for a brief moment just to breathe each other in. Wes broke them apart and knelt to comfort Callie.

"Bear!"

Maggie's broken cry of panic sounded through the Fairgrounds, over the distant sound of sirens approaching. She shoved her way through the crowds of people, customers and performers alike, to throw her arms around Bear with a sob. Bear held her tighter than he ever had, wishing more than anything that he could sink into her and just go to sleep, and they'd wake up and this was all a nightmare. He couldn't get close enough to her.

With his lips pressed against her neck, Bear murmured: "Did Atlanta find you?"

Maggie was silent, slowly pulling back to look at him. "She's not with you?"

Bear's stomach dropped. He ripped out of her grip, scanning the crowd. People were huddled together, trying to comfort and clean each other. Bear felt the earth drop.

Projecting his damaged voice as best as he could, ignoring the pathetic way it cracked, Bear called: "Does anyone have Atlanta?"

He knew the answer even before he bothered to ask. His fellow performers started to look around under their own feet. Worried chatter rose up and Bear couldn't distinguish one voice from another, his bad ear ringing terribly loud.

His feet were moving on their own accord. Back towards the fire, back towards where the Big Top was collapsing in on itself. Bear heard Maggie's shriek moments before he felt multiple pairs of hands grabbing him. Wes, Roy, and Maggie herself were all on top of him, looking all shades of concerned, devastated, and in Roy's case: pissed.

"What are you doing?" Maggie wailed.

"Don't," Roy bellowed, fighting against Bear's attempts to get free.

Bear shoved them away, his vision blurring with tears. "Fire has taken everything from me!" He stressed. "It will not take her."

Roy deflated, and after a moment of consideration, where his burning blue eyes matched Bear's tearful brown ones, he stepped back with an empty look of defeated horror. Maggie was stricken, her gorgeous face warped by heartbreak. Wes grabbed her to pull her back and she screamed, begging and weeping out Bear's name. Bear allowed himself to stare into Roy's eyes for a moment longer, and he nodded.

He wouldn't be stopped.

Ignoring Maggie's keening, Bear raced back to the Big Top.

* * *

<u>CALLIE</u>

Dee was trying to block her from seeing Bear disappear, but Callie could still hear everything. Maggie's gut-wrenching sobs drowned out Wes' attempts to comfort her. Callie peered from around Dee's shoulder.

The clown had sunk to the ground, bringing Wes with her, while Roy stood over them, completely defeated.

Fire engines sped up and stopped next to the Big Top, sirens blaring. Men and women swarmed around, some checking on people while the EMTs arrived shortly after, but most of them got to work trying to put out the fire. Hoses attached to the tanks equipped in the trucks, and powerful sprays of water were shot at the Tent.

Callie heard Roy approach the Chief and say: "One of my kids is still in there. He went back for his dog."

The Chief shot back: "He's an idiot." He gestured to some of his crew, passing on the news. As they rushed to put on the proper equipment to hunt Bear and Atlanta down, someone shouted for their attention.

A shadow of a body streaked out of the Big Top, barking. Callie's heart soared as Atlanta broke free of the fire, seemingly unharmed. She howled for a few seconds before turning around and diving back into the flames. The firefighters nodded to one another and followed the Shepherd without question. Within a matter of seconds, they returned, the leader holding Bear up by the shoulder, Atlanta striding loyally at her owner's side, nudging him along with the occasional gentle touch of her nose.

Behind them, the Big Top caved in on itself like it had been swallowed by a sinkhole. A tsunami of ash exploded and the firemen ducked, shielding Bear's body and their faces. Atlanta didn't seem to notice it as she lapped the soot off of her owner's hand.

Maggie broke free from Wes only to be stopped by firefighters. EMTs shoved past her and they hauled him onto a stretcher. Even from a distance away, Callie could hear Bear denying that he needed to go to the hospital.

His voice was weak and unconvincing, and he was unconscious by the time he was strapped in.

Taking advantage of Dee being distracted, Callie slipped around her and joined Maggie and Wes by Bear's side, releasing a shaky gasp of horror when she got a look at his face. It was covered in ash and redness; his eyes were closed peacefully like he was simply sleeping. His breathing was shallow and coming at random. At their feet, Atlanta whined, putting her two front paws up on the stretched by Bear's head, licking at his sweaty hair.

"Can she go with him?" Roy asked. His voice was breaking. "She's a service dog."

"The dog can come," An EMT said after a moment of hesitation. Atlanta jumped fully onto the stretcher, laying her long body across Bear's. From here, Callie could see her muzzle and paws suffered the most: the skin had been burnt off to expose pink skin and bloody pads.

Her nose briefly touched to Bear's and she whined. He didn't even stir. Atlanta cried and barked, settling her head down on her owner's chest, nuzzling under his chin. Callie felt sick with heartache, knowing damn well if the roles had been reversed, Atlanta would've rushed the fire for Bear, too.

The EMTs loaded Bear into the back of an ambulance, one of them turning to Roy with an unspoken question. Roy looked torn: go with the boy he loved like a son, or stay with the tragic remains of his Circus. Dee stepped up before he had to decide, putting a gentle hand on Roy's shoulder and nodding. Roy thanked her with a hug before she clambered into the back of the ambulance.

A choked off sob stopped the EMTs from shutting the backdoors. Maggie was trying to shove her way forward, caught around the middle by Roy. She reached desperately for Bear, her legs buckling again and bringing Roy with her.

"Bear!" Maggie wailed. The ambulance doors slammed closed and it sped off without a care in the world about the bawling girl clawing at the ground like she might be able to pull them back to her. Roy stayed in the dirt with her, his strong arms holding her to his chest as he rocked her gently.

The performers stood in a disheveled huddle, wide eyes and ash covered faces. Wes was crouched a few feet away, listening as the sirens grew distant. Callie could see him trembling from yards away. She turned to watch the fire fighters finish putting out the fire, a few police officers comforting guests who looked stricken. Seeing their horrified, sad faces made Callie irrationally angry.

What did they lose? They'd get their money back, and none of them were hurt. They didn't even get trampled exiting the Big Top thanks to the carnies well-orchestrated guidance. Around her, performers and workers were surrounded by the collapse of their home, their safe haven, the only place they ever belonged – and one of their most beloved comrades just got hauled off to the hospital on his death bed.

And if he died, the Circus in its entirety would go with him.

Frustrated, exhausted, confused, Callie stomped her foot and let the sob she'd been holding back consume her entire body. Paris tried to come over and comfort her but she spat for him to stay back. She didn't need to be comforted, she needed Bear. She needed this entire week, from the moment she let Quinn slip from her grasp, to be one long nightmare.

Under the cadence of Maggie's heaving sobs, Callie sank to her knees, her hands covering her eyes, and just let herself cry.

FIRE WITH FIRE

<u>MAGNOLIA</u>

The first time Magnolia was in a hospital after the day she was born, she was eleven years old and getting a rape kit examination. She entered the hospital in her cheerleader uniform and left in a smock, no underwear, shrinking under her mother's heavy and hateful gaze.

The hallways are silent and loud all at once: a paradox that is ever so deafening. She knew, even back then, that had her father not confessed the reason for murdering her uncle, she wouldn't be there. There would've never been justice.

She hesitated outside of Bear's room. For whatever reason, the hospital and its maze of white tile corridors felt more real than they did when she was eleven. No clown make-up, no flashy tutu or frilly neck piece, Magnolia was exposed in the truest form – they might as well strip her down to her bare skin again. There were no coping mechanisms here, there was only the harshest of realities.

A faint reek of gasoline greets Maggie when she pushes the door open. To her surprise, Bear was sitting up, glaring at a book in his lap with intense concentration. His left arm was bandaged up and his long hair had been cut up to above his shoulders, and he was shirtless. Atlanta was curled up by his feet in an mass of black fur, her limbs indistinguishable from each other, and their breathing was synced to a slow, sleepy pace. Only Bear's head raised in acknowledgment when the door clicked shut behind her; Atlanta stayed still.

"Hi, love," He greeted, smiling softly.

"Hi." Maggie sat down on the seat by his head, resting a hand on Atlanta's scruff. "You look better."

The fire breather shrugged, motioning as best he could with his arm wrapped in gauze. Color was back in his face and the blisters around his mouth looked less irritated, even the bags underneath his eyes had faded slightly. He looked more like a person and not the shell of one. Maggie's heart ached, but in a good way.

"I feel better, I think." Bear's lips smacked together and he dog-eared the page he was on, closing the book with an exasperated huff. The eyes on the cover of *The*

Great Gatsby stared back up at them, as if to challenge its reader's unimpressed scowl. "I hate this book."

Magnolia smiled and swung her backpack into reach, her hands rummaged through the disorganized array of belongings until she found what she was looking for: an old, faded, wrinkled copy of *The Catcher in the Rye*. Bear's eyes lit up and he tossed *Gatsby* across the small hospital room unceremoniously; it slid across the room until it hit the back wall, and Atlanta still didn't stir.

Maggie dug her fingers into thick, black fur. "Is she okay?"

"Tired," Bear mumbled, eyes glued to the first page of his book. "She feeds off of you, you know?"

"I think she's feeding off of you."

The dog's muzzle was marred with burns and her paws were wrapped with gauze. Some of the fur on her ears was patchy, too, and her ribs were barely rising and falling with each breath. When she slept, her paws and tail would twitch with her dreams, occasionally accompanied by quiet huffs and barks.

Here and now, she was still as a statue and silent like a corpse. Maggie tried to bite back a shuddered breath of terror.

Bear reached out, placing his hand over Maggie's where it was buried in their dog's fur. "Hey," He said, waiting until Maggie made eye contact before continuing. "She's going to be okay. All of us, we are."

"I don't–" Maggie tried to begin, tears flowing out before she could take control of them. Panic was coming and her limbs felt weak and shaky as she tried to steady her now rapid breathing. "I don't know if I can keep living like this, Bear. The ointment, the sleepless nights, the smell of gasoline, wondering which show is going to be the one that finally kills you–"

A soft knock on the door interrupted her and Dee entered with a cup of ice in one hand and a hot coffee in the other. The woman looked disheveled and exhausted, bags under her eyes and make up removed; she didn't even look shocked to see Maggie there, she moved robotically to hand Bear his ice and settled down on the soft cushioned arm chair in the corner of the room.

"Magnolia," She said with a sigh. "Wes didn't come?"

Maggie shook her head. "He stayed with Callie."

Dee glanced over at Bear and dramatically covered her eyes with her hand. "Oh, my heart. I can't believe they cut your hair."

Bear picked at the hair behind his neck with a wrinkled nose. "The ends were horribly burnt, you know that. It'll grow back."

"I'll miss braiding it, that's all."

Maggie stood so fast she got dizzy. Exhaustion, dehydration from crying, and hunger all came at her at once and she had to plop back down in her chair heavily to avoid falling over. Bear and Dee were watching her with wide, concerned eyes. Face buried in her hands, Maggie's body tried to cry but no tears came out; she just convulsed with dry, heaving sobs that felt more like she was screaming, bent over to lay her forehead on the bed next to Bear's legs.

She needed to let it all out. Up until that second, she hardly realized she had so much pent up but it came bubbling over like a volcanic eruption. Bear rubbed her back and curled over like a lock of wavy hair to hug her, whispering gentle words of comfort.

Guilt surmounted everything else. For refusing to see her father again, for leaving Bear to see him in the first place, for not visiting Quinn before it was too late, for not trying to talk Judas out of leaving, for being jealous that he had the guts to. How had she lived so many lives thus far in twenty-one years, and could not feel a shred of belonging in any of them?

There was a soft knock on the door and Maggie lifted her head in a sharp movement, the muscles tightening in protest. A doctor entered with Dee's approval.

He was a man not much older than Roy, with tricky greys appearing in his otherwise dusty brown hair. Square, black frames slid down the bridge of his nose as he looked not where he was going, but instead at a clipboard in his hand. Bear's nose wrinkled in childish indignation when the doctor pinned him under a stern gaze.

"As much as I enjoyed our last powwow," The doctor began, "I'm displeased to see you back here so soon, Bear."

"Not super thrilled myself, Doc," Bear responded.

Maggie stood from her chair and joined Dee in the corner, keeping her head down. The doctor introduced himself to them as he sat down in a rolling chair. He brought it to Bear's bedside, just sitting there for a moment, looking over the burnt bundles in his care. After a few moments of what was assumed to be him assessing the situation, Doctor Hall turned apologetically to Maggie and Dee.

"I'm sorry, ladies, but could I have a moment alone with Bear?"

There was a moment where Maggie thought Dee might refuse to leave. Spine straightened and mouth set in a tight frown, the woman agreed reluctantly and tugged Maggie up with her. Peering over her shoulder, Maggie just barely caught the angry look on Bear's face before the door slammed shut behind her.

Dee's back thumped against the wall, the back of her head hitting it with a dull thud in perfect synchronization. Heavy bags clung underneath her eyes and her jaw was beginning to grow faint five o'clock shadow; Maggie wasn't used to seeing her so unkept or without make up on her chiseled cheekbones. A pang of sympathy shot through her already wounded heart.

Careful not to startle her, Maggie placed a hand on Dee's forearm softly. "Do you want to go back? I can stay here with him."

Dee brought a hand up to scratch her chin in thought. She pulled it away like she had touched hot metal when she felt the prickly hairs against her palm.

"I must not be the prettiest sight, huh?" The woman laughed, dry and humorless.

Maggie said with a frown, "I just want to make sure you're comfortable."

"I will only feel worse if I dare to leave him," Dee sighed. She looked at Maggie with calculating consideration. "Have you eaten yet?" Maggie hesitated to reply and Dee huffed with exasperation. "*Go*. Now – and that's a very aggressive order. I already have on kid in a hospital bed."

Eyes rolling, Maggie gave Dee a hug and turned to follow the signs towards the cafeteria.

On the way there, her phone vibrated in her back pocket. She pulled it out, noting that it was nearly dead from a few days off a charger. A text from Adele popped up on her lock screen: "Is now a good time for your father to call you?". Maggie paused in the center of the hallway without thinking about it, causing a nurse in a brisk walk to narrowly avoid colliding with her back. She apologized to him profusely and moved to lean one shoulder against the wall.

Fiddling a hangnail on her thumb between her teeth, Maggie imagined her father leaning against a wall as well, but one of dark grey concrete, in a hallway with multiple others waiting for a turn to use the phones. She swallowed the anxiety rising in her chest and sent back: "Yes".

Within a few moments her phone lit up with a New York area code. Maggie let it go for two ring cycles before picking it up.

"Hi," Maggie answered, her voice awfully quiet in the vast hospital corridors.

"Hey kiddo." Her father sounded excited but tired on the other line. "Everything okay? Adele said you had something come up."

Maggie's heart ached; Adele hadn't ratted her out as a coward.

"Bear got hurt," She said, thankful that it wasn't a lie. "I'm in the hospital with him right now."

"I'm sorry to hear that. Is he gonna be okay?"

Over the phone, it was hard to tell if Damien was being genuine or just forcing for the sake of conversation. At this point, she didn't care either way – she just wanted someone to listen.

"I think so," She responded softly. "I don't know what to do, Daddy."

His voice dropped lower and became more muffled, as if he had cup his hand over his mouth and phone. "Whatever your heart tells you, Magnolia."

* * *

<u>BEAR</u>

Doctor Hall looked at him from across the hospital room like Bear was a pesky chipmunk he finally caught in a trap. Arms crossed, clipboard rested against his pelvis, a solemn mask thinly vailing a twinge of victory.

His silence said it all.

I told you so.

He didn't say that though, instead he sighed inwardly, tilting his head towards his chest so his glasses slid down the bridge of his nose. Hall adjusted them, then shifted his feet.

"Do you want me to read off your chart?" The doctor finally settled to ask. "I already went through it with Dee."

Bear hesitated. "I don't know." His head was throbbing with a migraine he purposefully hid from Maggie.

"Well," Hall said, pulling up a chair to sit beside his bed. "Let's talk about something you do know, then. A few days ago, one of your comrades – Quinn – was released from this hospital with life altering injuries given to her by your beloved Circus." He hesitated, as if giving Bear a chance to argue or butt in. Cautiously, he continued after a moment of silence. "She will never get to return to the Circus, Bear. She's out, for good.

"The thing with Quinn is she didn't get a choice in that. Her injuries were the result of a freak accident, which was out of her control. You, Bear, have all the control in the world over whether or not you get to leave here and return to the Circus. You have something that Quinn will spend every day of her life wishing she had: a choice." Hall sat back in his chair, his professionalism deflating like someone popped a hole in a balloon.

Bear's aching mind struggled to keep up. "I thought most of my injuries were because of the Top fire?"

Hall shrugged. "The topical ones, yes, including some smoke inhalation. The real danger is, as we've discussed, the fire breather's pneumonia."

"Acute exogenous lipoid pneumonia." The words felt foreign on Bear's tongue, even though he had spoken them so many times before. They used to feel like nothing. Now they felt like cement drying in his mouth.

They felt more real.

A choice, huh.

"Yeah," Doctor Hall whispered, like he could read his mind. "What we're looking at here is potential respiratory failure."

"Which is...?"

"Fatal." A beat. "In most cases."

Bear almost spit out: *I'm not most cases* but something stopped him. Whether it be the migraine, the thickness in his lungs, or the burning in his throat, Bear was thankful for it.

"It's frustrating," Hall went on, "to have a patient who already knows what's killing them, and is so hesitant to do anything about it. I don't think I've had one yet, myself. Tell me, Bear, has there ever been a flame that just wouldn't listen?"

"Fire never listens," Bear murmured. "You just learn to speak its language."

There was a soft knock on the door.

Dee had returned, her hair brushed, her skin a little livelier, holding a cup of coffee in one hand, and a bowl of dry looking dog kibble in the other. Atlanta raised her sleepy head.

"This is all they had at the store across the street," Dee said apologetically, setting the food down on the cold linoleum floor.

Atlanta blinked at it, then lowered her head back onto Bear's legs. Frantic worry shot through Dee's brown eyes.

"Is she okay?"

Bear glanced warily at his dog. "Yeah," He rasped. "Leave it there, she'll eat when she's ready."

"Are you hungry?" Hall asked, head tilted to the side.

The thought of food made Bear's stomach roll over. "No, not really."

A nurse appeared behind Dee in the doorway. "Doctor Hall? Barrett has some visitors. Is that alright?"

"*Bear*," Hall corrected. "And yes, if you're up for it?" He turned to Bear.

Before he could answer, Wes and Callie shoved past both the nurse and Dee. Wes froze when he saw Bear, but Callie flung herself forward immediately, skidding to a halt an inch away from being fully on top of him.

"You're alive!" The young girl shrieked way too close to Bear's sharp headache.

"Easy," Hall chastised gently. "I'm sure his head is killing him."

"Yeah," Bear grinned at her, "it feels like Wes' big butt is sitting on it."

Callie laughed, her cheeks dusty pink as she bent her body down to hug Bear. He hugged her back with his arm that wasn't wrapped in bandage, and looked over her head to see Wes staring, emotions unreadable.

He stared at the doctor like Bear wasn't even there. "Is he going to be okay?"

Hall stood, vacating his chair for Callie, and merely shrugged. "We're still trying to figure that out, aren't we, Bear?" He went towards the door. "I'll be back in ten minutes, then I'm cutting off visiting hours so he can get some rest."

When he disappeared down the hallway, Wes rounded on Bear. "What the hell does he mean by that?"

"Nothing, except that he's a jackass." Bear shrugged, keeping his tone nonchalant.

Wes wasn't smiling. He looked like he was going to be sick, looking down at Bear like he was looking at his corpse in an open casket. Bear's stomach tightened. Is that how they saw him?

Before anyone could speak again, Maggie returned, stunned at the influx of people who joined while she was gone. The skin under her green eyes was puffy, and her phone was in her hand.

"We have company!" Her voice was its normal level of chipper, though. "Hi, guys."

She hugged Wes, a lingering embrace.

Atlanta finally clambered off the bed to greet Maggie.

"Hi, baby girl," Maggie murmured. She sat crisscross on the floor across from the Shepherd while the dog picked slowly at her food.

"You okay?" Callie's voice snapped Bear's attention away from the scene. He hadn't realized it, but his eyes were drooping and his head was resting heavily against the pillow.

"Just tired," Bear reassured her, smiling softly. "How are you?"

"I can't believe *you're* asking *me* that."

"What? I can't be concerned for my friend's wellbeing?"

"In this instance," Dee chimed in, "no you can't."

Bear let their chorus of laughter – minus Wes' – shower over him. All this time, he thought he was doing it for them. All the blood spilled, all the toothbrushes shredded, and all the burn ointment – he had been telling himself that his body belonged to the Circus, so the Circus could continue to belong to them.

Now he knew the greatest gift he could give them was getting out of that fucking hospital bed.

* * *

CALLIE

She rode the elevator down with Maggie and Wes flanking either side of her, stiff and silent like statues, and a wad of money stuffed into her denying hands by Dee with instructions to get food and go straight home

252

"I couldn't eat if it was shoved down my throat," Maggie murmured as they stepped out of the elevator.

"Watch where you're going," Wes hissed at a man who was looking down at his cellphone as he followed the flow of people entering the elevator.

Maggie placed a guiding hand on Wes' shoulder until they were out of the automatic doors and stepping into the harsh sunlight of the June afternoon.

Despite the sickness she felt, Callie's stomach rumbled, reminding her that she had yet to eat.

"We have to go somewhere," She mumbled when Maggie and Wes looked at her quizzingly. "Dee will know if we don't, and personally, I could skip that lecture today."

She walked off without waiting for them to answer, hoping to avoid an argument she didn't have the energy for. In the week they'd been here, Callie had only explored as far as the train tracks, the grocery store, and the hospital; she turned down back alleys and streets, seeking out a local restaurant to splurge their money on.

Maggie and Wes followed a few paces behind, not speaking or doing much more than letting their feet lead the way.

Callie understood. She felt the same way when she had to leave Quinn behind at the hospital: like she had left without something. Without Bear and Atlanta, it felt like walking with not one, but *two* missing limbs.

Somehow, the absence of their weight only made everything heavier.

They rounded a corner onto Main Street and stopped dead, face to face with a giant mural advertising Bear's cocky, lopsided smile, unrealistically smooth-skinned face. Maggie choked on a muffled whimper behind Callie.

"Funny how the barkers don't paint on his blisters," Wes said, reading Callie's mind.

"They aren't very appealing, I guess," Callie said with a shrug.

Frankly, she couldn't understand why Wes and Maggie were acting like Bear was already dead. He was alive and laughing with them less than an hour ago.

"Do you really want to be a firebreather, Cal?" Wes asked quietly, still staring at Bear's giant painted face.

Callie frowned. "I think so. But I don't want to end up like Bear. Isn't there a way to do something at the Circus and not let it kill you?"

When Maggie responded, it was laced with bitterness. "If you figure it out, let me know."

Standing a few paces back from the wall, Callie watched Maggie and Wes maneuver to rip the poster down. One corner of the canvas wouldn't rip off despite Maggie's greatest efforts to pull on it. Wes stepped back as she yanked once, twice, and the heavy-duty glue the barkers used didn't budge.

"Maggie," Wes warned, voice low. "Maggie."

Callie caught a glimpse of Maggie's cheeks stained with tears, her face flush red with her straining, her teeth bared in frustration as she kept pulling.

"Maggie!" Wes snapped, more forcefully.

Whether caught by surprise or out of strength, Maggie's grip slipped on the canvas and she stumbled backwards, landing on her tailbone on the asphalt. She sat there for a moment before bursting into tears; tiny bits of gravel were stuck in the heels of her palms, and her elbows were grazed.

Wes knelt down beside her, brushing the dirt off her hands and helping her to her feet. "It's okay to ask for help," He whispered to her, and Callie wondered if he caught the irony in that at all.

He kept one arm around Maggie's shoulders as he tore down the canvas with one, easy yank. "See?" Wes said, so tenderly that Callie was taken aback. "Here."

Maggie held the poster to her chest, her cries subdued into nothing more than a steady stream of silent tears. "Thank you," She said. Her face left wet marks on Wes's shirt.

Wes placed a kiss on her head, then looked at Callie. "Where do you want to eat?"

ENCORE

<u>BEAR</u>

Two weeks since the burn down, and Bear had just been released from the hospital an hour and a half ago. Two weeks of doctors fluttering in and out of his room, taking blood tests, x-rays, cat scans, hooking him up to heart monitors. Two weeks of Doctor Hall looking at him with those sad, unreadable eyes.

On the fourteenth day, he kept it straight: "You're going to die soon, Bear, if you keep this up. By all standards, you should be dead now."

Bear had raised his chin defiantly to the halo of doctors and nurses surrounding his bed at his feet. "Thanks, Doc, but I think I'll be the one who decides when I die."

Hall tried to explain to him that's not how biology works at all, but Bear wasn't having it. He wanted to go home. So, when he got discharged, he didn't wait for anyone to be called down to pick him up.

With Atlanta at his side, he trekked the entire way back to the Fairgrounds. Each breath he took was a reminder, each increasingly weaker step was a sign. No one can fight fire with fire.

Not even Bear.

Wes had blocked him at the bottom of the hill with the pick up, spitting out a string of curses about how Bear should've just waited the fifteen minutes until he showed up. The trapeze artist hopped out of the truck, rounding the hood to stand chest to chest with Bear, cheeks flush with anger.

Bear had stared at him, ready to defend his right to walk. There was a moment where they both stood there, separated by an invisible line drawn in the sand, ready to yell at one another over something as trivial as Bear walking home from the hospital.

They never made it that far. Neither of them made the first move, they moved in unison, like two puppets on the same string.

It was sloppy, un-orchestrated. They were skilled in their crafts but fumbled with this; their teeth clashed, and Wes' hand gripped the baby hairs on the back of

Bear's neck with fierce intensity. They kissed like they were going to float away if they didn't.

The distance Bear had felt, the emptiness he sought to fill, it all made sense now. He couldn't get close enough. His lungs wanted air and his body ached from his long walk, but the thought of stopping this filled him with such terror that he gripped Wes tighter, closer.

I know you, and you know me.

Wes pulled back before Bear was ready to let him. They stared at each other, blinking in the bright sunlight.

For the first time, Bear looked into those ocean blue eyes and didn't feel like he was drowning.

He felt, instead, like he had finally come up for air.

"Can you taste gasoline?" Bear whispered.

"No," Wes replied.

With no Big Top to shelter it, the stage was bare to the sky.

Bear stood in the center, Atlanta between his legs, and took deep, long breaths. He relished in how easy the task had become since his stay in the hospital. Buzzing around him, the carnies were taking measurements and jotting down notes on the dimensions for a new tent. He reached down and trailed his fingers over the tips of Atlanta's ears, hyper-focusing on the feel of her prickly fur against his nerve endings to drown out the hectic sounds surrounding him. The world slowed down.

If he tried hard enough, and closed his eyes gently while his fingers dug into the thick fur around Atlanta's neck, he could hear the crowd's applause. It was louder in his bad ear. He made sure to center himself and keep his breathing rhythmic; if he slipped up, the cheers became sirens and the warmth of the fire he imagined was not his own.

Atlanta whined in warning, pressing up against his legs. Bear shook out his head and realigned, inhaling and holding his breath until the sirens disappeared. He opened his eyes, the sunshine bright enough to cause him to squint, and tried to count the carnies he could see. Fifteen. Atlanta licked his palm.

Cody, with hair finally long enough to put back in a man bun, used his hand as a visor to glance in Bear's direction. "Can't get enough of it, huh?"

"Never."

"I hear you, brother."

Bear watched Cody heave a charred metal beam out of a pile of ashes, his muscular arms tanned and streaked with charcoal.

At the far edge of the stage, sprouting from a pile of died-out embers, a single dandelion was tugged gently by the breeze. Bear knelt down to pick it from the base, losing a few white seeds in the process. Atlanta cocked her head to the side, watching curiously as he dug around for the pack of matches he had stuffed in his pocket.

He struck one. The tiny fire licked towards the delicate flower and at once it exploded into its own mini fire ball. The seeds, once so full of protentional to create more flowers, burnt up within seconds.

Roy approached from where he had been speaking to Dee by the entrance. He was taking a swig from his flask and smoking a cigarette, two habits he swore he was going to break by the end of the summer. Bear reserved judgement. He still craved the burn of gasoline in his throat. The Ringleader paused at the edge of the exposed stage.

"Barrett, walk with me." He beckoned Bear onward without waiting to hear the name complaint.

Bear didn't bother, figuring he had bigger fish to fry, and followed his Ringleader down through the Fairgrounds. They weaved through the food booths and past the rides, where carnies were working to rake together hidden piles of ash.

They walked until they reached the furthest back part of the field, up a short incline to the top of a hill just tall enough to gaze over the Fairgrounds in their entirety. Where the Big Top was now looked like an ugly wound in the landscape, like someone had freeze branded a perfect circle right in the middle. The beige, flat stage interrupted the lush green grass and colorful vendors that scattered amongst the meadow; a bleak and depressing reminder.

Roy pocketed his flask and stomped out the tiny remains of his cigarette. Checking over her shoulder for Bear's approval first, Atlanta wonder away from them, sitting calmly amongst a patch of wildflowers and watching the bugs play in the grass by her paws. Bear tried to picture himself holding any significance in the Fairgrounds below – and he just couldn't. It didn't matter how many posters and fliers displayed his face; it didn't matter how many guests said they came only for him. The fear of being ordinary was just too hard to shake.

"My ancestors," Roy began, just in time to cut off Bear's overactive intrusive thoughts, "created a Circus for one purpose: income. They wanted to be rich – they wanted to be showmen like Barnum. It sickens me that it worked, that people would pay such large sums to see such wild displays of dehumanization."

Bear listened, images of people in cages or behind glass walls flashing through his head. It was worse then, but when he thought about Quinn or Wes' parents, he wondered if it were any better now.

Roy continued. "I often find myself overthinking about what they would've done to you had they been the ones to get you. You'd be the biggest star in the world, no doubt about it. They'd have you richer than a king and everyone would know your face. People would pay dozens the amount they pay to see you now. That's your dream, right? To be the best."

There was no way Bear found fit to respond; he stumbled over his words when he tried. "I don't know. I think so, but then I think, what if that led me away from here? What if I can't have fame *and* this place?"

"I get it. That's why I left, too."

"But you came back."

"Who knew what would happen to this place if I didn't?" Roy shot back. "The hypotheticals I just gave you would probably still be true, I suppose. I've done nothing but hold you back and not allow you to reach your potential because I feared what your potential would do to you. Let me ask you something, Bear. Do you feel held back?"

"No," Bear said, and he didn't even realize that's how he felt. He suddenly remembered the recruiters from the night of Quinn's accident. Their offer had slipped his mind long ago. "I have a roof over my head, and a bed for my dog to rest hers. I have Magnolia. I used to think I had to be alone on that stage to prove myself. The truth is, being the only person up there while the Big Top was coming down on me, I realized it's the loneliest place in the world."

"You have no regrets?"

A question weighed heavy on Bear's mind. "Do you?"

"I bring children here to die," Roy said grimly.

"No, you bring them here to live."

Roy turned to him, the beginnings of a smile on his aging face. "You know, when the public found out you were alive and well, the first thing they asked for was an encore. Dee couldn't believe it. I could."

Bear raised an eyebrow. "Really? Will we give them one?"

"You will." Roy dug around for his pack of cigs, pulling one out and offering a second to Bear. Bear took it but denied a light. "I just spoke to Dee. I'm retiring."

Bear chewed on the end of the unlit cigarette, each word rolling over slowly in his head. When workers retired, they'd go back to lives of working in garages or body shops. When performers retired, they stayed comfy in their trailers and got to sleep through jump days – or, like Judas, they found a new life somewhere else. What did Ringleaders do?

"Dee is taking over," Roy said as if he had been reading Bear's mind. "She'll be wonderful. She already knows the job, she's been in the industry, and she cares with every fiber of her being."

"Why...?" Bear didn't get it. He *couldn't* get it. Confusion was starting to manifest as some petulant version of anger.

"I'm tired, son."

"Take a damn nap, Roy."

"Not that kind of tired."

Bear huffed, biting down hard on the cigarette. Tobacco leaves exploded all over his tongue and promptly spit them out in disgust. He stuffed what remained of the cigarette in his back pocket to avoid littering.

Atlanta had rejoined Bear's side. She sensed his turmoil and pressed up against his legs, wet nose nudging his hand to get his attention.

"Dee told me you had recruiters reach out to you recently," Roy said. "Is that true?"

"Yeah." Bear couldn't pick up on any notes of judgement in Roy's tone. "The night of Quinn's accident, actually."

It occurred to him that he was wearing those same pants. Bear reached into his back pocket and sure enough, found the business card. It was wrinkled at the edges and the text had faded thanks to its run through the wash, but it was there.

Bear took Roy's lighter and held the little flame over the corner of the card, watching it eat away at the paper until it was burning his fingertips and finally disintegrated in his hand.

Roy watched with a look of contentment on his tired face. "I'm guessing they couldn't win you over?"

"They're pitch lacked any effort. I'm not sure they've ever had to *convince* someone before."

"And you're the most stubborn son of a bitch around."

"Something like that."

"Look, Bear." Roy sighed and faced him, forcing eye contact that Bear didn't want to maintain but couldn't look away from. There was a serious note in his voice that almost reached desperation. "You have talent, not to mention an image that people just *eat up*. But more important than all of that – in my eyes at least – is your heart. You could make it big, and you could do it quickly, but you'd probably find that–"

Bear interjected. "Everything I ever needed was right here."

Roy smiled. "Yeah. Exactly." He hesitated for a moment and then added: "That's not to say I don't think you should go for it. If you want to, you should. I don't want you to feel held back."

"I don't," Bear assured him again. "I'm not even sure where I go from here."

"You don't have to know," Roy said softly. The first strokes of orange on the horizon were appearing as the sun prepared to set, both on the Fairgrounds and on Roy's time as Ringleader. "You just have to have faith in the process."

Tears began to form in Bear's eyes without warning. A wave of sadness overtook the lingering anger and he met Roy in the middle for a bone-crushing hug. The older man held him tightly like he might turn to ashes in his arms like the business card beneath his lighter. Bear's tears remained silent and unaccompanied by sobs; he let them flow while he buried his face in Roy's neck.

"Thank you," Bear whispered into his skin, muffled and wet. "You've given me everything. I could never repay you."

And he meant it. Everything he cared about was given to him or protected by Roy. There was no way to settle that debt or explain the level of gratitude he felt for the man who worked so, so hard to give a life worth living to so many kids just like Bear.

But Roy was shaking his head. "No, son. Thank *you*. You've brought my vision to life. Every continued breath is repayment ten-fold."

"I'm going to miss you," Bear rasped.

"I'm not going far," Roy promised, pulling back to cup Bear's face in his rough, calloused hands. He grinned despite his tears. "And I will always be the boss of you."

They both laughed, though it was weakened by sadness.

Bear stepped back and wiped his cheeks on the back of his hand. He looked over the Fairgrounds, watching as the lights began to come on as the sky took its time to darken. The Ferris wheel towered lonely above the rest of the structures, no longer competing with the Big Top. Bear noticed it turning slowly and figured some of the performers and workers decided to watch the sunset from the cabs.

"I know the time is right," Roy breathed. "So why is it so hard?"

"You're doing what so many of them don't have the courage to do. You'll set an example."

"A good one?"

"I think so."

"I'm proud of you, Bear."

"I'm proud of you, too."

Roy's retirement announcement was not entirely well received by the rest of the Circus.

Much like Bear, the general reaction began with anger and denial and descended into sadness and confusion. Several performers insisted they would leave, a few threatening to join other circuses. To Bear's surprise, they only became more distressed when Roy tried to slap a band aid over it.

"Dee will be taking over, you guys! You love Dee!"

Wes called out, "Dee isn't much younger than you, how long until she decides to retire too?"

Frightened by the image Wes planted in their minds, more indigent wails rose from the ranks. Roy looked exasperated and Bear felt a pang of sympathy. A decision that was hard enough to make was becoming even more difficult thanks to his rag-tag army of young adults terrified of change.

"What will we do then?" Allie asked no one in particular, yet everyone all at once. Her voice, naturally high pitched, was shrill with irrational anxiety.

She got a slew of different answers as everyone spoke up at the same time, their mass of exclamation drowning out Roy and Dee's pleas for order.

Bear sat silent with Maggie, Callie, and Paris, who all looked vaguely worried but refused to succumb to the mob mentality. After a few moments of letting the chaos unfold, Bear had enough. They were giving him a headache and causing a low hum of white noise in his bad ear – and quite frankly, it had been a long fucking week, and he was *over it*.

He glanced down at Atlanta, who was laying by his feet watching the crowd with dark eyes. The dog waited obediently for a command and Bear held four fingers up to his chin.

Atlanta leapt to her feet and barked, loud and demanding for attention. The noise cut off like someone pulled a plug.

"Shut the fuck *up!*" Bear bellowed across the crowd. He waited until he had two dozen pairs of wide eyes on him before he continued. "Roy isn't going anywhere, really. He'll still be around and even if he wasn't, we can trust Dee. And if she decides to retire, you know what we'll do?" He turned pointedly to Allie. The contortionist was sunken in on herself; he noted her skin clung closer to her bones. Bear softened his tone. "We'll be okay. No matter what – because we are here and we are together."

Those eyes continued to look uncertain, but the fear had left them.

Bear tore his gaze from them to Roy. "He has given us everything," he reminded them. "Accepting this decision is the first step in repaying him."

A murmur of agreement and apology rose from the once rambunctious group. Dee and Roy visibly relaxed, shooting Bear grateful smiles. Bear nodded to them and sat back down without another word.

* * *

<u>MAGNOLIA</u>

Over time, Bear's blister scars faded. The tissue on his ear and neck never fully healed, but the skin around his mouth recovered so well you could hardly tell it was ever oozing pus and blood. When he spoke, he could do so without cracking open old blisters, and he could drink and eat whatever he pleased and didn't have to worry about lacerating the sores within his throat. He slept through the night, and when he woke up, he didn't scrub his mouth with a toothbrush until the blisters were flat.

Instead, Bear woke with the sun and was able to drink tea out on the steps, warming his palms with a mug that had dogs of all kind playing around the face. One particular morning, Maggie noticed his dark brown roots sneaking up on the firetruck red as his hair finally grew back past his ears. She offered to dye it for him but Bear had shaken his head, saying they could another day. Another day didn't come for many months.

Bear traded splatters of coughed-up blood on his hands for splashes of paint. He sucked on the ends of pens, not cigarettes, and displayed empty cans of kerosene above the small desk at which he sat cross-legged, hunched over a canvas or novel. Their camper began to smell of sugar cookie tea or cinnamon rolls fresh from the bakery, and Maggie would wake as late into the morning as she pleased to the sound of Bear humming a gentle song into Atlanta's ear.

It was different. It was foreign, unreal: a lucid dream they haven't woken up from yet, and Maggie stepped around cautiously, terrified of disrupting anything that might cause her to wake.

Bear, on the other hand, seemed blissfully aware of this new reality he created for them. Long gone were his days of existing so loud he could drown out the sounds of his past creeping up on him, replaced with a quiet version of his life before.

And he tried, perhaps harder than he ever tried with anything else, to get Wes to join him. Maggie didn't know the details of what they went through together while she was dealing with her own shit, but it shattered her heart to watch the boys drift apart. Wes got angrier than he had when Judas left; he shut down, locked himself in his trailer for days at a time, and when he emerged on those rare occasions he reeked of booze, cigarettes, and marijuana.

They all fear for a long time that the trapeze artist was past the point of return – that the weight losing his parents, Quinn, his brother, and now whatever Bear had become to him had finally cracked and shattered his spine. He would've had to be Atlas to bare it, and unfortunately Wes was a mere mortal.

Bear seemed to think he had it all figured out. He would sit patiently beneath Wes' window, reading him passages of whatever novel he had picked up that week. The efforts never went noticed or appreciated but he never quit trying.

"No one gave up on me," He said to Maggie when she caved and questioned him about it. "He shouldn't be given up on, either."

"No one's given up on him." Maggie frowned. "We're just giving him time."

"We all run out of that eventually."

If anyone could voucher for that, it had to be Bear.

It was an evening in July when Bear finally did figure it out. The air had cooled to the low seventies, a saving grace from the scorching afternoon. New Hampshire had two seasons of grey area and with two seasons of extremes between them, and Bear had set off that afternoon shirtless and in sandals. He returned with an oversized hoodie with the tags still on, hiding something beneath it when he slipped under the Big Top.

Wes was letting Dee give him a haircut. She had been begging to get at the mop on his head for week but he had always managed to avoid it, saying he was too tired or too drunk. With the help of Maggie and Callie, she found a way to corner him – now they sat in front of him on the stage floor, playing a game of Uno while Dee hummed a gentle tune and tamed his flowing locks.

Atlanta jumped up when Bear entered, her head cocked and her tail wagging slightly: unusual behavior for a dog who would normally rush her owner with glee. She approached him cautiously, like he held some rare and important bounty under the sweater, safe from prying eyes.

"Whatcha got, B?" Maggie asked, not sparing him more than a quick glance over her shoulder. The game was intense. Both her and Wes only had one card left and Callie wasn't far behind.

"Something for Wes," Bear replied. "If he wants him."

Maggie's eyebrows knit together, confused. *Him*?

She turned back around in time to see Bear pull a fox-red Golden retriever puppy out from his hiding spot. Callie squealed in excitement and leapt to her feet, sending the cards flying in different directions. In any other circumstance Maggie would've been boiling with annoyance, but she didn't even notice the destruction of her near victory because there was a puppy tumbling towards her on unsure paws.

Before he could reach them, Atlanta intercepted with uncontainable joy. The adult dog bounced up and down, barking and bowing to the puppy's nose level; running circles around him. The poor thing was getting confused by his larger assailant, so Maggie swooped in to rescue him, scooping the precious bundle up in her arms before Atlanta could nip at his back again.

"She hasn't seen a puppy in a while," Bear laughed, calling the Shepherd to his side. Reluctantly, Atlanta sulked over to him but kept her wide, brown eyes on the puppy. "She forgets how big she is, huh, girl?"

"Where did you get him?" Callie was cooing to the puppy and letting him gnaw on her fingers with his sharp teeth. One particularly hard bite had her pulling her hand back with a disapproving pout.

"Breeder." Bear handed Maggie his AKC registry paperwork. "Been in contact with them for a few weeks. They called me today about a match. Most of their dogs go on to do service work but they suspected he'd wash out." He flashed them a shit-eating grin. "Said he enjoys getting in trouble too much."

Dee rolled her eyes. "Sounds like a perfect match."

Wes had remained quiet. He eyed the dog with a blank look on his face. Bear didn't look discouraged, though: he lowered himself to the ground next to Maggie and scratched behind the puppy's orange ears. The retriever leaned into it with a tongue lolling out happily, using two big front paws to hold Bear's hand in place so he could chew on his thumb.

Bear looked at Wes pointedly. "He needs a name."

"Why me?" Wes didn't sound annoyed despite the accusatory way he worded his question.

"Dogs help," Bear said simply. As if to prove his point, Atlanta nuzzled into his shoulder, gazing at him with adoration in her amber eyes.

Maggie offered Wes the puppy with a welcoming smile. The trapeze artist took him after a note of hesitation. The puppy instantly went to nibble at his earlobe, exposed now thanks to Dee's haircut; Wes shrunk in on himself with a snicker and Maggie, Callie, and Dee all brightened with delight.

It was the first time they heard Wes laugh in weeks.

The unsure, awkward handoff turned into a full embrace as Wes held the puppy tightly to his chest, burying his face in the soft fur behind his head. Bear was smiling, not triumphantly like he won a contest against himself, instead like he had just come across the first springtime flower after a harsh winter.

"So, a name?" Callie pushed. "I already have several ideas."

"Lets hear 'em," Wes said. "I got nothing. I've never had to name a pet."

"Well," Holding up her index finger, Callie began listing: "Concord, because Atlanta is named after a state capital and Concord is the capital of New Hampshire. Maverick, because Goldens are water fowl retrievers. Fox, because of his color..." She trailed off, a finger for each name tapping her chin in thought. "Or Quincy. It's a sub peak of Mount Adams, which is the second tallest mountain in New Hampshire." With a sudden hint of shyness, Callie mumbled: "Also, for Quinn."

"Quincy is the obvious choice," Wes declared. He held the puppy out at arm's length. "Welcome to the Circus, Quincy."

The rest of them echoed with beaming grins: "Welcome to the Circus!"

AFTER

<u>BEAR</u>

The recruiters found their way back to the Circus a few weeks after Roy's retirement, as if they could smell the change in atmosphere like coonhounds on a hunt.

Dave had lost weight: that was the first thing Bear noted as they approached where he leaned against the base of the Ferris wheel. He flicked away the butt of his cigarette, aiming purposefully close to Greg's shiny dress shoe. It did nothing to discourage the artificial smiles on the men's faces.

"Morning, Bear," Greg greeted, extending a hand out.

Bear just looked at it. "What do you want?"

"Wow," Dave laughed. "You sound just as excited to hear from me as my ex wife."

"I'm sure her and I would get along wonderfully."

"Nah, she's a bitch."

"And you're a dick," Bear hissed. He repeated stronger: "What do you want?"

Greg pinned him under an icy stare. "Same thing we wanted the last time: you."

Pursing his lips, Bear ran his eyes over the men in front of him, trying to read their body language and how it differed from their forced expressions. Greg had returned both of his hands to his pockets when Bear denied him a shake; Dave had recoiled in on himself at Bear's insult. He had to give it to them: they put up a good front, and they're chemistry and charisma probably won over lots of malleable targets.

But they would not win over Bear.

Dave pushed harder before Bear could respond. "We heard about your Ringleader getting outta dodge after that fire. Can't handle the heat, get outta the kitchen – or, circus." He trailed off with a nasally laugh-snort combination.

"We're worried about what this means for your career advancements." Greg pulled out a cig and gestured for a light. Bear lied about not having one.

"What if *I'm* not worried about my 'career advancements'?" Bear shot back. He fought the urge to whine like an overtired toddler. "I almost died, still kind of processing that."

"You're lucky to be alive," Greg agreed, "and I'm sure your doctor gave you the whole spiel about how much time you have left if you keep it up like you have been."

"Not a lot."

Dave got a wicked twinkle in his eye. "Don't you want to make sure you go out with a bang? After spending your last few years living like royalty?"

These sick fucks.

There was a moment his brain felt a jolt of thankfulness that they went for him and not someone who shared their values, like Wes. He was also glad they offered at this point in his life and not when he was rabid for fame. Like car salesmen, they were insatiable – but instead of pushing for a hatchback, they were trying to convince Bear to give up longevity for prosperity.

And even more unlike car salesmen, they weren't very good at it.

"Actually," Bear cleared his throat, absentmindedly reaching up to twirl around a lock of hair, only to remember with a tinge of sadness that it had been cut short. "I'm retired."

He said it to get them off his back, but he found he liked the way the words flowed off his tongue. *Retired.* Bear was tired.

The recruiters' outer layer of forced enthusiasm melted away like candle wax. Greg moved past the slack-jawed state of confusion before Dave did, his dark eyebrows nearly touching above his nose as they furrowed in a disapproving scowl.

"Don't joke around like that," Dave said, chuckling nervously. His round face had become flushed and pink, like raw meat.

"You can't retire," Greg said low and steady. "You're in your prime, Bear."

"Wasn't it you who just agreed I'm near the end of it?" Bear countered, his irritability growing and patience shrinking. Atlanta was somewhere with Maggie, and his anxiety was left unmanaged. Deep breaths.

"An end that could be extraordinary if you choose to let it."

History tends to swallow ordinary people.

Bear had been the one to say that, sprawled out on Dee's floor, trying to remember what breathing unencumbered by pain felt like. That fear was something genuine, something Therapist Jen had pinpointed in one of their last sessions together. Just weeks after his family died, their names were forgotten. They had no friends, no family other than Bear, no jobs – they were ordinary, and the passing of time had absorbed them.

His family were bad people though. They stole, beat their children and their spouse, spent what little money they had on drugs rather than food for their kids. Maggie had been the one to raise the question: "Were they forgotten because they were ordinary, or were they just unworthy of being remembered?"

Bear realized he had been quiet for a long time, and Greg must be beginning to think he was winning him over. Bear flashed the man a genuinely apologetic smile.

"I'm sorry," He said, and meant it. "If you got to me a few years ago, I would've been all yours. Growing up sucks."

Greg sighed. "Yeah. It does."

Now Bear shook his hand, firm and polite. He did the same for Dave, whose palm was clammy and unpleasant to hold.

"The industry will be sorry to see you leave," Dave said.

"But we'll be glad to see you live," Greg finished, and like Bear, it sounded like he was telling the truth.

Bear watched them go with a skip in their step that wasn't there before. A wet nose nudged his fingers and Atlanta was nuzzling up into his hand, accompanied by Maggie a few paces away.

"Who was that?" Maggie asked, looking beyond him to where Dave and Greg were getting into a BMW.

"Fans," Bear said, and pulled her into his chest, breathing her in. Maggie laughed as she rested her head under his chin.

A voice calling their names broke them apart.

Callie, Paris, and Wes were jogging towards them with huge smiles on their faces, being trailed by Quincy who was still figuring out how to run on his too-big paws.

"We have news!" Callie announced proudly, skidding to a halt right before she crashed into Bear. He steadied her with a hand on each of her shoulders.

"Good news, I hope," Maggie lamented. "I don't think I can handle any more bad."

"Really good," Paris assured her.

"I decided," Callie began, looking at Bear as she spoke, "that fire breathing isn't really my passion–" *Duh.* "–and I want to return to acrobatics. But I need a partner–"

"And that's going to be me!" Paris finished, sticking out both of his palms like jazz hands. Wes was beaming over their shoulders, arms folded across his chest and looking well-rested for the first time in a long time.

Bear's heart warmed. "That's wonderful!"

"I'm so glad you found your place." Maggie wrapped Paris up in a hug, kissing the top of his head. "And I don't mean acrobatics. I mean here." She opened her arm for Callie to join the embrace, too. "I'm so proud of both of you."

Clearing his throat, Bear said: "I have some news too." The attention snapped to him like a flipped switch, and varying levels of concern appeared on his friends' faces. "I'm retiring from fire breathing," Bear announced. It felt harder to say to them; his throat tightened up and his chest constricted, but nonetheless he persisted.

Silence.

It was harder to say, but easier to imagine. Deep down, he knew he was done when he woke up in the hospital for the second time and saw Atlanta's charred fur. He had tried to ignore how the smell of gasoline now made his stomach roll over, or how the sight of his torches only made him remember the burns on the corner of Callie's mouth. There was a lesson learned that was a long time coming.

No one could fight fire with fire. Not even Bear.

Wes' look of contentment shifted into something darker: fear and slight ripples of sorrow. *I'm sorry,* Bear wanted to say, hoping his eyes expressed it for him. They must've, because the trapeze artist was the first one to speak again.

"Thank God," He breathed, blue irises beginning to swim with happy tears.

Maggie flung her arms around Bear's shoulders, and then Callie and Paris, and finally Wes. Bear laughed, overcome with a joy he never felt before, and found that it was easier to breathe with everyone squeezing him than it ever was when he was eating fire.

They pulled back after a long minute, so it was just Maggie cupping Bear's cheeks. "Are you okay?" She asked, and she was so, so beautiful.

Bear felt Atlanta pressed against his legs, her heartbeat matching his own, and the black fur on her paws entirely grown back. Surrounding him were rows of fairy lights hung like conga lines of fire flies, red and white tents that were erected in carefully calculated positions, and the comforting reek of fried food that traveled on the breeze. He was surrounded by everything he came to represent, the image of a man who wanted to be good, not rich.

Yet, somehow, all he could see was his Magnolia. It was for her that he had laid down his torches: he never wanted to be the reason she cried ever again. He wanted to live to witness all of her accomplishments, just as he had held her back long enough for the sake of his own.

He wasn't sure if he believed in love.

But, if he did, he'd love her the most.

"Yeah," Bear's smile favored the left side of his cheek. "I'm going to be okay."

Above them, the Ferris wheel stood tall and mighty against a bluebird sky.

* * *

<u>MAGNOLIA</u>

It was late September when she left the Circus.

She did not leave in secret, but she refused to have a big exit. New York City could not stop calling to her and eventually her heart gave in. Roy had dipped into the Circus' fund and set her off with enough money to *buy* an apartment in Soho, a cozy one-bedroom above a coffee shop and nestled between a bookstore and a speakeasy. It was an easy commute north to Mohawk: a trip she swore she'd try to make once a month.

Roy helped her move in. He brought his old furniture from his pre-Ringleader days out of storage to fill her empty apartment, and dished even more cash out to get her a king-sized bed and a mattress of her choice. Maggie begged him to let her repay him but he denied every offer.

"You just do your best out here, kiddo," He said, wrapping her up in a hug. "And call if you need anything at all."

Maggie had started to cry. She couldn't explain to him how she needed to go back and never return all at once. She couldn't even begin to understand the emotions herself, let alone have the energy to beg someone else to make sense of them. Her apartment didn't smell like sugar cookie tea or cinnamon rolls, and worse even - it didn't smell like gasoline.

(Her most embarrassing moment thus far would have to be stumbling into a corner store drunk with eyes puffy from crying, asking if they had air fresheners that smelt of kerosene.)

She had sobbed in Roy's arms and didn't stop crying for a week. As some sort of training exercise, everyone at the Circus had made her agree not to call them for the first few days in case she was tempted to

come back prematurely - and although it was
heartbreaking, the logic was not flawed. If she heard his
voice, she would've found a way back to New Hampshire
on foot.

She tried not to think about him. He sent her off
with his headband and a dog collar with a name
embroidered in pink and a heartbreak she'd never
recover from. It was an inevitable part of life, he
promised her. He knew it was coming and accepted it
long before she did. Is that why it had been so easy for
him to let her go?

It wasn't easy. Maggie knew that.

True to her character, she buried him deep within
her and wouldn't even let herself think his name. Every
now and then she dreamt vaguely of bright red hair, or
caught a glimpse of a stranger with a smile that favored
the left side of their face. She stopped watching TV and
movies because, apparently, torches were a common
prop, and national geographic was doing a weekly special
on grizzlies.

Painting became her go to activity. It was the
perfect mix of familiar, calming, and validating. It was
something she was good enough at that she didn't have
to think too hard about it. Canvases with mountain
scenes or flower patches lined the walls in her
apartment; the goal was to cover up every inch of boring
beige with colorful daydreams.

Her favorite hung above her bed. She found the
biggest canvas at the nearby craft stores and looked at it
everyday, contemplating what was good enough to turn
it into. It began with a base of blues and the rest of it
followed as naturally as the beating of her own heart. A
towering, mighty Ferris wheel against a bluebird sky. She

washed the paint off of her hands and wiped the tears off of her cheeks, humming a Circus tune.

Life became ignoring cat calls or strangers trying to sell her a mixtape.

Maggie walked with her head down and her jacket pulled tightly around her body to fend off against the autumn chill. Teetering on the edge of a curb, staring down into the murky water of a street puddle, she let taxi cabs speed past just inches from her nose. The sun was setting on her ninth day in New York and she had yet to find a job of any kind – writing or otherwise. Across the street she spotted a dingy looking diner with neon signs and big, panoramic windows that had people moving languidly beyond it like characters on a big screen. Woman in short skirts and tight grey t-shirts served men raging from homeless, to tourist, to executive.

Pie was the best medicine for a broken heart, Maggie decided.

A little bell dinged pleasantly above her head when she pushes her way through the door, getting blasted in the face by warm air. The door shuts behind her like a vacuum seal. Above her head florescent lights flicker in desperate need of new bulbs, and all eyes in the room turn in her direction. Instinct told her to shrink in on herself but Maggie forced her chin up as she strode over to the long counter, slipping up into an end seat. A waitress, a middle-aged woman with Botox in her lips and poorly applied blue eye shadow, offered her a welcoming smile.

"Good evening, sweetheart." Her accent was Boston-esque and sent a pang of missing New England through Maggie.

"Good evening," Maggie responded. She took her hands out of her pockets and rubbed her palms together, trying to shake the chill on her fingers. "You got cherry pie?"

"With your name on it, sugar." The waitress winked before walking off towards a glass display case, her hips swaying.

Cupping her hands, Maggie exhaled hot air onto her numb hands and swept her eyes around the diner. It reminded her a lot of the one she had her first dinner with Bear at with its antique car decor and quiet 70s music playing over the speaker. A loud group of men were laughing over some burgers and fries in the corner, an older couple shared a piece of pie and in the booth behind them, two girls knocked their foreheads together sipping out of the same milkshake.

Aside from a middle-aged man sitting a few seats down from her at the counter, Maggie was the only single person in the restaurant.

The waitress – her name tag said Sally – returned with a large slice of pie with cherries spilling out of the dough, a dollop of whipped cream already melting down the sides. Maggie smiled from ear to ear, thanking her wholeheartedly.

"Anything to drink, love?" Sally asked, leaning up against the counter with one arm. "Coffee, milkshake, maybe just water?"

"Water would be great," Maggie said, and on second thought, added: "Do you have Earl grey tea?"

"Cream and sugar?"

"Actually, black is fine."

"You got it, gorgeous."

Maggie picked at the pie slowly, savoring the sweetness she allowed herself to indulge in. She worried about staying in shape now that she had left the Circus and Dee's homemade cooking behind – already she had become obsessed with the convenience of New York fast food. A wad of Roy's cash sat heavy in her breast pocket, encouraging her to get a second piece.

Sally slid a glass of water and a mug of tea across the counter with a smile. "Haven't seen you around here. You new to the neighborhood?"

Maggie glanced up. "New to the city, kind of. Grew up here but I moved away. Been back about a week now."

Pencil thin eyebrows shot up in interest. "Yeah? Where'd you move to?"

The man a few seats down was listening now, his body angled towards the conversation as he sipped on his black coffee. Maggie pushed a cherry around her plate with the prongs of her fork, torn on how to answer that. On one hand, she could lie and just pick a state. Through traveling she obtained enough knowledge on some of them to uphold a conversation. On the other, she could tell the truth about her years spent at a traveling Circus and be the most interesting person in this diner.

She decided she was too tired to put energy into a lie.

"I joined a traveling Circus," She said. Waiting for the shock on her audience's faces to die down, Maggie stuffed her mouth with a forkful of pie and whipped cream.

"Wasn't expecting that one," The man laughed, putting his mug down. "What'd you do?"

Maggie swallowed and wiped her mouth on her denim sleeve. "I was a clown. Not the coolest thing there, but it worked for me."

"Why'd you leave?" Sally asked, her eyes wide with awe and disbelief. "I mean – what could be better than being in a *circus*?"

Despite herself, Maggie choked on a chuckle. "I want to be a writer. And being in the Circus wasn't all fun and games. It was hard work, and some of the shit I saw..." She trailed off, thinking about Quinn, thinking about... she shut her mind off before it could conjure up an image of his face. This diner wasn't the place for a breakdown. "It was great, though." A smile found its way back onto her face as her blood warmed with happy memories to drown out the horrific ones. "Best decision I ever made."

The man was staring at her with a strange look in his eye; he grins, slow and considering. "Sally," He gestures to the waitress, "top me off, would you?" Sally nodded, grabbing his mug and bringing it back around to the coffee brewers. To Maggie, the man held out a hand. "I'm Will Young."

"Magnolia Mendoza." She shook his hand firmly.

He dug around in his suit jacket pocket when the handshake broke, lips pursed with thought. When he found what he was looking for, he slid it down the counter blank side up, like he was passing notes in class. It was a small rectangle, and when Maggie flipped it over, she realized it was a business card.

"I'm a writer's agent," Will explained. "And this is your lucky day."

Sally returned his coffee mug completely full and slipped out to check on other costumers, but Maggie

could see her eyes occasionally flittering over to her and
Will. Maggie held the business card in her hand like it
might evaporate if she gripped it too tight. She could feel
eyes on her yet all she could focus on was the future she
had in the palm of her hand.

Will cleared his throat after a few moments. "I'd
love to work with you. I feel like you got a lot of
interesting material for me, coming from where you're
coming from."

"More interesting than anything that's happening
in New York City?" Maggie questioned, unsure. It felt too
good to be true, like there must be some ulterior motive.

Hands raised in mock surrender, Will shrugged.
"There's more than eight million people in this city, all
telling the same stories about the same streets. You gotta
have something really good to stand out at this point –
and a girl returning to the city after an affair with a
circus? Shit, Magnolia, they'll eat you up."

That made enough sense. Oddly enough, through
all of Maggie's brainstorming sessions, writing about the
Circus never occurred to her. It had felt too real, and
such a normal part of her existence that she couldn't
fathom being able to write more than a paragraph of
interest. There was so much of it unprocessed and
writing about it might be the key to finally accepting that
she had lived it, and now she wasn't.

She didn't even realize she had started crying until
Sally snuck back over and handed her a pile of napkins.
Maggie tried to keep up with the tears pooling out of her
eyes but they were faster than she was, so she gave up
and let them flow. They weren't tears of sadness, though.
As if carried by a nonexistent breeze, the faint smell of
gasoline drifted under her nose.

Her last image of him weighed heavily on her mind. Shoulder to shoulder with Wes, their dogs tumbling on the ground around their feet, a pair of matching smiles on their faces. Rest had done good for them. They had looked their age for the first time in a long time: youthful and less like the victims of never-ending sleepless nights. His hair, bright with a fresh layer of red dye, was finally long enough to braid against his head.

It hurt like an open wound.

There was a brief moment where Maggie thought he might come with her, right after she announced her plans to leave for New York. She wanted to believe it could work if they went together, but she knew his heart was waging a war. They belonged in different worlds – at least at this point in their lives. He wouldn't be happy if he followed, she wouldn't be happy if she stayed.

But he wanted her to go.

So, she watched him disappear over the bend as she hung out of the window of Roy's pickup truck. As she settled back in the passenger seat, bottom lip quivering with suppressed sobs, they heard a sharp, confused bark.

The shadowy figure of a Shepherd streaked around a corner, following the truck as it thumped along the winding road. She nearly caught up to them before she stopped dead, as if by some invisible force field, loyal to a command Roy and Maggie couldn't hear.

Only then did the sobs come, like a dam finally breaking, when out of the rear view, they saw the lonely figure of her dog sitting in the middle of the road.

Will waited patiently for Maggie to stop sniffling, which was a long time to wait. He put her pie and tea, and refills of both, on his tab, and moved down to sit in the chair directly next to her.

Maggie dug around in her pockets, seeking out the only bit of fabric that might bring her comfort. His headband was wrinkled from being balled up for so long and it was beginning to smell less of kerosene and more of denim and Manhattan subways. Maggie had doubted her heart could shatter any more than it already had, but apparently it could, tenfold.

One day, everything will fall into place.

"So, what do you say, kid?" Will asked gently, eyeing the artifact with interest. "You got a story to tell?"

Maggie nodded, holding the headband to her heart. For a long time, Maggie trained herself to use the means of escapism to bury what hurt her down as deep as it could go. Somewhere along the way, she learned that the only way to heal from it was to grow from it.

Maggie took a deep breath.

I hope we fall together.

"Yeah. It's about my friend, Bear."

The end.

Author's Note

While circuses have fascinated me my entire life, I never went to one because of the corruption I knew lied within the foundation of them. The lack of humanity both people and animals faced beneath the big tops hurts my heart. But I could not shake the feeling that I needed to write about one.

I worked at a haunted hayride for a few years and acted in a carnival scene with people who have become my closest friends. We were clowns together and birthed some bizarre comradery through our characters that extended into our lives when we took our make up off. This only deepened my connection to circus performers.

Through reading about various acts, I stumbled upon fire breathing. Instantly, the beginning images of Bear popped into my head; I felt like I struck gold.

First, I tried to stuff Bear into different narratives, still trying to pull myself away from the fantasy idea of a circus – something that doesn't appeal, something that wouldn't sell. He didn't feel like he belonged anywhere else, no surprise there. So, I fleshed out this character: a troubled boy, driven by the death of his parents to become the best version of himself he could be, even if it costed him his life. The rest of the characters and story evolved around him, like a Big Bang.

Originally, this story was far different. It was told only from the perspective of a long forgotten about character: Roy's nephew. In the first versions, Roy was an awful ringleader who exploited Bear far worse than he did in the final version, and it's up to his nephew – who comes to work at the circus for the summer – to stand up to him and save Bear's life. In that version, Wes is a ticket taker, Magnolia is a side character, Judas doesn't exist, and Atlanta is a wolf salvaged from the last of the animal acts.

It was a good story, and if you're reading that and thinking "man, I would've rather read that!", I'm sorry! I hit a major roadblock in the beginning stages; I figured if I couldn't get past the first chapter, how could I write the entire thing? The issue was so simple: I had no desire to write about the nephew's (Jesse's) life before he went to the Circus – and then it hit me as to why.

The Circus is the story, and the characters there deserve to tell that story themselves.

So, Jesse was pocketed. Wes was turned into a performer, and after reconnecting with a friend of mine (named Judas), he got a twin brother. Magnolia got her own story. Atlanta became a police dog, and then an Army dog. The Circus became the center of the universe again, and it was less about Jesse's conflict with his uncle Roy, and more about the conflict between performers and the Circus itself.

The characters all carry a piece of me. Bear's insatiable need to be better, Maggie's strained relationship with her father (which, originally, was going to be a strained relationship with an abusive ex-boyfriend, pulled right from my own reality. Then, I decided that ex-boyfriend of mine did not deserve a place in this story, so he was nixed, too), Wes' fear of change, Judas' polarizing wanderlust.

These instances, surrounding these characters, felt necessary to take root in a Circus. Where every act could relate to their traumatic experiences. I hope it resonated.

Acknowledgements

First and foremost, to River, who believed in me and this story more than anyone ever did. For the longest time, Bear existed only within our text bubbles; it was with your constant pushing that it ever came to life beyond that. Thank you for being my muse, my cheerleader, and one of my dearest friends. The world isn't ready for the talent and beauty your novels will bestow upon it, but I cannot wait.

Mr. Stoncius. I promised you in eighth grade that I would dedicate my first book to you, so here you go. You were the first person to ever truly believe that I could put something like this out in the world, bound and published, and I won't ever forget that.

Zak, my wonderful editor and proofreader. Thank you for your continued support and wonderful advice. I can't wait to steal your Oscar.

Auntie Lesly, my other editor and proofreader. The strongest, most beautiful soul in the entire world. If I could one day be half the woman you are, I will be good enough.

And finally, to Bear himself. I hope everyone else finds you as wonderful as I have. Letting you go into the world feels very much to me like fire

breathing to you: this is an extension of my soul.
You have existed inside me as many different
characters under many different names – I'm glad I
could finally find a way to share you with whomever
is bold enough to journey with you.